WHO IS
ROBIN?

WHO IS ROBIN?

A NOVEL

JON DIJON

NEWMARK PUBLISHING COMPANY

Published in 1993 by
Newmark Publishing Company
South Windsor, Connecticut 06074
(203) 282-7265

Designed by Irving Perkins Associates, Inc.
Typeset by Pagesetters Incorporated
Printed and Bound by The Book Press
Manufactured in the United States of America

10 9 8 7 6 5 4 3 2 1

Library of Congress Cataloging-in-Publication Data

Dijon, Jon
Who is Robin?

93-084590

ISBN 0-938539-77-9

AUTHOR'S NOTE

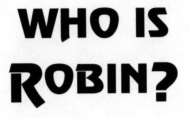

WHO IS ROBIN?

CHAPTER

1

Dr. Scott Perkins delicately incised the skin and subcutaneous tissue in the patient's left groin area with the scalpel.

Stacy Sharp, the scrub nurse, filled Scott's hands with surgical instruments as he looked straight ahead, concentrating on the operative field. Stacy had to anticipate Scott's every move and to know what instrument he wanted by closely watching the operation in progress.

There was a deadly silence as Dr. Perkins deftly cut the tissue, clamping and tying the blood vessels as he worked. His eye-hand coordination was perfect and he worked methodically with no wasted motion. Occasionally the silence was broken.

"Metzenbaum scissors."

"Pick-ups with teeth."

"Halstead clamp."

Finally, Dr. Perkins had dissected the area down to the diseased tissue. Rather than looking like a bunch of grapes, the tissue looked like a bunch of plums that were glued together.

"Stacy, you'd better have a few vascular clamps ready, just in case," said Dr. Perkins.

He dissected sharply below the diseased tissue against the abdominal musculature. Suddenly there was a fountain of blood in the wound.

"Put the suction tip over here." He pointed to Joe Barry, the surgical resident assisting him, as he placed a gauze pad and applied pressure over the red streak of blood.

As the suction sucked the blood out of the wound, Scott visualized the bleeding source and quickly clamped the open vessel. A silk suture ligature was placed around the artery and the major bleeding stopped. Several other small blood vessels were clamped and tied. Finally the mass was removed. He handed off the specimen to Joyce, the circulating nurse.

"Call for a pathologist," he said. "Well, Joe, you've seen the tissue. What do you think?"

"It looks like fish flesh. I'd say it's probably a lymphoma."

"You're probably right."

Joe Barry, the chief resident assisting Dr. Perkins, spoke up hesitantly. "Sir, could I close up the wound?"

"Sure. You'll be doing these cases not too far in the distant future. I'll assist you."

The two surgeons changed positions at the operating table.

Stacy handed Joe the needle holder with the silk suture in it and he started sewing the tissue together.

Scott looked up at the clock. It was close to 3:00 P.M. It had been a full day and he was exhausted. He had an office full of patients that he still had to see.

Suddenly, he felt the rubber glove over his left forefinger penetrated by a needle.

"Ouch!" he hollered. "You got me!" he shouted. "For gosh sakes, be more careful!"

"Sorry, sir," said Joe.

"My fault. I was looking at the clock."

Scott stepped back from the table, took off his gloves, and saw where the skin on his finger had been penetrated and was bleeding. The circulating nurse poured an antiseptic solution over the area and a Band-Aid was applied.

The scrub nurse assisted Joe Barry in closing the wound.

Scott sat down on a metal chair. A few moments later, a pathologist came into the operating room with the resected tissue.

"What've you got?" he asked.

"Does this patient have AIDS?" Dr. Roberts, the pathologist asked.

"Why?"

"Because the tissue shows florid follicular hyperplasia, which is often seen in AIDS patients."

"Why, the bastard! I've just been inoculated with this guy's blood. What a way to get AIDS! Who'll ever believe me?"

"What about me?" asked the anesthesiologist. "I had difficulty passing the tube down his throat. With all his coughing and spewing of mucous, he coughed all his infective crap into my face. Those AIDS bugs can be inhaled, you know."

"He lied to me," said Scott. "He said he was a straight arrow and that he was happily married. I met his wife, in fact."

"And he's a lawyer," said Paul Aronson, the anesthesiologist. "You can't trust anyone these days."

"Ask him as he comes out of the anesthesia. Maybe with the sodium pentothal, he'll tell us the truth," said Scott.

"I don't thinks that's legal," said Aronson.

"He lied to me—anything is legal."

The endotracheal tube was removed, and as the patient started to wake up, the anesthesiologist started to quiz him. The patient was glassy-eyed and groggy.

"Mr. Sousa, Mr. Sousa, have you ever taken drugs in the past?"

"Huh? Huh? Sure, I tried coke and heroin when I was in law school in New York City. I was young and foolish then. I don't do that anymore. I'm a straight arrow."

"That's great," replied the anesthesiologist. "I suppose you frequented the bathhouses down in New Jersey."

"Only a few times," he replied. "I did get involved with some of those sexy massage parlors. It was fun. I was raising hell—just like the rest of the boys. I had a few sexual contacts in some of them. Why are you asking me all this stuff? I've been straight since I got married six months ago. Hey! What's going on here?"

The lawyer was rapidly regaining consciousness.

"We're just finding out what a straight arrow you are," said Aronson.

Attorney Sousa became red in the face and started to struggle. He tried to sit up. The anesthesiologist roughly pushed him back down on the operating room table.

"It's your past we're worried about. You told me an outright lie," said Scott.

"The reason I lied was because I was afraid you wouldn't operate on me if you knew about my past. That's why I lied! I didn't want some inexperienced jerk doing my operation. I wanted the top man to do the job."

"Some doctors wouldn't operate on you! It's people like you and with your life style that created this problem!"

"I'm sorry. I didn't want anyone to know about my past."

"You're a lying fucking lawyer," said Aronson. "I should have given you an overdose of anesthesia. You're a plague on our society. We'd all be better off if you were dead! It's lifestyles like yours that are fucking up this world!"

The lawyer looked the anesthesiologist straight in the eye and pointed his finger at him. "I've got just as much right to do what I want to do with my sex life as anybody else. Read the Bill of Rights in the Constitution. Besides, you're a doctor and the Hippocratic Oath says you have to take care of me."

"The Hippocratic Oath doesn't say I have to risk my own life to make you well! People with your sexual orientation have given us AIDS. You ought to be put out of business."

"Arguing is not going to get any of us anywhere," said Scott. "We all have a problem. It's a big one! I'd better check in with Dr. Dick Scranton, head of the Infectious Disease Department, and see what he suggests. All I can say is that this is one hell of a way to get AIDS. You've made my day, Mr. Sousa."

"I guess we'll both have to get a blood test for AIDS now," said Sousa. "What am I going to tell my wife?"

"That's your problem," said Scott. "I suppose you lied to her, too!"

CHAPTER

2

When Dr. Perkins got back to his office after surgery, he called his secretary, Judy, into his office.

"Judy, get Dr. Scranton on the phone for me. Also, shut the door so the patients and other office personnel can't hear my conversation with him. I want you to stay in here. I have a big problem related to one of the surgical cases I did today."

Judy looked at Dr. Perkins. He didn't look like he usually did. He appeared quite nervous and had beads of sweat dripping from his forehead. It was most unusual to see him this way. Usually when he came back to the office after surgery, he was quite relaxed, and often had a sandwich or a cup of coffee with her, and would discuss what had transpired in the operating room. He also usually asked if there had been any important phone calls.

"I'll get Dr. Scranton for you right away."

The phone call went through and Scott picked up his phone.

"Dick, this is Scott Perkins. I had a big problem in the operating room about an hour ago. I was operating on a young lawyer with a mass in his left groin and, as the tissue was being studied by the pathologists, I told my surgical resident that he could take over and sew up the wound. In the process of closing, the resident nicked my left forefinger with a needle, breaking through the rubber glove and causing bleeding."

"I wouldn't worry about that," interrupted Dr. Scranton. "Wash the wound well with an antiseptic solution and put yourself on a broad spectrum antibiotic. That should handle it."

"You don't understand," replied Scott. "Let me finish. When the pathologist came back with the frozen section diagnosis, I almost had a heart attack."

"What happened?"

"He asked me if the patient had AIDS. He told me the tissue was diagnosed as florid follicular hyperplasia, often seen in AIDS patients."

"Hmm. That is a problem and it could be a serious one."

"That's why I'm calling you. I was inoculated with this guy's blood. The anesthesiologist is pissed off, too. He had trouble putting the endotracheal tube down this guy's throat and he coughed all over him and spat in his eyes and face."

"Well, you have a more serious problem than the anesthesiologist. Do you know anything about the patient's previous life-style?"

"He looked different when I first met him. He had a ponytail and seemed effeminate. I did ask him if he was a homosexual. He was taken aback by that and denied it. He said he was a straight arrow and was happily married. As he was coming out of anesthesia, Dr. Aronson, the anesthesiologist, asked him about his life-style. He admitted shooting drugs and fooling around in the bathhouses down in New Jersey when he was in law school. He could be HIV positive."

There was silence in the other end of the phone. Finally, Dr. Scranton spoke up.

"Other surgeons have gotten nicked in the operating room many times, but now that AIDS is on the scene, it's a much bigger problem."

"I need your advice. What should I do now?" asked Scott.

"You'll have to test your patient's blood to see if he's HIV positive," said Dr. Scranton. "What did you say his name was?"

"Attorney Robert Sousa. He's a patient on the surgical wing, North 1023."

"Well, you're going to have to get a blood sample from him some way and test him for AIDS. He's going to have to sign permission."

"What if he refuses?"

"Then you have a bigger problem. You might have to go to court and have the judge force him to consent to a blood test."

"You've got to be kidding me. I'm trying to save this man's life, he lies to me, and I need to get him to sign a release so I can sample his blood to see if he has AIDS, so I can save my own life? What's this country coming to, anyway?"

"They're trying to prevent discrimination," said Dr. Scranton. "If he's positive and the news isn't kept confidential, he could lose his job and be ostracized."

"What about the rest of the people? If he's positive, he should be identified so the rest of the populace can be protected from getting AIDS from him. What about the hospital personnel who have to take care of him? Shouldn't they know he's got AIDS so they can protect themselves? What about me—as a surgeon? I've got as much, if not more, to lose than he does."

"Obtaining a blood sample from the patient is not the complete answer," said Dr. Scranton.

"What do you mean?"

"If Attorney Sousa tests positive for HIV, and you were inoculated by that needle stick, it could take at least six weeks before antibodies against the virus can be detected in your bloodstream. In some cases, it may take a year or more."

"Shouldn't we test his blood for HIV now?"

"Yes," said Dr. Scranton. "But you're going to have to be diplomatic. You also may have to sweat it out. You may need to get another blood sample in six months or a year from now, too."

"This gets more complicated the longer I talk to you," said Scott.

"Why don't I just order some blood tests on him and have the lab do the HIV test?"

"Because it's a crime if it's done in that manner. It's an invasion of privacy."

"My life is not worth anything and his is worth more, you're saying. I'm the victim because he lied to me."

"If you went to court, the defense would say you should have protected yourself better."

"What? I suppose I should wear metal nonpenetrating gloves

when I operate on patients? That's impossible! As it is now, I have to wear rubberized sterile gowns that can't be penetrated by body fluids, a special helmet, eyeglasses, and boots to prevent absorption of blood through the feet. This is just another way to increase the cost of health care."

"I realize that," replied Scranton. "That's why surgeons are at the greatest risk for AIDS."

"How many health personnel have gotten AIDS from a needle prick?" asked Scott.

"Maybe twenty or forty," replied Dr. Scranton. "There are probably more that we don't know about."

"There's another question I'm afraid to ask you, but I've got to know. If Sousa is HIV positive now, and I won't know whether I acquired AIDS through that needle stick for possibly a year or longer, should I stop doing surgery?"

"That's a tough question," said Dr. Scranton.

"If I stop doing surgery now I'll be wiped out financially. My family will be stigmatized and my surgery practice will be destroyed."

"I don't think you need to stop unless you become HIV positive," said Dr. Scranton.

"Should I be taking those new drugs that may prolong my life, AZT and DDI?" asked Scott.

"You'll have to make that choice yourself. There can be some toxic side effects from those drugs. I'm not so sure there are too many scientists who can give you good advice as to what you should do in this situation."

"Thanks a lot! This accident wouldn't have happened if I knew in advance this patient had AIDS. I think every patient admitted to the hospital for surgery should have their blood tested for AIDS. I'm willing to have mine tested, if patients are willing to have theirs done."

"I agree with you," said Dr. Scranton. "Come over to my office tomorrow. I want to do some blood studies on you for a baseline."

"Don't be in such a hurry. I'm going to have to think about it before I let you draw blood from me. In that regard, I'm no different from Sousa. Everyone in the hospital will know if it's positive or they might ask, 'What's Dr. Perkins doing having his blood tested for AIDS?' "

"I never thought of that," said Dr. Scranton. "Maybe you should go out of state to have your blood tested."

"That's a great suggestion! This gets more and more complicated," replied Scott.

"I think the first thing you have to do is get Attorney Sousa's blood tested for AIDS."

"I'll go talk to him as soon as I finish office hours this afternoon. I'll keep in touch with you," said Scott, as he hung up the phone.

Dr. Perkins looked over at Judy. "Well, you've heard it all. One needle stick can destroy my career and my life."

"I think it's horrible!" replied Judy. "The public should be aware of the risks that surgeons face every day. There's got to be a better way. No one is going to want to be a surgeon in the future."

"Well, Sousa is a prime example of how there are cracks in the system. A lawyer, who is supposed to defend justice, lies to a doctor, a surgeon, who is supposed to take care of the sick and the maimed. The wires got crossed somewhere. That's just the beginning of the problem. The lawyers control our political system and make the laws. Some of them are gay, just like Sousa."

"That's one of the biggest problems this country has to face. I think they should quarantine all AIDS patients, just like they did for smallpox, to protect everyone," said Judy. "Why don't they do an AIDS test on everybody?"

"That would be too expensive and the public would become needlessly alarmed. It would be necessary to pass a federal law. Besides, some of our representatives and senators might have positive AIDS tests and that might prevent them from getting re-elected. Some of them are homosexuals or lesbians and readily admit it. Others are hiding their sexual habits in the closet. I don't think that law will ever be passed."

"Well something has got to be done about the AIDS problem or it will be worse than the bubonic plague," said Judy. "It could wipe out a nation."

As Judy looked at Dr. Perkins, she could tell he was deeply disturbed by what had happened. He was wringing his hands and was visibly shaken. He looked as though someone had punched him in the stomach. He finally looked up at her and said, "We'd better get back to work and see the patients who are in the waiting room. Life goes on, at least for a little while."

After seeing twenty patients, he walked over to the hospital to see Attorney Sousa. His wife was at his bedside. Should she be in on this conversation? thought Scott. I think not.

"Mrs. Sousa, I'm going to examine your husband again briefly. I wonder if you would mind stepping out to the waiting room for a few minutes?"

"She can stay," replied Sousa.

"I'm the doctor, I determine that," said Dr. Perkins.

"I'll step out," said Mrs. Sousa. "I'd like to talk to you after you're through though," she said as she walked out of the room.

"Bob, I think we have to have a frank talk."

"I think so too," said Sousa. "You had no right questioning me when I was under anesthesia."

"You had no right lying to me," said Scott. "You're a lawyer. You know better than that."

"I wanted my past to be completely confidential. My wife doesn't know about it."

"That's one of the reasons I asked her to step out. Have you told her?"

"No," said Attorney Sousa. "That would open up a can of worms. I should sue you for what you and that young anesthesiologist did."

"I hope it doesn't come to that. Everyone would get hurt then. There's something very important I have to tell you. I'm here to tell you that the tissue I removed from your groin is florid follicular hyperplasia. This type of tissue is seen in AIDS patients."

"Oh my gosh! Do I have AIDS?"

"We don't know yet," replied Scott. "Yes. You could have AIDS."

"Oh, this is horrible. My wife is expecting a baby."

"Well, that puts a new wrinkle in it. That makes it a bigger problem. There's something else I have to tell you. While I was operating on you, my finger was stuck by a needle and I may have been inoculated with your blood. I need to know if you test positive for AIDS."

"What if I refuse to let you do a blood test?"

"I don't think you will," replied Dr. Perkins.

"I know the law. You have to have my written permission."

"I know that."

"Would you like me to sue you?"

"Would you prefer we go to court and have it all over the newspapers? I'm sure it would sell a lot of papers."

"I wouldn't want that. I've got to think about this."

"Aren't you interested in protecting your wife and your baby?"

"Of course I am. I'm not as interested in protecting you, though."

"Thanks a lot. I operated on you in good faith to determine why you were sick and now you tell me this. Do you want me to discuss what has happened with your wife?"

"No, not at all. Besides, I haven't given you permission to talk to her."

"Here we go again. You're talking like a lawyer. Aren't you concerned about your own welfare? If you have AIDS you should be treated now. Your wife could have AIDS and so could your unborn baby. If you test positive for HIV I'd also like to get some treatment and protect my own family."

"I have to give this some deep thought," said Sousa. "I know I need to be tested for AIDS. I'm worried about keeping the results confidential. I need to earn a living too. My wife doesn't know anything about my past. This will certainly be a real test of her love for me. I don't know how to tell her."

"Just tell her the truth," said Dr. Perkins. "Stop lying."

"That's easier said than done," said Sousa.

"I'll tell you what. I'm going to discuss this with my wife. I'll give you my decision in the morning."

"Do you want me to be around when you talk to her?"

"No. It will be pretty sticky between she and I. It could be messy!"

"OK. I'll see you the first thing in the morning and we'll draw that blood sample. Have a good night's sleep."

"I don't think I'm going to sleep tonight."

First thing the next morning, Scott walked over to the hospital and went to Attorney Sousa's room. He wasn't in the room.

He's probably in the john, thought Scott. He walked out to the nurses' station and asked the head nurse, "Where's Robert Sousa?"

"He signed out against advice at 4:00 A.M. His wife picked him up. We notified your answering service, doctor."

CHAPTER

Scott was quite upset when he walked down the hall to his operating room to start his 8:00 case. He felt he was in big trouble because the bird had flown the coop.

The only people aware of his problem about possibly contacting AIDS were his wife, his secretary, and Dr. Scranton, the chief of infectious disease at Jefferson Hospital. The resident surgeon and anesthesiologist, who had scrubbed on the case and Joyce, the circulating nurse, were also aware of the significance of the needle puncture, but they didn't know the patient had signed out of the hospital against advice.

The acute stress was beginning to overwhelm Scott, because as a doctor, he was aware of the significance of that needle stick—he knew too much.

Sousa had to be found quickly and, in some way, convinced to have his blood tested for HIV. Scott was aware that the blood test would not completely relieve his anxiety, but it might ease some of his immediate apprehension. Dr. Scranton had told him the attorney could have AIDS but test negative.

When Scott arrived outside his operating room he spoke to Joyce, who was waiting for him to get last-minute instructions concerning the cases scheduled for that morning.

"Joyce, I have to get in touch with Judy as soon as she gets in. I want you to start calling my office at 8:30. She usually arrives between 8:30 and 9:00."

"I can handle that," replied Joyce, sensing that something important was up. "I'll start calling her at 8:30. Is there anything else you want me to do?"

"Yes," replied Scott. "Do you know what time the medical chiefs get into the hospital?"

"Around 9:00. Usually they get in later than the surgeons, unless they're on service and have to make teaching rounds with the medical residents."

"They have a better lifestyle than surgeons, don't they?"

"Not all of them. The cardiologists don't get much sleep sometimes when they have a bad heart case. If the gastroenterologists get a bad bleeder, they too, can be kept hopping."

"Well, I guess there are some exceptions. We do have some hot-shot medical docs around here. I also want you to call Dr. Scranton, the chief of infectious disease, as soon as he gets in."

Suddenly Joyce realized what this was all about and it showed on her face. She had been in the operating room when Scott had had his finger stuck. She wondered if there was something big developing.

"On second thought, forget it. I'll have Judy handle this." Scott began to realize that too many people might become aware of his problem, although he trusted Joyce.

"Anything I should know about the cases we're doing today?" asked Joyce.

"No, except that I have to get out of here as early as possible," he replied.

Joyce walked into her operating room, where the anesthesiologist was preparing the patient for surgery. He had put an intravenous line in place and was getting ready to pass an endotracheal tube down the patient's throat.

She felt compelled to say something to the anesthesiologist and to the scrub nurse, Amy Johnson, one of the older experienced operating room nurses. She spoke up loudly so they could all hear. "Amy,

Dr. Perkins doesn't look like he's in a good mood today. I'd be a little careful. Try to stay ahead of him."

"Wouldn't you know," replied Amy. "I requested this scrub because it's a challenge, and you come and tell me this. He can be a bitch if he's mad."

"I'm not interested in you climbing under the woodwork. All I'm saying is that it looks like he's disturbed about something so keep on your toes and be on your best behavior," replied Joyce.

"Thanks for the info," said Amy.

After Dr. Perkins finished his ten-minute scrub he entered the operating room and put on his gown and rubber gloves.

Once the case was started, there was an unusually deep silence in the operating room theater. Usually there was some good-natured chit-chatting to be heard—but not today. Dr. Perkins was all work and no play. He was intense, rapidly incising the tissue and concentrating on the operation.

The patient was a young white male with a large black malignant melanoma of the back. Scott rapidly and meticulously dissected the tumor, his hands working mechanically. He rotated a large skin flap into the defect. He methodically did all the surgery himself and was obviously in a hurry. He did not take the time to teach the resident about the operation. The resident would have to take a back seat today and learn by watching.

Just before Scott put the last stitch in place, he spoke up, directing his comments to the anesthesiologist, Bill Michelson. "Bill, I'm sort of in a hurry today."

"I noticed," he replied. "Your scrub nurse was having trouble keeping up with you."

"Do me a favor and don't take a long coffee break between cases."

Bill was perturbed by his remark. It was unusual to hear something like that from Dr. Perkins. He wasn't about to challenge him, however.

"I'll try to expedite the change between cases," he replied. "They still have to clean the room and Joyce has to set up the instruments."

"I understand," Scott replied. "I have a serious problem that needs to be taken care of. I'd appreciate your help. Joyce, have you been able to get my secretary on the phone?"

"Not yet," she replied. "The lines to your office are all busy. I called the hotline and the outside lines."

"I hope Judy hasn't gone to take orders over to the hospital."

Scott went back to the doctor's locker room and tried to call his office. The phone finally rang through.

"Dr. Perkin's office. Would you please hold?"

Finally, Judy came back on the line. "May I help you?"

"This is Dr. Perkins, Judy. I need your help. That lawyer I operated on yesterday left the hospital. He signed out against advice. I want you to call Dr. Scranton and tell him I have to see him today. Try to set up an appointment for me when I get through in the operating room. If necessary, cancel out some of my patients."

"I'll try," said Judy. "It might not be that easy. I'll call Joyce back and let her know."

"OK. Thank you."

Scott was not enthusiastic about starting his second case. It could be a long, drawn-out affair and he had too much on his mind. Fortunately, he had a chief surgical resident to assist him.

The case was an exploratory laparotomy on a very sick, jaundiced patient. The patient was as yellow as a turnip and had been referred to him from a small outlying hospital. The referring doctor thought the patient had a pancreatic or bile duct cancer blocking the drainage from the liver, causing the retention of bile and the bright yellow skin discoloration. An ultrasound showed a blocked common bile duct. A CT scan revealed that the patient had a suspicious lesion in the liver. A needle biopsy was non-diagnostic. The gastroenterologist was unable to get a biopsy of the blockage area.

After the patient was prepped and draped, Scott made a large abdominal incision. Retractors were put in along the edges of the wound to open the area for visualization. He sharply incised along the area around the lower end of the stomach to expose the pancreas and bile duct that was obstructed by the tumor. He reached into the patient's abdomen and his experienced fingers palpated the area. He could feel a hard mass at the lower end of the bile duct. He looked up from the operating table and spoke to the visiting doctors who were watching.

"Since we don't have a biopsy, I'm going to open the duodenum below the stomach first and get a good look at the end of the bile

duct. I want to biopsy the tumor before embarking on a big operation that has a high mortality and morbidity rate. We have to
determine whether he needs a Whipple procedure to resect the
pancreas. The x-rays don't give us a clear picture as to what's going on."

He quickly made an opening in the gut where the bile duct enters
from the liver.

"This doesn't feel like a tumor to me. I'm going to split the
sphincter at the end of the bile duct so I can see what's going on in
here."

Using a scalpel, he quickly cut and split the sphincter over the
small hard mass and used a cautery to control the bleeding. He then
put light forefinger and thumb pressure with his left hand above the
incised area. A large yellow-black stone popped out.

"Eureka," he yelled. "Hallelujah! This guy doesn't have a cancer.
He's got a stone blocking his bile duct."

He took more x-rays to make sure there weren't any more stones,
and then sutured the opening in the gut. He then focused his
attention on the abnormality in the liver.

He quickly biopsied the abnormal area by placing two big
stitches through the liver and gently tied the sutures down into the
liver substance. He cut a piece of tissue out between the stitches.
The excised tissue was then given to a surgical pathologist for a
frozen section to determine the diagnosis.

A few minutes later, Dr. Calvin Oaks, a senior pathologist, came
into the operating room where Scott was working.

"Dr. Perkins, that liver tissue is a benign blood vessel tumor—a
hemangioma."

"Great! We'll let the patient keep his tumor. He'll be very happy
when he wakes up!"

As Dr. Perkins started to sew up the belly, Joyce came over to him
and, in a soft voice, told him that Judy had called and said that Dr.
Scranton would see him as soon as he finished the case.

Scott took an elevator to the eleventh floor where Dr. Scranton's
office was located and introduced himself to the secretary.

"I'm Dr. Scott Perkins. I believe I have an appointment with Dr.
Scranton."

"Dr. Scranton's on the phone. He'll see you shortly. Have a seat."

It seemed like an eternity before he was told, "Dr. Scranton will see you now. You may go in."

"Hello, Scott. What's on your mind? What's new with that problem of yours?"

"You remember that case I told you about—the operation where my finger was pricked and the patient was an attorney who might have AIDS? Well, there's been a horrible development."

"What happened?"

"I went over and talked with him in the hospital last night after I talked to you. I thought I had a good rapport with him. I told him the tissue I had excised showed that he might have AIDS and that a resident surgeon had pricked my finger with his blood on the needle. I suggested we both may need to have some blood tests done to be sure we weren't HIV positive. 'That's your problem,' he said. 'Not mine!' He was quite upset that we found out about his sexual background when he was coming out of anesthesia and threatened to sue me and the anesthesiologist. 'You lied to me,' I hollered. I got mad and threatened to sue him. It was a stand-off. His social history was now out of the closet. He told me not to talk to his wife about the possibility of his having AIDS. Evidently, she's pregnant and knows nothing about his past. I told him that because she was pregnant, she might need blood tests—not only for her protection, but for her unborn baby. 'My gosh. I didn't think about that,' he said.

"I also told him I would be glad to talk to his wife in his presence, if he wanted me to. He was vehemently opposed! He said he wasn't sure he would submit to a blood test because if it became known that he had AIDS he would be ostracized. His career as a lawyer would be ended.

"I was totally frustrated by his response. I suggested that my life was in his hands—also my career as a successful surgeon.

"I didn't like his reply. 'You're quite a bit older than I am,' he said. 'You've lived your life. So what if you do have AIDS and die a couple of years down the road? It's no big deal!'

"After that remark, I wanted to punch him in the nose. His attitude was terrible! He made me furious! I knew I had to control my temper but I had difficulty remaining calm. I had to try to get his cooperation. I pleaded with him and told him about my wife and four children. Didn't he have any morals or compassion? He said he could care less. He was only interested in what happened to himself and forbid me to talk to his wife. He said he needed some time to think and work things out.

"'I'm emotionally disturbed,' he said. 'I can't think clearly. I'll tell you in the morning if I'll submit to a blood test for AIDS.'

"I tried to reassure him. I told him we'd keep the blood test confidential and his name would not be on the blood sample container.

"'People eventually find out,' was his reply. 'I'm not sure I'll submit to a blood test. It's an invasion of my privacy.'"

"So what's the problem?" asked Dr. Scranton.

"The problem is Attorney Robert Sousa has disappeared! He left the hospital early this morning—he signed out against advice."

"Have you tried to call him at home?"

"Yes, I have. His phone's been disconnected."

"You really do have a problem," said Dick.

"That's the understatement of the year. I've been wracking my brain trying to decide what to do. I can't come up with any good answers. That's why I'm here."

"I've never faced a problem like this before," said Dr. Scranton. "It's going to require quite a bit of thought. Are you planning to go to the police to have them try to locate him?"

"That's no good. I'd have to tell them why I'm looking for him. I'd have to tell them I might have AIDS."

"Hmm, that's right."

"It would be on the docket then, and everyone would know."

"If you do find him, you may have to go to court to force him to submit to a blood test," said Dr. Scranton. "I've never heard of that being done before. If the newspapers get wind of that news item it might hit the headlines. You do have a predicament."

"Dick, have you talked to anyone in the hospital about my problem?"

"No. And I have no intention of telling anyone. In fact, I've handwritten my notes about your problem and kept them in my confidential locked file. My secretary can't even read the chart. She doesn't have access to that file."

"Well, I'm already worried about leaks. I've talked to the resident surgeon on the case who stuck the needle in my finger and he promised not to discuss it with anybody. I told him if he talked, it would mean his ass. I've also talked to the anesthesiologist, who's shitting in his pants worrying that he might have AIDS from inhaling the lawyer's bloody mucous. He's also a basket case. He's talking about seeing a psychiatrist. I told him to keep his mouth shut. A psychiatrist would be the worst person to talk to. It would only add another person at the hospital who knows about the incident. I told him to take some tranquilizers or have an extra martini.

"To make it more complicated he's got another problem. He's recently married and his wife is crawling all over him. She's got real hot pants and he's afraid that if he's got AIDS he'll give it to her. They've already had their first big fight. She's accusing him of not loving her because he won't put it to her. He says he's in trouble if he does and he's in trouble if he doesn't. This incident has a domino effect. It affects more people the more you think about it."

"Why doesn't he just tell her that he's been exposed to an AIDS patient? If she loves him, she'll understand."

"He's thought about that and he's not so sure. How do you tell your new bride that you've just been exposed to the AIDS virus and you're afraid that if you have intercourse with her she'll get AIDS?"

"Why doesn't he just use a condom?"

"Because they're both older and they decided before they got married that they would try to have children. If he suddenly starts wearing a condom she's going to wonder what's going on."

"That's a tough one!"

"What would you do in that situation?"

"I think he probably has to come clean with her and tell her the truth. If he doesn't, it could lead to a divorce."

"Now that this guy's disappeared, what do I do? I don't know if I have AIDS. Should I stop doing surgery? Am I infective to my patients?"

"Don't go any further. I can answer that question," said Dr. Scranton. "As long as you test negative, you should be able to do surgery. However, you're going to need frequent blood tests. If you come up with a positive test or show signs or symptoms of AIDS, you'll have to quit."

"Should I double-glove myself to prevent spreading something I may or may not have?"

"That's up to you."

"I've tried double-gloving already and it doesn't work that well. I pride myself in the dexterity of my hands. Double-gloving makes my fingers stiff and I can't operate as well. I suspect some of the OR personnel already know about that needle stick incident. If I start double-gloving they'll wonder why I'm the only surgeon doing it."

"Well, don't get too paranoid about this," said Scranton.

"I think if it were you, you might get a little paranoid," replied Scott.

"You're probably right about that!"

"Should I start taking AZT and assume that I have AIDS?"

"I can't answer all your questions," replied Scranton. "What are your thoughts? What do you plan to do? Your biggest problem is trying to locate that attorney and see if he'll submit to a blood test."

"I realize that. This AIDS problem is going to drive me nuts! My practice is as busy as it's ever going to be. I'm doing more than enough surgery and now the shit hits the fan. I worry about my wife and family just like anyone else. I've decided to have frequent blood tests so I'll protect my patients and my family. That's no problem. However, I've decided that I'll drive out of town and have a reputable laboratory do the testing. I'll have them send the reports to you under an assumed name. That way there will be no question as to my honesty as to whether I should continue my surgical practice. I also feel I must find that lawyer and talk to him again. I'm thinking of hiring a private detective to locate him. If and when I find him, I hope to convince him it'll be valuable for both of us to have frequent blood tests for AIDS."

"That sounds like a good idea," said Scranton. "Keep in touch and let me know if there's anything I can do to help."

"Thank you for your time and suggestions," said Scott. "I'll be in touch."

CHAPTER

That evening, as Scott walked out of Jefferson Hospital, he heard a voice behind him.

"Scott, Scott Perkins, I want to talk to you."

He turned around and saw Dr. Paul Aronson, the young resident anesthesiologist who had given anesthesia to Attorney Sousa.

"Hi, Paul. I've been meaning to call you."

"I want to talk to you, too. I think we'd better find a place where we can't be overheard. We can go up to my office. It's empty right now," replied Scott.

They walked over to the Professional Building together and took the elevator up to Dr. Perkins' suite of offices. They went into his consultation room.

"I'm a basket case," said Aronson. "I don't know how you can look so calm and be in so much trouble."

"It's a façade," replied Scott. "It's probably because I'm a surgeon. I'm supposed to be able to face severe stress every time I operate and calmly handle the problem."

"Has that guy gotten his blood tested yet?" asked Aronson.

"No. That's something I've got to talk to you about. He's flown the coop."

"What do you mean?"

"Just what I said. I spoke to him after the operation and told him that my finger was pricked and I was inoculated with his blood. And that because of that interrogation we did when he was coming out of anesthesia and the information we found out, we both needed to have our blood tested for AIDS. He was pissed off! He wasn't sure he'd have his blood tested."

"Why, that bastard. I'll squeeze the blood out of him."

"That won't help. That's no good now."

"What do you mean? Did he die or something?"

"No. I went over and spoke to him after the operation and he told me he'd give me his answer this morning after he'd had time to think about it."

"So. What's his answer?"

"That's the problem. Early this morning, he signed out of the hospital against advice and he's nowhere to be found."

"You've got to be shitting me! He can't do that!"

"Well, he did. It looks like you and I are in big trouble—only I'm in bigger trouble than you are. I got my finger stuck with his blood."

"I'm not so sure," replied Aronson. "He coughed all of his fucking blood-tinged mucous in my face. I probably inhaled some of his blood. I got a snootful of his crap. I'd like to kill the son-of-a-bitch. I could be just as infected as you might be."

"What do you base that on?"

"Well, you surgeons wear gowns, masks, and gloves to prevent direct contact with the patient's secretions. Anesthesiologists don't."

"Well, that's your own fault, then. Maybe all anesthesiologists should wear gowns, masks, and gloves."

"That's really not what I'm worried about. I'm worried about lung secretions that I might have inhaled. He spat all over my face when I tried to put a tube down his throat. A lot of these AIDS patients have severe lung problems that are caused by the virus. He could have pneumocystic carini pneumonia. A lot of AIDS patients get that."

"What are you talking about? He didn't look like he had any lung problems," said Scott. "His preoperative chest x-ray was negative."

"Well, animal studies suggest that pneumocystic carini pneumonia is transmitted through the air. You can have that problem without any big x-ray changes. There's also some evidence that you can isolate the AIDS virus from the tears of AIDS patients. I don't believe our infectious disease specialists know what they're doing. Besides, that bastard lied to us completely," said Aronson.

"Yeah, and he's a lawyer," said Scott. "Well, he's gone and the problem is how do we find him without letting the world know about *our* big problem?"

"What a revolting development!" said Aronson.

"I do know that we have to find him some way. But once we find him, what if he refuses to have his blood tested?"

"You can hold him down and I'll draw the blood from him."

"That's not a realistic answer," said Scott.

"I know. I talked to some of my medical colleagues in hematology today. The test itself can be inaccurate. Not all patients with AIDS have positive tests. A positive test for HIV antibody in an asymptomatic person can be due to a subclinical infection, immunity, or cross reactivity with other viruses. The test can also give false-positive results due to laboratory error."

"There's not too much doubt in my mind that Attorney Sousa will have a positive AIDS test. After all, his groin lymph nodes showed follicular hyperplasia," Scott reminded Aronson.

"That's right," said Aronson. "Sometimes there's a disadvantage to being a doctor. We know too much. That's why I've got pains in my stomach, chest pains, and on top of that, severe diarrhea. I'm even taking medication for all three maladies."

"Hopefully Robert Sousa won't test positive for AIDS, and all of our anxieties will be for naught," said Scott.

"It's not that easy," said Aronson. "AIDS has been reported as long as eight years after exposure."

"How do anesthesiologists protect themselves from getting the virus?"

"There is some good news. I've been doing some reading," said Aronson. "The viruses that cause AIDS are susceptible to many disinfectants, including 40% ethyl alcohol, 1% Lysol, 5% phenol and Clorox. When you wash your hands, if you use a chlorinated or halogenated soap, it's adequate to get rid of the organism."

"So, that's why I smell Clorox around the operating rooms after they've operated on an AIDS patient. They use Clorox to help sterilize the rooms. It stinks around there after they finish cleaning up. It actually smells like a swimming pool."

"That's right. That's why we're also using more disposable anesthesia tubes and other equipment in the operating room."

"That's another way of keeping the cost of medical care down, right?" said Scott.

"Well, how are we going to find Sousa?"

"I'm going to send you on a long train trip to look for him."

"Which direction do I go?" asked Aronson.

"That's the problem. I've decided to hire a private detective to locate him. Once we find him, we'll both present him with our problem."

"That sounds like the best idea. I hope it works and we find him before it's too late."

"I hope so, too."

CHAPTER

Scott gave it a lot of thought before hiring a detective to look for Attorney Robert Sousa. He had quite a few lawyer friends who he played golf with at the country club. One was the state's chief prosecuting attorney, John Adams. Scott spoke to him privately and he suggested hiring an experienced private investigator by the name of Harry Gray.

Scott called Mr. Gray and made arrangements to meet him at his office on a Saturday morning when no one else would be around and they'd be able to talk privately.

Harry Gray was a tall, gray-haired, middle-aged man. He was quite handsome with a gray-black mustache. He was approximately six feet tall and looked like he may have been a linebacker for a professional football team. He was also a bachelor.

Scott found out that he was a retired New York City detective and took jobs on consignment. Starting at the age of twenty he had worked with the New York City Police Department. He had a noticeable bulge over his left shoulder where he carried a .38 Smith and Wesson revolver.

Scott decided he wasn't going to mention anything about the AIDS problem when he talked to Harry Gray.

"Mr. Gray, I'm Dr. Scott Perkins and I need your help. You were highly recommended by a prosecuting attorney, John Adams."

"That's an interesting referral," replied Mr. Gray. "You must have a big problem or you have a lot of political clout."

"Not really, although I did operate on his wife. I guess that may have helped. I want you to try to locate someone for me. One of my patients skipped out of the hospital and he may have a serious health problem."

"Why don't you go to the State Health Department or the police about it?" he asked. "You don't need me."

"Yes, I do! You don't understand. It's actually quite complicated. You see, I want you to locate him and then come back and tell me where he is so I can talk to him about his health problem."

"This sounds fishy. You mean you want me to locate him and not bring him back?"

"That's right."

"That's not the way I usually work. What's wrong with this guy anyway?"

"It's not necessary for you to know that."

"Well, if I'm going to work for you and it's going to cost you money, you're going to have to be more explicit. What's this guy's name and what's he done wrong?"

"His name is Robert Sousa and he works in town for one of the big law firms. He signed out against advice from the hospital and he's left town. He could be very sick. You could be helping him also."

"Looking for a lawyer can be a tricky situation. My fee has to be higher."

"Just what is your fee?" asked Scott.

"I work two ways," replied the detective. "I can work as a bounty hunter and accept a certain set amount—say $10,000. Or I can work on a salary basis for which I'll need to be paid $750 a week plus expenses."

"How long do you think it will take you to find him?"

"I need more information before I can answer that. Is this guy dangerous? Does he carry a gun?"

"I don't believe he has a past criminal record but I'm not sure," replied Scott.

"Well, I'll need to get as much information about him as I can get. Where does he live? Where does he work? Do you have any photographs? I can also use any personal information you can provide."

"I think I can get some information from his hospital records. I do know he has a new left groin scar where I recently operated on him."

"Do you have any other identifying characteristics?"

"He's about five-feet, seven-inches tall and weighs about 140 pounds. He has blonde hair, blue eyes, and a small, upturned nose. He wears his hair in a ponytail."

"A lawyer wearing a ponytail?"

"That's right," replied Scott. "He looks quite effeminate. I asked him about that. He said back in the American Revolutionary War days, all the men wore ponytails—even George Washington."

"That's an interesting analogy. Do you happen to have his social security number?"

"That should be on his hospital record or in my office records. I should be able to get that for you."

"Am I hired?" he asked. "If you hire me, I'll need an advance for my expenses. How do you want to do it?"

"There's a time element involved here. I want to find Attorney Sousa as soon as possible. What's your bounty fee?"

"Ten thousand dollars," he replied. "Five thousand up front. I'll guarantee I'll find him within six weeks."

"I'll give you a bonus of $5,000 if you find him in three weeks."

"Fair enough," replied the detective, as his eyes lit up.

"You really want this guy bad, don't you?"

"Real bad!" said Scott. "How do you want me to make the check out?"

"Make it out to Harry Gray, Dunbar Detective Agency."

Scott wrote out the check and handed it to him.

"I'll have my secretary make copies of Robert Sousa's hospital record and my office records for you Monday morning. However, there will be nothing in his records about his medical history. I also want to remind you that everything you do for me is to be held in strict confidence. No one is to know what you're doing. Do you understand?"

"That's OK by me."

"Also, you're to report to me once a week on Friday at 5:30 P.M., after my office help leaves."

"That will be fine with me."

On Monday morning, Scott went to the hospital record room and got the shock of his life. Attorney Sousa's records were missing.

"Bring his records up on the computer."

"They haven't been typed up yet," replied the secretary.

"How about his admission records? They should be on the computer."

The secretary typed in the name and birth date. Nothing came up on the screen. "Are you sure of the name?" asked the secretary.

"Yes. What the hell's going on here?"

After seeing that, Scott went directly to the head of the record room, Mrs. Egan.

"Mrs. Egan, I operated on a patient Friday and he signed out against advice on Saturday and they can't find his record. In fact, his name isn't even on the computer."

"That's odd. There must be some mistake. Let me try. What's his name?"

"Robert Sousa."

Mrs. Egan tapped his name into the computer. Nothing came up but an error message.

"It's either been accidentally erased off the system or some other mistake has occurred. I'll see if I can find out for you."

She dialed a phone number and found out there had been no problem with the hospital computer system.

"I'll have to check this out, Dr. Perkins. I don't know why this happened."

He got on the phone and called his secretary, Judy. "Look in the files for Robert Sousa's chart."

"Hold on for a minute," said Judy.

She came back on the phone. "That's funny. His chart is here but the material inside is missing. It's got to be around here somewhere."

"That's great! I've got a bigger problem then I realized. They've lost his hospital records too!"

When he got back to his office, he called Detective Gray and told him what had happened.

"Looks like you have a dangerous attorney on the loose. He's really trying to cover his tracks—steals his hospital chart and breaks into your office to get your records. He has to be clever to do that in such a short period of time. Don't worry about it. I have some friends at the State Tax Department. I'll get his social security number and other information over there. If I have any difficulty, I'll give you a call."

"No, Mr. Gray. I think I want to meet with you today and discuss this recent development," replied Scott.

"I'll be at your office at 5:30," he replied.

At 5:30, Detective Harry Gray walked into Dr. Perkins' waiting room. The office was completely empty except for Dr. Perkins, who was visibly nervous when he saw the detective.

"I'm in a quandary. I don't know what to do after these recent developments," Scott remarked.

"Well, don't get too upset. After your call I went over to the law firm where Attorney Sousa worked. There's some good news! The senior secretary knew me and was very cooperative. I've dealt with that law firm before. I was able to get Sousa's social security number. She also located a photograph taken for his security identification card. He's in trouble with the law firm, too! He was working on a couple of sensitive tax cases. He took some confidential papers with him when he left. They're as mad as you are."

"Well, if they're so mad maybe they'll help me pay for some of your expenses."

"They're not that mad. They want to find him and the records just as much as you do but they're unwilling to pay."

"How do I know you're not working for them, too?"

"You don't. But if you don't trust me, you'd better get someone else to work for you."

"I didn't mean to offend you. I'm sorry. I'm a little on edge. How do you plan to go about finding this guy?"

"I'm going to do some snooping around here first. I think this guy is acting like he's going to get out of town. He's definitely on the lam. I'll check with some friends of mine at the cab company. Sousa's car is still in the garage at his condo. It's a piece of junk. I checked on that. I got the security guard at the condo complex to let me look at his place and it's ransacked and he's gone! Most of his clothes and personal belongings are gone—including all his wife's stuff."

"Give me a call if you find out anything."

"Don't worry, I'll be checking in with you often, since you're paying the bills."

Three days later, he called Dr. Perkins. "I'm flying to Dallas. I think I got a good lead on Sousa and his wife."

"What's up?" asked Scott.

"I found out from the security guard at the condo that Sousa and his wife took a Yellow cab at about 6:00 P.M. on Wednesday. I contacted the Yellow cab people. The drivers have to call in their destination every time they pick up rides and it's recorded at the base. I showed the ID picture of Sousa to a bunch of cabies and one of them recognized him. I greased his palm and he told me that he had dropped them off at the Delta airline departure area at the airport. I checked with Delta and found out that Sousa's destination was Dallas. I'll be going to Dallas."

"Well, good luck. Keep in touch. I hope you find the bastard."

"Dr. Perkins, Dr. Bill Clark, the new chief of surgery, is on the phone," said Judy.

"What does he want?"

"He didn't say. He mentioned something about a committee they were forming."

"Tell him to hold while I finish taking these sutures out of Mrs. Robinson."

After he finished, Scott picked up the phone.

"Hi, Bill. What can I do for you?"

"Scott, we have a few problems developing in the hospital concerning the AIDS virus and how it affects the hospital personnel. Some of the young doctors, nurses, and IV people have a lot of questions."

"Tell me about it. So do I—no one knows the answers, unfortunately."

"That's why we're forming the committee."

"What's that got to do with me?"

"We had a meeting of the executive committee today and it was decided that we should form a new committee to deal with the problem. I want you to serve on that committee. A lot of AIDS patients die from cancer and you have expertise in that area."

"I need to take a crash course about AIDS myself, for personal reasons. How often will the committee meet?"

"Once a month, or as needed," replied Bill.

"When are they having the first meeting?"

"Friday at 5:00 P.M. We have a problem that needs to be resolved."

"I'll be there."

"Judy, call the Medical Library and tell them to do a Medline literature search on the AIDS virus for me. Tell them I want the material stat. I need to read up on the subject."

The next day, Judy went to the library and picked up the data and Scott took it home. The material was an eye-opener. Most of the literature was from the Center for Disease Control in Atlanta, Georgia. It was scary. Some of the statistics were estimated because it was impossible to accurately tell how many people were actually infected with the human immunodeficiency virus (HIV).

It is thought that almost a million people in the country are infected with the AIDS virus—half of whom would develop AIDS within eight years. The AIDS virus has been isolated from blood and body fluids of infected individuals. The infection is transmitted through homosexual or heterosexual contact, by contaminated needles or blood products, and from an infected mother to her child in the prenatal period.

After reading the material and being personally involved with the AIDS problem, Scott decided to talk to Bill Clark. He also decided he wouldn't tell him about his own problem with the needle stick.

"Bill, I didn't realize what a big problem this AIDS virus is creating. It looks like it's going to be worse than the bubonic plague. From looking at the research literature, physicians and health care workers, particularly surgeons, nurses, and intravenous personnel who have contact with blood are at the greatest risk to get AIDS."

"That's right," replied Clark. "That's why I want you on that committee. We have a lot of big problems developing right here at this hospital. The number of AIDS cases being admitted is increasing every year. It's already hit home in our department. One of our best surgical residents is going to quit the surgical training program because he doesn't want to put his wife and kids at risk if he acquires the AIDS virus."

"Has he been tested?"

"No. But he's been exposed to seven patients with AIDS who had to have operations. He can't handle the stress associated with the job. He claims he could have the AIDS virus right now and his blood test could be negative."

"He's right," replied Scott. "Unfortunately! This AIDS problem is escalating. It hits at home, too! I had a recent personal problem and I also had a problem in my office just the other day with my office personnel.

"Dr. White, one of the medical oncologists, referred an attractive young lady who needed some lymph nodes in her neck biopsied for a possible tumor (lymphoma). I took the nodes out and the pathologists said her glands were suggestive of AIDS. Dr. Scranton from the Infectious Disease Department saw her and did a blood survey and she tested positive for AIDS."

"What's that got to do with your office personnel?"

"I have two nurses who work part-time for me in the examining rooms when I see the patients. When they found out the patient had AIDS they refused to work in that examination room."

"What did you do?"

"I had to have the room disinfected with Clorox. That cost me a few bucks!"

"That's ridiculous! The AIDS virus can't fly over and bite them."

"You know that and I know that because we're doctors, but try to convince the public and the personnel who work in medical offices."

"The biggest risk for health care workers is the transmission of AIDS by accidental needle sticks."

"Tell me about it," said Scott. "Surgeons get stuck all the time."

"I know," replied Clark.

"How are we going to prevent the transmission of the AIDS virus to surgeons?"

"We have to have universal precautions on all patients to prevent exposure to the virus. Masks, waterproof gowns, eye coverings, and gloves have to be worn."

"A needle can go right through a glove and even double gloving doesn't protect."

"That's right. That's just one of the problems. The cost of all this precautionary equipment will raise the cost of health care. The liberal politicians will scream," said Scott.

"In the future, nobody's going to want to be a surgeon if the risk for getting AIDS gets too high. The smart college students will all want to be lawyers or brokers—they can complete their education in seven years. Look at you, Scott, how many years of postgraduate education did you take to become a cancer surgeon?"

"Sixteen years," said Scott.

"You're a dying breed. The risk factors are increasing rapidly. They outweigh the rewards for the surgeon. Besides, laws have been passed to prevent identification of AIDS patients to preserve their confidentiality and prevent discrimination."

"I don't agree with that law," said Scott. "I think all patients who are admitted to the hospital and all doctors should be tested for AIDS."

"That'll never happen. There are too many homosexual politicians making the laws," said Clark.

"Once the public becomes provoked about these problems they'll force the politicians to change the laws."

"I don't think so. It's that same old problem—gridlock in Washington and gridlock at home."

"After our discussion, I see I've made a good decision in putting you on that committee. I'll see you at the meeting on Friday."

When he finished office hours on Friday, Scott went to the hospital boardroom to meet with the committee. There were nine committee members: the chief of infectious disease, two medical oncologists, three surgeons (including Scott), the director of nursing, the head of the IV Therapy Department, a hospital administrator, and Bill Clark.

A brief summary of the developments at Jefferson Hospital was presented to the group by the chief of infectious disease, Dr. Scranton. His comments were ominous.

"The number of patients with AIDS being admitted to Whitestone Hospital is rapidly increasing. The cost for universal precautions is significant—close to one million dollars a year. Most of that cost is for gloves, disposable gowns, and receptacles for disposing of blood and waste products. There is also a significant number of inadvertent needle sticks. Problems in nursing care for AIDS patients are developing. Many AIDS patients have insufficient insurance. Most of these patients are young. Many are black men in the 25-to-45 age group. Some patients with AIDS are drug abusers who give birth to infants with AIDS. Until those infants die, the cost of caring for them is prohibitive. The cost of caring for any AIDS patient is rapidly increasing. Drug costs are exorbitant."

After Dr. Scranton finished talking, the head of the nursing department, Mrs. Mason, spoke.

"We've had a problem recently in regard to care given to AIDS patients in this hospital. As you all know, we cannot identify AIDS patients without their permission and many of the personnel, including nurses, do not want to take care of these patients. Their attitude is that these people created their own problem by their actions and the nurses don't have very much sympathy for them. Also, you have to have written permission from the patient in order to test for AIDS. However, it doesn't take too long for the hospital personnel to figure out which patients have AIDS because they're usually the sickest ones. Unfortunately, some patients have AIDS and you can't tell. Two weeks ago we had a crisis concerning an AIDS patient on North 31. I'll try to describe what happened.

"When the night shift came on, three of the nurses had called in sick. Float nurses had to be assigned to cover that floor. There were only two float nurses available, so one of the supervisors helped out. Unfortunately, there were some sick patients on North 31, including two AIDS patients who were in end rooms. One of the float nurses was six months pregnant. She was assigned to take care of one of the AIDS patients who was dying and had pneumocystis (lung disease) and needed constant suctioning of mucous.

"The nurse refused to take care of the patient once she realized he had AIDS. She said she didn't want to expose her baby to the possibility of getting AIDS.

"The night supervisor told her she was fired if she didn't take care of the patient. She told the supervisor that if she would help take care of the patient, she'd do her job. The supervisor refused. The young pregnant nurse walked off the floor."

"That's a tough one to handle," said one of the surgeons.

"That's not the end of the story," said Mrs. Mason. "The nurse got a lawyer and we received a letter. She wanted her job back. The girl was a good nurse and an excellent worker. When the word got out to the rest of the nursing staff, the staff nursing council said she ought to be reinstated. The letter mentioned the possibility of some type of job action if she wasn't rehired. Her case went to arbitration and she got her job back."

"I can understand that young nurse's attitude," said Scott. "She wasn't just worried about herself, she was worried about her unborn baby."

"The problem is not as simple as it sounds," said Mrs. Mason. "A lot of our nursing personnel don't want to take care of AIDS patients. Period! We can't discriminate and ration care. It's a real problem."

Joyce, Karen, Kim, Sally and Lillian were sitting on the edge of two of the operating room stretchers shooting the bull and relaxing before the operating room schedule began. Robert Potter, a new addition to the OR staff at Jefferson Hospital, sat on a bench near the stretchers. He was the new instrument engineer.

As usual, the operating rooms were all prepared with sterile instrument set-ups for each case, packaged and covered with sterile drapes.

Karen, one of the senior head nurses, spoke up. "What's your surgeon up to today, Sally?"

"He's booked in to do a pelvic exenteration, one of those horrendoma cases! You know, they take the colon, bladder, and the female organs out."

"What's left?" asked Joyce.

"The brain, heart, and lungs. Not much more."

"Why does he do it?"

"It's a surgical challenge," replied Sally.

"You mean he's on an ego trip."

"You might consider it that," she replied.

"Would you have it done?" asked Kim.

"Not me. I'd have a scotch and water drip."

"What do you mean?"

"Just what I said. I like drinking good scotch and water. I'd have them put it in an intravenous line in my veins and just let it run."

"That's not a bad idea," said Sally.

"With those big exenteration cases, there's nothing left to really live for. No sex, no thrill out of a good bowel movement and lots of difficult peeing."

"But the patient's alive," said Karen.

"Where did your surgeon learn how to do that operation?" asked Kim.

"Out of books and working on patients," said Sally.

"Did he train at a cancer center?"

"Not that I know of."

"Don't the patients ask about his training background?"

"They're too scared to ask, but they should."

"I'd want to know all about my surgeon's background before I'd let him operate on me," said Kim.

"Has your surgeon had good results with those pelvic exenterations?" asked Joyce.

"I can't answer that. I never see the patients once they leave my operating room. I do know the surgical residents don't like to take care of them, though."

"Why?"

"Because they get every complication in the book, and they catch hell if they don't take care of them properly."

"Don't you have any good news today?" asked Joyce.

"Yeah. Most of my surgeons' cases are inoperable. I hear this one is a good possiblity. It means I'll have a long coffee break between cases. I'll be thinking of you."

"I'll bet you will," said Joyce.

Lillian, an OR technician, broke into the conversation. She stuck out her chest and said, "We're going to be doing laparoscopic surgery today in my operating room! It's the wave of the future— Star Wars, I call it. We're going to pluck out a few gall-bladders."

"Sounds spacey," said Sally.

"And expensive," replied Joyce.

"Complicated," said Robert Potter. "I've got more video monitor screens scattered around these operating rooms than they use at NASA."

"That's the only equipment that's not disposable," said Lillian. "That's one of the reasons why the cost of health care is soaring out of sight."

"It's got to be disposable," said Potter, "because of all those lethal infections floating around. Would you want to get AIDS from contaminated instruments?"

"Nope. If I get AIDS, I'm going to get it from sex."

"You can get hepatitis from contaminated blood," said Kim. "That can kill you too! It destroys the liver and then you bleed to death."

"That might be better than dying from AIDS or cancer," said Joyce.

"Where are the surgeons learning how to do all these laparoscopic operations?" asked Sally.

"They learn by operating on pigs. They take two- or three-day courses somewhere down south. The surgeons call it Band-Aid surgery because they no longer have to make those big, muscle-splitting incisions. They cut a few small holes in the abdomen so they can put a light and camera inside. The camera is attached to a video monitor, which gives them a close-up view of the area to be operated on. Then, they put CO_2 gas into the belly to blow it up like a balloon so they have more room to see. Delicate, sophisticated, disposable surgical instruments are inserted into other holes in the belly so they can cut the gallbladder out, cauterize, and clip the blood vessels to prevent bleeding."

"Are all the surgeons doing these operations?" asked Joyce.

"Some of the older surgeons are having trouble. The younger hotshots seem to do better," said Karen.

"Well, you can't teach an old dog new tricks," said Lillian.

"That's not the reason," said Joyce. "It's because they're in a different generation—you know, the generation gap. As kids, the new surgeons grew up with pinball machines, Pac Man, and Nintendo games. That's how some of them learned good eye-hand coordination."

"Have you seen any complications yet?"

"Yep. There's a learning curve for the surgeons. If you're a patient, you'd better not be at the beginning of that learning curve."

"I know that one of our surgeons, the one we call Slow Motion, got into big trouble the other day. He was shoving one of those big trocars into the belly through the umbilicus. You know, that sharp-pointed instrument they use to make a hole to pass the laparoscopy scope through. Well, he pushed it in too fast and too far and made a hole in the aorta."

"What happened?" three of the girls asked in unison.

"The shit hit the fan," said Joyce. "Suddenly there was so much blood in the belly that the surgeon couldn't see anything on the monitor. Luckily, he cracked the abdomen open immediately. 'Get a vascular surgeon, pronto,' he screamed. 'We got a big hole in the aorta!'

"Dr. Chu, one of the vascular surgeons, was down the hall and came right in and repaired the hole. Her belly was full of blood."

"It's a good thing Slow Motion saw the bleeding. I'm surprised he responded so quickly."

"I don't think we're going to call him Slow Motion anymore after that episode," said Joyce. "He finally woke up. He almost had a heart attack."

"Did the patient make it?"

"Yep. But now she's got a scar that goes from her chest to her pubis. It's like a long zipper."

"Well, at least she's alive."

"I read in the newspaper that some of these laparoscopic patients have bled to death and others have had to undergo multiple surgeries to reconstruct the biliary drainage system from the liver."

"I wish you people would hush up!" said Lillian. "I've got lots of small stones in my own gallbladder."

"When are you going to have yours taken out with a laparoscope?"

"Not until that learning curve gets better, honey. I might never have it done. Lots of people die peacefully with their gallstones still in that gallbladder sac."

"Quiet down, girls," said Karen, the OR supervisor. "Let's get back to work. Here comes three busy surgeons down the hall: Popeye, Big Mac, and Hot Knife."

"Well, there are three millionaires," said Sally.

"Wait a minute. Oh! Oh! The Grim Reaper's walking behind them. Who's got him today?"

"I do," said Kim. "I'm already getting a splitting headache."

"What's Hot Knife up to?" asked Karen.

"He's doing a liver resection for cancer."

"Who's giving anesthesia for you today?" asked Sally.

"Dr. Nelson," said Joyce. "He's in the room setting things up.

Dr. Perkins is going to use a fancy new device to cut through the liver. It uses an argon beam that coagulates and cuts the tissue."

"Things have really changed in surgery, haven't they?" said Lillian.

"You can say that again," replied Joyce. "Everything is getting more mechanical. It's almost like robot surgery. I was around when Dr. Perkins did one of the first successful liver resections in this hospital twenty years ago. At that time, you really had to know your anatomy and how to operate to get a liver patient off the table.

"Before you did any cutting, you had to meticulously dissect and tie off the arterial blood supply to the liver segment being removed, tie off the venous drainage and bile drainage, and then individually tie the blood vessels as you cut through the mushy liver."

Just then Dr. Perkins arrived outside his operating room and stopped to talk to Joyce. "Joyce, how are you today?"

"Fine, Dr. Perkins. I see we have a big case."

"That's right. There'll be some visiting doctors in to watch. I'm going to use that new argon beam coagulator to cut through the liver. Did the technicians from the company set up the equipment?"

"Yes. They were here at 6:00 A.M.," answered Joyce.

"We'll do an anatomical dissection first to tie off the major blood supply, just to be safe, in case that new equipment doesn't work. That Argon beam coagulator worked beautifully in the laboratory last week on some of the dogs we did, so it should be all right."

"How are the dogs doing?" asked Joyce.

"They're all alive and well," replied Scott. "They regenerate their livers better than humans."

"The patient you're doing today is young to be having a liver resection."

"She had a colon cancer operation done three years ago at St. Mary's Hospital," he replied. "Now she's got a tumor mass in the right lobe of her liver. Make sure we have enough blood on call in case we need it. We also may need the surgical staplers."

Stacy, the scrub nurse, helped dress the surgeons. Scott was handed a sterile towel to dry his hands and arms.

The chief resident surgeon prepped the patient's entire chest and abdomen with a Betadine cleansing solution. Sterile drapes were then placed around the surgical area.

After Dr. Perkins and his assisting resident surgeons were completely dressed by the chief scrub nurse, Scott spoke to Dr. Joe Pike, who would be across the operating table from him, assisting in the operation.

"Joe, why don't you briefly tell these visiting doctors about this patient's problem."

"Yes, sir," replied Dr. Pike, as he turned and faced the visiting doctors.

In a loud voice he said, "Mrs. Collins is a 49-year-old white female who had a colon resection for cancer three years ago at St. Mary's Hospital. The tumor was large and had penetrated outside the wall of the bowel and a few glands around the tumor were involved with cancer. A CT scan done at that time was negative for spread of her tumor to the liver or other areas of her body.

"As most of you know, there is a new test now used to follow these patients, that is sometimes helpful in determining spread. It is particularly helpful in colon cancer cases and is called a CEA blood test for chorioembryonic antigen. If that test is done and the levels rise dramatically, one should look for a recurrent cancer.

"This patient had a rising CEA six months ago, and an exploration was done by another surgeon at St. Mary's Hospital and nothing could be found.

"Two weeks ago, a CT scan was done and showed a single large tumor in the right lobe of the liver. A complete work-up was done, looking for other areas of involvement and there were none. Radiologists then did a needle biopsy. The needle, with a cutting edge at the end, was directed into the mass in the liver under x-ray control, and a piece of the tumor was removed.

"The tissue was examined by a pathologist and was similar to the colon cancer that had been removed from her bowel three years ago. Dr. Perkins plans to do a complete right hepatic lobectomy."

Scott took his place on the right side of the operating table. The head scrub nurse, Miss Sharp, was opposite him to hand him instruments as he worked. He glanced over at the senior anesthesiologist and said, "OK to start?"

"Yes," replied Dr. Nelson.

Scott's right forefinger went out and a scalpel was firmly placed in his hand. He quickly made a large T-shaped incision, first going across the upper abdomen and then into the chest, cutting the diaphragm. He placed two vascular loops around the major vein (vena cava) placing one loop above and one below the liver. If a tear or a hole occurs in that vein, the loop can be tightened down to cut down on the blood loss.

Then he dissected down to the major arterial, venous, and biliary drainage areas of the liver. Since the right lobe was being resected, he isolated the right hepatic artery, right branch of the portal vein, and right hepatic bile duct and tied them off.

"I'll take the Argon beam coagulator."

He slowly manipulated the device through the capsule of the liver in the middle, and began cutting through the soft, mushy substance. There was very little bleeding except for a few large veins and sinuses that he closed with suture ligatures. As the operation proceeded, his assistant gently rotated the liver to the left so Scott could see the small veins on the undersurface that drained into the large vein going to the heart. Special vascular clamps were applied as he gently tied and divided the veins. The gallbladder had already been removed. He completed the resection. The chief resident surgeon was told to close the wound and Scott retired to the doctor's lounge.

"That's a neat device, that Argon beam coagulator," said one of the visiting doctors.

"Yes, it is," replied Scott. "Some of these new devices are making bad surgeons look like good surgeons. There's one problem though. It isn't 100 percent foolproof, so the surgeons had better know how to do the operation the old way, in case the gadget doesn't work. That also applies to all those laparoscopic cholecystectomies. You'd better know how to do a removal of the gallbladder—the old-fashioned way—in case there's a problem."

"What's the five-year survival rate on liver resections?" asked one of the visiting surgeons.

"About twenty-five percent," replied Scott. "Not great. But it beats dying."

"I'd agree with that."

CHAPTER

"Dr. Perkins, Dr. Brenda Sawyer is on the phone," said Judy.

"Who is Dr. Sawyer?"

"She's a new medical oncologist on the staff who trained at the Dana Farber Cancer Institute in Boston. I hear she's really smart."

"Thanks for the briefing," he replied as he picked up the phone. "This is Scott Perkins."

"Dr. Perkins, I have a patient who needs surgery and is requesting your services. She's a sophomore college student at the University of Pennsylvania."

"What's her problem?"

"She's been working at a summer job and has had chronic fatigue. She's developed some enlarged glands in her left neck."

"I could do a needle biopsy if you want me to," replied Scott.

"I've already done the needle biopsy. Dr. Blackstone, the cytologist, says the biopsy has mixed cellularity and is not specific for tumor. I want you to take a gland out so we can really study the tissue."

"Is she in your office now?"

"Yes. Her parents are with her and they're frantic."

"Send her down and I'll work her in this afternoon. I'm in suite 411."

"That's great."

That afternoon, Scott saw the patient, Ellen Ross, a pretty blonde college student, 20 years old, with a trim figure and broad smile.

"Tell me about your problem. How long have you been sick?"

"About six weeks. I feel lousy. I don't have any energy. I'm tired all the time."

"Has Dr. Sawyer done any blood work on you?"

"Yes. She said they were all pretty normal. She told me I don't have infectious mono."

"Have you noticed any other symptoms? Any fever? Any burning on urination or any stomach upsets?"

"Not at all, but I do have some glands in my neck. Dr. Sawyer stuck a needle into one of them. I guess that's why I'm here."

Scott took a closer look at her. She looked like a typical college student.

"Do you take the birth control pill?"

"Every girl in my freshman class takes the pill."

"That's interesting. Do you have a boyfriend?"

"Nothing permanent," she replied. "I don't date too much. I've had to study. I'm not the brightest student and I don't want to flunk out. My education costs too much."

Scott did an indirect laryngoscopy, looking in her throat with a light and a mirror. Her oral cavity appeared normal. He felt her neck and could feel enlarged glands on both sides. The glands in her left neck were bigger than the right and were easily palpable. He examined her abdomen and thought he could feel the tip of her spleen. She certainly was a suspect for a glandular cancer—a lymphoma. She looked chronically fatigued and sick.

"When do you have to be back at college?"

"In two weeks."

"Hmm. That presents a little problem. It might take us a few days to get you into the hospital and on the operating schedule. You will need a recuperative period after the surgery."

"Could I have it done in Philadelphia? I don't want to miss my classes."

"It's all right with me if it's all right with your parents. I have a good friend who trained with me in New York who's professor of surgery at Jefferson Medical College—Dr. Richard Knight."

"That sounds better for me."

Dr. Perkins discussed Ellen's problem with her parents in his consultation room. They were quite anxious and, at first, were reluctant for her to have her surgery in Philadelphia.

"It's really a minor operation. They take a gland out for analysis and she has a few stitches in the left neck."

Ellen and her parents finally agreed on Philadelphia.

"Please have Dr. Knight send me a follow-up note about his findings," Scott requested.

As Ellen Ross left the office, Judy spoke to Dr. Perkins. "What do you think her problem is?"

"I think she's got a lymphoma. She'll end up getting chemotherapy and radiation. She may need a staging procedure also to see if she has any cancer in her abdomen. Who's our last patient today?"

"George Hayes, a good friend of yours. He called yesterday and said he wants to talk to you about a personal matter."

"Did he give you any idea what it was about?"

"No, and since he is a close personal friend I didn't pursue it."

"Well, have Karen bring him down to my consultation room."

George Hayes was the president of a computer company that designed programs for large corporations. He was Scott's frequent golfing partner and occasional dinner guest at his home.

As George walked into Scott's office he looked quite anxious and disturbed. He shut the door behind him.

"Scott, I've got a horrible problem and I need your advice and help. I want everything I tell you to be kept in strictest confidence."

"Of course, George. What's this problem that you think is so horrible?"

"I'll try to make it brief. Six weeks ago I flew out to a computer convention in San Francisco. Margie wasn't with me. I was staying at that beautiful hotel—the St. Francis. The second day I was there I was sitting in the lobby area in those soft chairs where they have the piano player and girls dressed in Japanese kimonos serving you fancy drinks.

"Well, this gorgeous young thing came along and sat down in a lounging chair next to me and I bought her a drink. One drink led to another, and another, and then I took her out to dinner. She wasn't a routine pick-up. She was quite intelligent and a good conversationalist. She was beautifully dressed and was very pretty and athletic-looking. She also had a high-rise apartment overlooking the San Francisco Bay area. I spent six evenings sleeping and making love to that young lady in her apartment. She was gorgeous and knew all the tricks. I learned a few new ones, too. It was an exhausting, but tremendously satisfying, week."

"It sounds like you had a good time."

"Well, I did. This girl had a beautiful body—about five feet six inches tall, 130 pounds, and full, upright, firm breasts. She had narrow hips and a flat belly, beautiful curves to her buttocks, and long sinewy legs. On top of that, her face was beautiful, with full luscious lips and gorgeous teeth. When she kissed me, I felt it in the tips of my toes and when she rotated her moist, sharp-pointed tongue—man, I felt like I was on a trip to the moon."

"You really don't have to go into all the intimate details," said Scott. "I hope you used condoms."

"No. Damn it! She said she was on the pill. I did use some of those antibiotics I had left that you gave me when I went to Europe last year. By the time the week was up she didn't want to leave me and I didn't want to leave her. She said she was madly in love with me and wanted to fly back East. Man, I knew if I stayed another week, I'd be dead. She knew more different ways and positions to have sex than anyone I ever knew. I couldn't satisfy her. She said she had been so frustrated the last six months before her divorce that she would have slept with a gorilla if she could. I think she was a nymphomaniac. She really knew how to rotate her butt. She couldn't get enough of me. 'Let's get married. I think I could be happy with you,' she said."

"George, I told you you didn't have to go into the intimate details to make your point!"

"But you need to know the full background," replied George. "I told her that getting married was an impossibility and that I was already happily married. She told me about her divorce settlement and how she'd received over a million dollars, including the apartment overlooking the bay.

"I'm fifty-three years old and she was a young-looking thirty-four. I had a fleeting thought of quickly retiring and moving out to San Francisco. I suppressed that thought but did give her my business address and phone number."

"It sounds like you had a gal with hot pants. Why are you telling me all this?"

"Well, when I got back home, I tried to forget about her but it wasn't easy. That is, until two days ago when I got a phone call from her. It was a real bombshell."

"What? Is she pregnant?"

"No. Much worse than that. She said that she had tested positive for AIDS and she was accusing me of giving it to her."

"Holy Christmas!" said Scott. "You sure she isn't trying to con you out of some money?"

"It's not that simple. She's scared me shitless. If she's got AIDS then I could have AIDS! When I got back from San Francisco, Margie and I got together like we usually do after I've been on a trip. Do you realize that my wife could have AIDS too, if I got it from that girl in San Francisco?"

"Yes, I do," replied Scott. "I also happen to think that you have a lovely wife."

"What should I do now? You're my buddy and you're a doctor. You've got to help me!"

"I'll call Dick Scranton, the Chief of Infectious Disease, and see if he can see you and give you some advice. I think you have to get a blood test to see if you do have AIDS."

"Anything you say, Doc. What should I tell Margie?"

"I think you have to tell her. Make a full confession. I also think you need to get a lawyer."

"What a mess!" said George.

"That's the understatement of the year."

Six months later, George Hayes called Scott and told him that he had tested positive for AIDS. His wife was negative, but for how long, no one could tell.

Scott received a letter from Dr. Knight in Philadelphia about Ellen Ross. She also had AIDS. The glands in her neck were the tip of the iceberg. Multiple blood tests all came back positive. She was in the advanced stages of her disease and was started on AZT and DDI. Ellen had been sleeping with a former marine captain who had been discharged from the service and was a graduate student at the university. He was a bisexual. He knew he had AIDS when he dated her. She had lied about her cohabitation and had been sleeping with the marine captain all during her freshman year.

CHAPTER

7

Scott had a busy operative schedule. In a short period of time, he learned quite a bit about AIDS—but nothing that could help him.

He didn't hear from Detective Gray for seven weeks. He was pissed off. He was supposed to hear from him every week on Friday afternoon.

Finally, he received a collect, long-distance call from Dallas, Texas.

"Dr. Perkins, this is Detective Gray. I think I'm on to something big here in Dallas."

"It better be good," said Scott. "You were supposed to call me every week. Where the hell have you been?"

"I was on Sousa's trail and I got close, but the prey slipped away. Before I flew to Dallas, I checked on his friends from when he was at New York University Law School."

"How did you do that?"

"I drove down to New York City and stopped at the New York University Law School. Whenever a law school graduates a class, they photograph all the graduates and put them into a yearbook. I was able to make a copy of the names and photographs.

"Sousa's former roommate lives in Dallas, Texas. He's an assistant state's district attorney down there by the name of Bill Carroll.

"I thought Sousa might want to look up some of his old friends. I slipped the security guard another twenty dollar bill to let me look around again in his condo. Some recent unpaid phone bills were lying around. I checked some long-distance phone calls he made. There were three recent calls, all to the same number in Dallas. I called the number. The person who answered said, 'Attorney William Carroll's residence.' That's all I needed. I hung up, flew to Dallas, looked up the address, and staked out the place.

"Evidently, he's one of those, if you know what I mean. He's a faggot. He likes boys instead of girls. There was a whole stable that kept coming to his house—no females. This guy's a real queer. In fact, he's running a male den of iniquity.

"I kept looking for someone who looked like Sousa but no one fit the description. Finally, early one morning, a man came out of the place who looked like Sousa and got into Carroll's car. I followed him. He drove to downtown Dallas and went into the district attorney's office. I was in a dilemma as to what I should do. I couldn't confront him there.

"I didn't have a subpoena and I remembered that you wanted me to call you to give you his location. I waited for him to come out. It was Sousa! He came out with a guy who fits the description of Bill Carroll and I followed them to the Dallas-Fort Worth Airport. I got in line behind them and listened to their whole conversation. The two took an American Airlines plane to New Orleans where they were going to the American Bar Association's annual meeting. Evidently, Sousa's wife was going to meet them there. The plane was full so I couldn't get a seat. I'm calling from the Dallas Airport. I've got a reservation on a flight tonight. Fortunately, I found out what hotel they're staying at."

"How'd you find that out?"

"I called Carroll's secretary and told her I was an attorney who went to school with her boss and I was going to be in New Orleans. I needed to contact him about the reunion.

" 'That's simple,' she said. 'He's staying at the New Orleans Hilton at 2 Poydras Street on the Mississippi River.'"

"You mean she gave you all that information without asking who you were?"

"I told her I was the district attorney from Manhattan. That opened her mouth."

"Do you want me to fly into New Orleans?"

"Not yet," said Detective Gray. "He's up to something. When he stays put, I'll call you."

"Well, it sounds like you're finally doing your job. Don't lose him!"

Three days later, Scott received a call from New Orleans.

"I think we've got our man," said Detective Gray, "but he's up to something or else he's really sick."

"Oh no. I hope he doesn't have AIDS," said Scott. "Why do you think he's sick?"

"I followed him in a cab to the professional building next to the Tulane University Medical Center on Tulane Avenue here in New Orleans. He saw Dr. Jonathon Smith, a surgeon. He was in his office for about an hour and a half."

"Hold on for a minute. I have a directory of specialists in my office. I'll look up that Dr. Smith."

Scott looked through the medical directory and found Dr. Jonathon Smith. He was listed as a member of the American Board of Plastic Surgeons.

"Dr. Smith's a plastic surgeon," he told Gray.

"I wonder if Sousa's going to get a face lift to change his identity."

"Are you sure it's Robert Sousa?"

"One hundred percent. He's escorting a young lady around who looks like she's pregnant. It's probably his wife."

"Is she a blonde or a brunette?" asked Scott.

"She's a brunette."

"That's her. It's got to be him. I'll cancel my surgery and fly down tomorrow."

"What are you going to do?" asked the detective.

"That's my problem. I've got to talk to him. I'm going to confront him and ask him to agree to a blood test."

"What's that for?"

"I'll tell you about it when it's all over. Keep an eye on him until I get down there. I'll call you in the morning before I leave the hotel and tell you what time I'm arriving."

Detective Gray decided to sit in the lobby that night to make sure Sousa didn't check out. Around 8:00 P.M. he saw Sousa and his wife come into the lobby with Bill Carroll and go to the main ballroom of the Hilton where the American Bar Association was having their annual banquet.

The men were dressed in tuxedos and Sousa's wife was wearing a long black and gold gown. Around midnight, Sousa came out of the ballroom alone and went up to his room. An hour later, he came down to the bar in the lobby, and had a drink with what looked like two other lawyers. He went up to his room again around 3:00 A.M. Sousa's wife and the assistant D.A. from Dallas came out of the ballroom around 3:00 A.M. and took an elevator. I decided not to go to bed. I stayed in the lobby and snoozed in a chair. Around 4:00 A.M. I saw Sousa get off the elevator. He looked like he was in a hurry. He grabbed a cab. I decided to follow him in another cab.

Sousa's cab went to the New Orleans Airport and Sousa caught an early American Airlines flight to San Francisco. He was alone.

Gray called Perkins from the airport. "Attorney Sousa's flown the coop again."

"What do you mean?"

"He checked out of the Hilton and got on a plane to San Francisco."

"Well, I guess I don't need to fly down to New Orleans. Are you planning to go after him?"

"I'm not sure. I may have to. Unless you want me to wait around here. I'm sure he's going to come back to his wife eventually. I could tail her for a while."

"What do you think is best?"

"I think I ought to stay here. A bird in the hand is worth two in the bush. I wouldn't know where to look for him in San Francisco."

"That makes me nervous," said Scott.

"There's something else I have to talk to you about. Wire me some more money. This Hilton Hotel is expensive," said Gray.

"How much do you need?"

"Send another five grand."

The next afternoon, Scott got an urgent call from Detective Gray. He shut his office door and took the call.

"There's been a horrible development down here in New Orleans."

"What's wrong? What happened?"

"It's all over the newspapers."

"What do you mean?"

"The assistant district attorney from Dallas and a young, attractive brunette were found dead in bed in the nude at the Hilton. They were each shot behind the ear. It's front-page headlines. The story says that they're looking for the killer. Robbery was not a motive because no money or jewelry was missing although there was no identification found on the woman. I'm sure it's Sousa's wife. The lady was approximately five months pregnant. What do you want me to do?"

"What do you mean?"

"Well, I know who did it. If not, he's a prime suspect. He's on his way to San Francisco. The New Orleans police should be told."

"Do you think they'll believe your story? What are you going to tell the police? I might be dragged into the investigation," said Scott.

"I don't think they'll believe my story. I'm sure the police have identified the body of the Assistant D.A. from Dallas. It was in the paper. It's only a matter of time before they identify the woman's body. They'll call Carroll's office in Dallas and find out who he was meeting at the Hilton in New Orleans.

"That will help identify the woman's body. They'll probably go looking for Sousa right after that. He and his wife might have registered under an assumed name, however."

"What do you want me to do?"

"Nothing. Unless you want to call the police from a phone booth and tell them that Sousa's headed for San Francisco. Don't identify yourself."

"I don't believe you're going to need my services anymore because the New Orleans police and all the other police in Dallas will be looking for Sousa," said Detective Gray.

"You're right. Head back East and send me your bill."

CHAPTER

Scott spoke to Joyce, the circulating nurse in his operating room. "Who's giving anesthesia for us today?"

"Dr. Paul Aronson, the young attending. I'm sure you remember him," Joyce said as she looked directly at Dr. Perkins.

"Oh, yes. I remember him." He hesitated for a minute and then said, "We've got an elderly male who has a cancer in his lower bowel. I'm going to try to save his rectum. It could be a tough case. The anesthesia will be important because this guy had a coronary three years ago."

"Well, I'm sure they'll have the monitors on him," replied Joyce.

"Got a good scrub nurse, I hope."

"Sharon's going to scrub. She's that black girl with gray hair. She's excellent. You might have trouble keeping up with her."

"You don't really mean that, do you?"

"Not really. I don't want your ego to get too big, though."

"Did they assign me a good resident or have I got a budding psychiatrist who thinks he wants to be a surgeon?"

"The chief's on tap, Dr. Norman Green, that tall, skinny resident. He's good!"

"Great," said Scott, as he walked into the scrub room to scrub before surgery. His cap, mask, and glasses were all in place.

Everything was all set as he gowned up and took his place next to the operating table. He gave his hand signal to Sharon and she placed the scalpel in his right hand.

Scott took the knife and made a long midline incision in the abdomen. The bleeders in the muscle were clamped and tied and then he cut through to enter the abdominal cavity. He felt the bowel below the bladder and announced, "This patient's resectable. I believe we'll be able to rehook this guy up. He's not going to need his entire rectum taken out."

Using long surgical scissors, he gently cut the gray thin covering over the bowel and along the lateral edges of the abdomen. Using his gloved fingers and a sponge stick he freed up the bowel. He gently lifted it out of the belly. Using special clamps, he clamped the blood supply to the segment to be resected and tied the vessels. He stapled both ends of the bowel. The segment containing the tumor was then removed.

Scott then used the mechanical stapler to bring the two cut ends of the bowel together. He tied a pursestring suture around the mechanical device and his assistant activated it down below in the rectal area. It neatly cut the two edges of the bowel and stapled the ends together. It took about five minutes. This was done so the bowel was back in continuity for normal bowel content flow.

Scott used a syringe filled with brown-colored Betadine solution and injected it up the rectum to see if any of the solution leaked out above into the abdomen. There was no leak, meaning the two cut ends of the bowel had been stapled together properly.

"That stapler is really great. It certainly cuts down on operating time," he commented. "We'll need muscle relaxation so we can close," he told the anesthesiologist.

"I'll give him some relaxing medication," said Dr. Aronson.

Within seconds the abdominal muscles relaxed and Dr. Perkins pulled the cut ends of the abdominal wall together and quickly closed the defect.

"I'd like to see you in the doctor's locker room when we're through," said Aronson.

"OK. I'll be there," replied Scott.

A few minutes later, they met in the locker room.

"What's on your mind?" he asked.

"Have you heard any news about our friend, Robert Sousa?"

"The New Orleans police are getting nowhere in trying to find him," said Scott, "if that's what you're interested in."

"I am," said Aronson. "It's almost six months now since he took off. There's two people dead. It's kind of scary. I've had every symptom associated with the AIDS virus and more. I think we have to find that guy before I go nuts."

"What do you suggest we do?" asked Scott. "I've thought about going down to New Orleans or Dallas or San Francisco. I wouldn't know where to start, however."

"Maybe we should rehire Detective Gray if he's still around."

"Yep. He's still around. You can help pay his salary now that you're making all that money as an attending anesthesiologist. I saw one of my patient's anesthesia bills the other day. The bill was more than my surgery bill."

"Now, you know how important anesthesia is."

"Sure it's important, but you guys are paid too much," said Scott.

"I'm guilty. I'll contribute," replied Dr. Aronson, as he raised his hand. "We've got to get this monkey off our backs. I still get diarrhea thinking about it, and I don't want to get a bleeding ulcer. I'd swear I've got AIDS."

"We could both meet with Detective Gray and see if he's got any more thoughts about finding Sousa."

"Set up the meeting then," said the anesthesiologist.

Three days later, Dr. Perkins and Dr. Aronson met with Detective Harry Gray in Dr. Perkins' office. Scott started the conversation.

"We're still interested in finding Robert Sousa."

"I thought you would be," replied Mr. Gray.

"Do you have any thoughts about that?"

"Yes, I do," said Gray. "I hate being a loser. I still think I can find him. Besides, I could bring him in now. He's a killer and there's Texas and Louisiana bounties on his head."

"What do you mean?" Scott asked.

"The Dallas police are mad as hell. One of their assistant D.A.s has been killed and the murderer is at large. They got the state to put up a $20,000 bounty for information leading to Sousa's arrest. That's another incentive for me to find him."

"I'll help pay your travel expenses," said Aronson. "Where would you go first?"

"To the Hilton Hotel and the police department in New Orleans. I want to see what their investigation found."

"I'll contribute another $5,000," said Scott. "I hope you catch him. You'd better be careful. Don't forget he's a killer!"

"I didn't get those medals for bravery when I was a police lieutenant in New York City for nothing," replied Gray. "I'll make a plane reservation."

One week later, Scott received a phone call from Detective Gray in New Orleans.

"Dr. Perkins, I think I'm on to something, but I need your help."

"What's that?" asked Scott.

"That plastic surgeon, Dr. Jonathan Smith, who Sousa saw before the killing, may know something. I went through the police investigation report and there was no mention made about the doctor. Remember I told you I saw Sousa visit the doctor? I want you to fly down here and ask Dr. Smith some questions. He might talk to another doctor, someone like you—a fellow surgeon."

"I'll have to make some arrangements, but I can be down there in a couple of days."

Scott flew to New Orleans and was met at the airport by Detective Gray.

"I'm going to wire you when you go to see that plastic surgeon."

"Why do you want to do that?"

"Because he may say something that we may want to use to make him talk."

"What if he finds out I'm wired?"

"He won't—I don't think. You'll pop in on him unannounced so he can't be prepared. In fact, you're going to be one of his new patients. You'll tell him you need a face-lift. Once you get into his office to see him you're to identify yourself as a surgeon and tell him why you want to talk to him. Ask him about the Sousa case. I'll tell you exactly what I want you to ask."

"Is there any risk for me?"

"I don't know."

"How am I going to get in to see Dr. Smith promptly? Sometimes it takes weeks to get an appointment with those plastic surgery guys."

"You're to tell his secretary that you're from New England and that you heard about his reputation and you want him to do a face-lift. Say one of your friends told you about him. If he's got an ego like most plastic surgeons, he'll see you within three days."

"I'll try it," said Scott.

Sure enough, the plastic surgeon's secretary told Scott she just happened to have a cancellation and Dr. Smith could see him in two days.

Scott smiled—that detective was right. What a bunch of bullshit!

The beautifully manicured office with expensive artwork on the walls and exquisite leather furniture suggested that Dr. Smith was making a bundle and some of it was being spent on his office furnishings.

After twenty minutes, his secretary announced, "You may go in now."

When Scott entered the walnut-paneled office, he shook hands with a distinguished, tall, good-looking doctor appearing to be in his middle fifties. He wore a white lab coat with his name embroidered over his left breast pocket.

"What can I do for you?" he asked.

"I'm interested in getting a face-lift."

"Hmm," he said, as he moved Scott's face from side to side and up and down with the palms of his hands. "Face-lifts are not covered by routine insurance. It can become an expensive operation."

"How expensive?"

"It depends on whether you have your eyelids fixed, the cheek muscles tightened, and/or the chin bulge removed. I might also recommend some special dental work."

"Give me a ballpark figure. Money is no object. I'm a successful surgeon."

"The total job would be between $15,000 and $45,000. I'll have to take some photographs first—front, back and sides. Then I'll give you my recommendations."

"Why do you have to take pictures first?"

"I take pictures of all my patients before I do face-lifts. I want them to see the beautiful change for the better—before and after pictures."

"Well, I'm going to have you do the operation, but first I want to talk to you about something else. You saw a friend of mine, Robert Sousa, about a year ago. Would you happen to have his pictures in your file? I believe he also wanted a face-lift."

"All my patient's records are confidential," said Dr. Smith. "I can't and will not release that information. Why do you want to see those pictures?"

"Well, he's missing and his family's looking for him. I'm a good friend of the family and one of his children is very sick."

"What's this got to do with you wanting a face-lift?"

"I want you to understand, I still want you to do the face-lift, but I'm also trying to help the family locate their father."

Dr. Smith pressed a button on his desk and his secretary came into the room.

"Jean, look in our office files and see if you can locate the file and pictures of a man by the name of Robert Sousa."

A few minutes later, the secretary came back with a folder and there were three 8 × 10 photographs in the file. He showed the pictures to Scott. There was no doubt the photographs were of Robert Sousa. There were also some other records there which he didn't let Scott see.

"Mr. Sousa never came back," said Dr. Smith. "He paid for my consultation fee in cash. I remember him very well. He said he was moving to San Francisco and he didn't like the way he looked. He was a pleasant normal-appearing male with some feminine characteristics—delicate facial features, thin, with long slender fingers, and probably weighed about 140 pounds.

"He expressed some thoughts to me about having some transvestite tendencies. He said he was dissatisfied with his body and thought he might want to see what life was like on the other side. He mentioned that when he was young and played with his friends he enjoyed dressing up as a girl. It made him feel more natural. He also said that almost all his life he had a sense of being a female and was disgusted with his male characteristics."

"I can't believe what you're telling me. Sousa was a known homosexual in law school. He frequented the New Jersey bathhouses and had a live-in boyfriend."

"I don't believe that," said Dr. Smith. "People who have gender dysphoria have a marked disdain for any homosexual behavior."

"Unless he has a big reason to change," remarked Scott, "and I think he's got a big reason!"

"I don't understand," said Dr. Smith.

"It's a long story. There's something else I have to ask you. Have you ever done a sex change operation?" asked Scott.

"Yes, I have. That's one of my specialties. Before I operate on those people, however, they have to be evaluated by a psychiatrist. If you convert a male to a female, you have to amputate the male organs and there's no going back once that's done.

"There's another problem too," said Dr. Smith. "You sometimes run into someone who has a schizoid personality. These people don't really know who they are—male or female—and they might request a sex change in an attempt to handle severe stress associated with functioning in today's society.

"This can be dangerous for the plastic surgeon. If the patient doesn't like what they are after the sex change, they can make an attempt on the doctor's life. I had one of those. That's why I have a gun permit."

"Did Sousa want a sex change?" asked Scott.

"No. He was more interested in a face-lift and wanted a hurry-up job. I refused to do it. I do not do hurry-up jobs! I consider myself an artist and sometimes it takes time to create a Rembrandt. I'm sorry, my secretary's buzzing me. I've spent too much time with you already. I can do your face-lift in about six weeks. You'll have to decide what kind of face-lift you want and she'll set it up for you. You also have to pay fifty percent up front with a certified bank check or cash. It sounds like this Robert Sousa was one hell of a mixed up guy."

"Yes, he was and still is," said Scott. "Is there anything else in his file that would help me find him?"

"I'll look," said Dr. Smith as he leafed through the manila folder. "Here's something. He asked me for the name of a good plastic surgeon in San Francisco. I gave him the name of a classmate of mine, a Dr. Marshall Kelman. He does a lot of plastic surgery on the West Coast Hollywood people. He's one of the best in the business."

"Doctor, thank you for all your information. I'll be calling your secretary to set up another appointment."

CHAPTER

Scott met with Detective Gray later that afternoon and told him about his conversation with the plastic surgeon.

"No wonder no one can find that son-of-a-bitch. Everyone's been looking for a male attorney and he could possibly be a female—or a transvestite."

"What's our next step?"

"I think I should go out to San Francisco and snoop around. He's probably hanging out in Finnoccio's, that restaurant that has the male-female impersonation shows. Besides, that guy's dangerous. He's a murderer. He's already killed once and he could kill again. He's not going to be an easy one to catch and bring in. However, I'm sure Dallas will pay the $20,000 bounty if he's dead or alive."

"For God's sake, don't shoot him! I'd still like to know if he's got AIDS. I'd still like him to have a blood test."

"Well, if I shoot him, I'll shoot him through the heart and collect some of his blood for you to test. Will that make you feel better?" asked Gray with a smirk on his face.

"That's not funny."

"For all we know Sousa has had a sex change and is probably walking the streets as a prostitute just to see what it's like to be on the other side. He's what you might call a double-double queer. He's a candidate to get AIDS as a homosexual and as a transvestite. That's a new twist. If he tests positive now, it ain't going to mean too much," replied Gray.

"That's not true. You haven't found him yet. You don't even know if he's had a sex change. You also don't know if he's a transvestite. Knowing Sousa, he could still be practicing law under a different name. The only thing we do know is that he's done a good job hiding from the law. When do you plan to head out to San Francisco?"

"Next week. I'm going to use the same approach on that plastic surgeon in San Francisco that you used in New Orleans. I'm going to get evaluated for a face-lift."

"You could use one," replied Scott.

"That's not funny!"

"Well, I hope it works. I still want you to call me once a week."

"I will."

Scott got a phone call from San Francisco three weeks later.

"I got in to see that plastic surgeon, Dr. Marshall Kelman. You ought to see the office that doctor's got! Your office looks like an outhouse compared to his. He's got three young assistant surgeons who follow him around like little puppy dogs. He must have ten-thousand square feet of office space, fully carpeted and sound-proofed. Just the furniture in that office must have cost a hundred thousand."

"I'm not interested in the furniture in his office. Did you find out anything about Sousa?"

"Yes, I did. I flashed my badge and he was cooperative. Sousa's changed his name."

"How did you find out about that?"

"It was easier than I thought. This Dr. Kelman gets referrals from all over the country and his secretary keeps track of all his referral doctors. She looked up Dr. Jonathon Smith from New Orleans and pulled the file. Kelman did a face-lift on Sousa and he took before and after photographs just like that other plastic surgeon. I must say he did a beautiful job. He pulled his ears back so they weren't so prominent, did an eyelid plasty, straightened his nose a little, and made his face look much thinner."

"Did you find out where he lives?"

"Yes. He was staying at the Sir Francis Drake. I checked it out. He's not there anymore. I also found out something else interesting. He asked Dr. Kelman about having a sex change. Evidently that's a real expensive job—fifty-thousand or more—and you have to be evaluated by a psychiatrist at a San Francisco hospital before he'll do the job."

"Did he have it done?"

"Dr. Kelman said he didn't, but I'm not sure I believe him. He was quite nervous when I asked the question. He told me he sent Sousa, now known as Robin Cooker, to a psychiatrist who evaluated him for a sex change and that was the last he saw him."

"So, Attorney Sousa has a face-lift and a new name, Robin Cooker. That's interesting. What are you planning to do next?"

"I'm going to go see the psychiatrist. However, Dr. Kelman wouldn't give me the psychiatrist's name."

"Why not?"

"He said he had told me too much already and it was an invasion of the patient's privacy. Sex changes are very sensitive plastic procedures and many times the patient wants the change to acquire a complete new identity. I flashed my badge again and he still wouldn't talk. I told him that Robin Cooker had killed people already and that he or she was extremely dangerous on the loose. He still wouldn't talk."

"I wonder if he had been threatened by Sousa."

"He denied that he had been. I told him I could get the San Francisco police involved. 'Doctor-patient confidentiality would stand up in court,' he replied. 'I don't have to tell you anything.' Not where there's three murders involved? I asked. 'I have to think about this. Why don't you give me a call tomorrow?' What time? 'Call me after office hours at 4:00 P.M.'

"I called him the next day and he still refused to talk. He said he had consulted his lawyer and his lawyer told him not to say anything. He could be sued by the patient if the patient found out. Besides, he said he had no proof that this individual had killed three people. I asked him if he wanted to make it four—making himself the next victim.

"He said he hadn't seen him since he sent him to be evaluated and he never got a follow-up note. He said that was eight months ago. And that was the end of my conversation with Dr. Kelman."

"It looks like you hit a dead end. I think you might have to contact the San Francisco police and get them involved," suggested Scott.

"I don't want to do that, yet. I'm going to try to get that plastic surgeon's daily log or I might even try to steal Sousa's records out of Kelman's office."

"You'd better watch your step. You could end up in jail yourself."

"I'll call you if I need to get bailed out."

A month went by before Scott heard from Detective Gray again.

"Dr. Perkins, the pot's heating up here in San Francisco," said Gray when he finally called.

"What do you mean?"

"I finally got the name of the psychiatrist who was to evaluate Sousa for a sex change."

"How'd you get that?"

"I found out that most of the doctors at that San Francisco hospital are on salary and everything they do is typed into a computer so the university can bill the patient. There are computers all over the place. All you have to do is type in the patient's name and it tells you all the information: diagnosis, name of admitting doctor, and the cost for services. It eliminates the doctors from having to dictate letters and the secretaries from typing them and then having to be mailed. That can all be very costly and time-consuming.

"I took a good-looking nurse out to lunch, told her my problem— with a little embellishment—she obliged with typing Robin Cooker into the computer for me. All I wanted to get was the psychiatrist's name and there it was, right on the computer screen next to Robin's name. Dr. Ted Lockwood. He was one of the head honchos in the psychiatry department. I wonder if you want to fly out here and talk to him? He'll probably give you more information then he'll give me."

"You're probably right. But why waste time? Why don't you just go to the police now and tell them what you've found?"

"Because we haven't found Sousa yet, and I can't give them a good reason why we're looking for him, either."

"OK. I like San Francisco and I don't mind spending a few days there. I'll call you tomorrow with my flight schedule. I'll try to get a reservation at the St. Francis Hotel."

Detective Gray met Scott at the San Francisco airport.

"How do you plan to get to see that Dr. Lockwood?" he asked Scott.

"I've already taken care of that. I called a surgeon friend of mine at that San Francisco hospital. He's a member of an international cancer society that I belong to. He set it up for me to talk with Dr. Lockwood tomorrow afternoon."

"Did you tell him what you are planning to ask him?"

"No."

"Good," replied Gray. "I found out something else from that computer. That psychiatrist must charge a lot, because there were some big bills on that computer. You might be able to find out if Sousa had that sex operation or not. Hopefully the psychiatrist will tell you something."

Scott went to see Dr. Lockwood the next afternoon. His office was in a medical office building attached to the hospital and was a typical psychiatrist's office; small waiting room with soft classical music playing and soft, comfortable furniture. Scott knew a few psychiatrists back home and knew how they operated. Usually they saw patients on an hourly basis, but it was really only 45 minutes. Fifteen minutes at the end of the hour was for phone consultations or family meetings. You have to be a good listener to be a good psychiatrist. When he got in to see him Dr. Lockwood seemed to be on the defensive before he could ask any questions.

"Well, Dr. Perkins, why did you travel across the country to see me?"

"It's a long story," replied Scott. "I'll try to give it to you in a nutshell. I'm trying to locate a former patient of mine who I believe you have recently seen in consultation. The patient's family, who are close friends of mine, have asked me to help locate an attorney named Robert Sousa. I also have an urgent personal interest in finding him."

"I've never seen anyone by that name," replied Lockwood.

"I realize that. The patient, who I believe you saw in consultation, is now called Robin Cooker. I believe Robin Cooker is interested in undergoing a sex change or may have already had it done. This is how this individual is trying to disappear."

"Before you go any further, I wish to make a comment. An adult, in their right mind, can do anything he or she wants to. We're the captains of our own destinies."

"I understand," replied Scott. "This man or woman, Robert Sousa or Robin Cooker, has a truly bizarre background. I operated on him two years ago in New England. I may have acquired the AIDS virus from him."

"That's impossible."

"Hear me out. Robin Cooker's real name is Robert Sousa. He's a known homosexual who tried to hide his sexual habits by marrying a twenty-three-year-old woman. He killed his pregnant wife and his law school roommate, who also was a homosexual, two years ago in New Orleans—for what reason we don't know. He is known to have come out to San Francisco and has been seen by Dr. Marshall Kelman, a plastic surgeon, inquiring about a sex change. He was referred to you for consultation and preoperative evaluation."

"Are you sure Robin Cooker is being sought by the police?"

"I'm absolutely sure! As a doctor of medicine myself, I can't understand how Robert Sousa, a known homosexual who liked and loved boys in the past, is now or is considering taking on the role of a female. I should think that would be repugnant to him."

"Not necessarily," said Dr. Lockwood. "As you may know, he has the gender dysphoria syndrome. He is so dissatisfied with his own body that he wants to change. Some people become transvestites— they wear the clothes of the opposite sex. Others want to alter their sex completely by surgery."

"You've lost me with that statement," replied Scott.

"He had an effeminate homosexuality. He was sexually attracted to other men and derived pleasure from his penis. After a while, he assumed a more feminine lifestyle. What Robert Sousa was seeking was a means to avoid the moral, financial, and social stigma of homosexuality. Some of these people take female hormones, which makes the penis inactive as a source of pleasure. Yes, I did see him and he is a female now! In fact, the plastic surgeon did a terrific job making the conversion.

"Robin Cooker's surgery was done by a plastic surgeon specialist in Los Angeles. A complete changeover was accomplished. I saw her after her surgery and she's a knockout! If you saw her walking down the street today she'd make your eyes turn. She was placed on high-dose hormones and developed beautiful, firm breasts. She wanted them larger so she had bilateral silicone breast implants put in place (the expandable type). Broad-based implants were used.

The implants were placed a little medially so she would have more cleavage. Robert Sousa, that is, Robin Cooker's, penis was amputated and a cosmetically acceptable functional vagina and vulva were constructed in the perineum. The vagina was made large enough to permit comfortable intercourse. She told me she's happier than she has ever been and that her vagina is as busy as she wants it to be."

"Do you have Robin Cooker's address?" asked Scott. "She's wanted for murder."

"That I can't understand. She was such a sweet young lady. Her last address was in Hollywood somewhere. I'll give it to you, but I understand she's not staying there anymore. She's traveling around the world on a yacht with some multimillionaire. You might have trouble finding her."

"Well, at least I've got to try. Thank you for your help."

CHAPTER
10

"Well, Dr. Perkins, what do you want to do now?" asked Detective Gray. "Attorney Sousa has passed through the transvestite stage, had a sex change, and is now out in the world as a female. We're having trouble catching up to that broad—or whatever you want to call him or her."

"I suppose we should call him Sousa or 'it.' I think we have a cunning murderer on the loose. Who knows what Robin's next move will be?" asked Scott. "She could kill more innocent people. I've decided to fly back home and go back to work doing surgery so I can pay your expenses. You'll have to fly down to Los Angeles and try to locate the bitch. We ought to alert the New Orleans and Dallas police as to what's going on. They might find Robin Cooker faster than we can."

"I doubt it," replied Gray.

"I think we should try to find out who the plastic surgeon is who did the sex change operation," suggested Scott.

"That ain't going to be easy. Do you have any suggestions? That

69

psychiatrist, Lockwood, doesn't know who it is. I've already asked him—or he may know, but won't tell me."

"He may be afraid to tell you because Sousa—Robin Cooker—has threatened to kill him if he talks."

"You may be right," replied Gray. "He swears he doesn't know which plastic surgeon did the sex change. There are so many sexual weirdos in that area, there's got to be quite a few plastic surgeons doing sex changes. It's a lucrative business out there."

"I'll bet it's somebody who has an office up around Hollywood. There are a lot of strange, eclectic people in that area. You might have to look around for a sex change for yourself to be able to find out who the experts in the field are," said Scott with a smile.

"That's not in my contract," said Detective Gray.

"You asked for a suggestion, so I gave you one. If you have a better idea, use it."

"This Sousa creature is getting under my skin. I'd like to kill it, when I see it."

"He's already gotten under my skin—in more ways than one," replied Scott. "I don't want you to kill Robin when you find her. I want that creature kept alive."

"You'll have to explain your reason for that to me pretty soon. I don't understand," said the detective. "Sousa's a murderer and you want me to capture her alive. It doesn't make sense to me. I'm sure I can arrest this creature now if we can prove it's Attorney Sousa."

"You may have trouble proving that Robin Cooker, a female, is Attorney Robert Sousa."

"You're right," said Gray. "However, we're dealing with a murderer and an extremely dangerous person."

"How are you going to prove who she is? You can get sued for false arrest, you know," said Scott.

"Those plastic surgeons take pictures before and after. I'm sure that Los Angeles plastic surgeon took some mug shots. I'd give one of my testicles to get my hands on those pictures."

"You'd better make sure it isn't more than one testicle you have to give," said Scott. "You might have to shave your mustache off."

"That ain't funny," said Gray.

"I'm heading East on a flight tomorrow morning. Keep in touch. Good luck finding out who did the sex change," said Scott.

Six weeks went by and Scott didn't hear from Harry Gray. Finally, he received a phone call from Los Angeles.

"Dr. Perkins, this is Detective Gray. I've got some more information about Sousa but it's not what you want to hear. I found the plastic surgeon in Los Angeles. He's a Dr. Rudolfo Von Salzen. He trained in New York and Europe and is considered the preeminent plastic surgeon in the country for sex changes. He does sex changes both ways—female to male and male to female. You could buy a Mercedes or build a small house for what he charges for one operation. I've got a quick question I want to ask you," said Gray.

"Fire away," replied Scott.

"I got an idea about how they make a man into a woman but for the life of me, I can't figure out how they make a woman into a man."

"I don't know all the details, but it's the same for both changes. Usually they see a psychiatrist first and are advised to live and work for one or two years as a man so they live like a man while they get psychological advice. They are given male hormones that change their physical appearance. Their voice changes and gets deeper and they grow hair on their faces. They have their breasts and female reproductive organs removed, and the plastic surgeon creates a penis for them. Usually they need a mechanical device to make the penis work. It's easier to make a man into a woman than a woman into a man. It's also very expensive surgery."

"It all sounds pretty complicated to me. I don't know why anyone would want to have that done."

"Neither do I, but a lot of people do have it done. Well, anyway, finish your story about the plastic surgeon."

"Well, he checks your bank account before you even get in to see him. The first visit is to determine eligibility for the operation and the ability to pay. This guy gets full payment before he even does the job—not fifty percent."

"How did you find him?" asked Scott.

"It wasn't easy. I had a stroke of luck. You know how I like to play golf. I was depressed because I couldn't find Sousa, so I went to a bar for a few drinks. I met a businessman at one of the bars at the Century Hotel in Los Angeles. We got to talking and the conversation turned to sports. I mentioned that someday I would love to play the Riviera Country Club where they play the Los Angeles

Open. That's where Ben Hogan won the U.S. Open quite a few years back, you know.

"He told me he was a golfer too and that it just happens he was a member of Riviera Country Club. I knew there was something I liked about that gentleman! The next thing I know, he invites me to play in a member-guest four-ball tournament the next week. Of course I didn't have my clubs with me, but I accepted anyway. I'd buy a whole new set to play Riviera."

"With what I'm paying you, you could afford to buy three sets of golf clubs. Since when do I pay for you to play golf at an exclusive club like that?" asked Scott.

"Let me finish my story," said Gray.

"OK, but this better be good."

"So, anyway, I bought a pair of golf shoes and rented a set of clubs from a guy who used to work at Nevada Bob's. That Thursday afternoon I played golf and I had one of my best rounds. We finished second in the tournament. He was ecstatic and so was I. Playing in the foursome was a plastic surgeon who worked at the U.C.L.A. Medical Center. We rode in the cart together. He knew this Dr. Rudolfo Von Salzen and told me he was also a member of Riviera Country Club. He said he'd set up a game the following week with Dr. Von Salzen. It was a real breakthrough!

"I had another good round and this Von Salzen was a regular guy. I'm not an intellectual like they are, but my golf game was better than theirs. I got to talk to him and told him I wanted to see him about some plastic surgery.

"You don't need plastic surgery on your face," said Von Salzen.

"I was surprised! I didn't expect that response. He eventually told me to call his secretary and to tell her that we had played golf together at Riviera and to give me an appointment.

"I called his secretary the next day and saw Dr. Von Salzen the following week. He turned out to be quite cooperative after I flashed my detective badge. He was also on an ego trip about this Robin Cooker. I told him about you.

"When I asked him if he had a patient by the name of Robin Cooker, his eyes popped out of his head. His reply was, 'Of course. That was one of my best triumphs. I could never forget that name. How do you know Robin?'

"I told him I knew Robin Cooker when she was known as Attorney

Robert Sousa. I told him I was hired by you to find Sousa and that when she was known as Robert Sousa, he had a pregnant wife. He said that was nonsense. It was impossible and he couldn't believe that.

"He said Robin Cooker told him he was not married and that he had been a homosexual and had tried being a transvestite in San Francisco. That wasn't good enough for him. It just mixed him up more mentally. He said he was evaluated by a psychiatrist at a San Francisco hospital and he told him that he wanted to be made into a woman.

"The plastic surgeon, Dr. Von Salzen, told him there was no going back once he was converted and tried to talk him out of it. He also told him that his insurance would not cover the hospital or surgical fee. Sousa's reply was there was no problem paying his bills. He told him he had plenty of money. The plastic surgeon had him re-evaluated by another psychiatrist, and he approved the sex change.

"Von Salzen did the operation and said it was one of the most successful operations he had ever done. The breast augmentation was perfect and the formation of a vagina and vulva flawless. He said Robin had the perfect body for a conversion. Her weight was 138 pounds before the operation. She slimmed down to 120 pounds and with her narrow waist, hips, and perfectly curved buttocks, and the use of estrogens all her facial hair disappeared. Her blonde hair had grown long down to her waist. She told him she went to a beauty parlor for a permanent and new hair style. Dressed in high heels and expensive tight-fitting dresses, she was a knockout. She showed him pictures of herself in bikinis. He said she could easily have won a beauty contest the way she turned out.

"I saw the pictures and he wasn't kidding. She was gorgeous!

"I asked him when was the last time he saw her. He said it was about three months ago. She flew in from Paris to see him and to have her breasts made larger. She was a 34C and wanted to be a 36D. She had the expandable silicone implants that you can increase or decrease. He told her he thought her breasts were perfect but she wanted to make them a bit larger so she would have a deeper cleavage when she wore low-cut dresses. She wanted to improve her décolletage.

"He asked Robin if her boyfriend knew why she was seeing him. She said she didn't think so. She had taken so many female hormones that she had a lot of breast tissue anterior to the silicone implants. Von Salzen said if you palpated her breasts they would feel normal, but firm and youthful.

"Then I asked him if he injected the implants and he said he did increase the size for her. He also said he recently received a card from her in Paris.

"I asked Von Salzen what she was doing in Paris. He said that when she first left Los Angeles she told him that she was going to become a prostitute in France, and he laughed.

"She also told him she was going to marry a rich Frenchman and if he couldn't satisfy her, she'd be someone's mistress. She made the comment that she wished she had been born a woman, but since she wasn't she was going to go to France to learn how to become one. She claimed to have French ancestors and that her mother was French. She said she planned to become a *femme fatale* and that after six months to a year in France she would become a true courtesan. She also said she was going to be very selective and wouldn't let everyone who wanted her make love to her."

"It sounds like Von Salzen had an interesting story to tell about Robin," commented Scott.

"Well, you haven't heard it all yet. She was interested in Paris fashions and the clothes that the French girls wear. She wanted to wear the latest styles to enhance her feminine elegance. She also told him she wouldn't be afraid to take her clothes off for the right man. He'd have to be very rich and attractive and then she'd give him total happiness.

"I asked Dr. Von Salzen how she looked a year and a half after her operation. He said she was beautiful. When he saw her three months ago she told him she was happier than she'd ever been. She always loved men when she was masquerading as a male homosexual. Now that she's a female, her fulfillment is complete."

"It sounds like she's a real weirdo," said Scott.

"You can say that again!" replied Gray. "Dr. Von Salzen said he was amazed at her self assurance when he saw her. Her self confidence exuded from her face and body. She had the self confidence that comes from being the center of attention. The clothes she wore were the latest creations from Christian Dior and Yves Saint Laurent. Someone who had big bucks was taking care of her. She spoke fluent French and, mixed with her English, it added to her sexual voice tones and attitude. She really had turned out to be a *femme fatale*.

"She was not alone when she flew in from Paris. She obviously had an affluent Frenchman in her stable. She was not in his stable—he was in hers. He said the man was a tall, handsome six-footer about forty-five years old.

"She whispered to Dr. Von Salzen in a soft voice, 'I ration his sex with me. I find it's better that way for both of us. It's more enjoyable when he wants me more. If he behaves, then I'm his special dessert. The French really know how to make love. I've learned so many different ways of sharing my body with his. I feel like the most beautiful flower in the world that has just bloomed after we make love.'

"Von Salzen noted that both their bodies were bronzed from frequenting the beaches of Monaco. She spoke fluent French when she talked to her companion. Dr. Von Salzen was introduced to the gentleman. He gave me his name. It was a long name—François Charles Victor Louis, etc. Unfortunately, he didn't give me his complete name. He was a handsome Frenchman with royalty ancestors and was very athletic looking.

"I asked if he had any information about where she's staying in Paris, but he didn't and wanted to know why I was asking.

"I told him Robin Cooker was being sought for the murder of three people. He said he didn't believe it. He said she was such a delicate, sweet thing that she couldn't hurt a fly.

"I told him he'd better be careful with her, because she could be a black-widow spider.

"Then he offered more information that I'm not too happy about. He said she may be changing her name again. The Frenchman wants to marry her. So far, she's said no. She'd rather be his mistress than get married. She seems to be enjoying his courtship.

"Robin told Dr. Von Salzen that she learned a lot spending a year in France. She said that what makes a French woman different from the rest of the women in the world is that French women are witty and enjoy playing the game of love. She said she's enjoying every minute of it. She enjoys the courtship and has learned to be a French coquette and enjoys the favors of the Frenchmen—who are different from Americans. She likes their attention and admiration and feels like a complete woman in their presence."

"Good for her!" replied Scott. "It certainly sounds like she's enjoying her new life. Did you ask Von Salzen where she lives in France?"

"Yes. She wouldn't tell him. He thinks she lives in some château and travels all over the world."

"Did she say when she'd be coming back to the States?"

"No, but she did say she missed San Francisco."

"Did you get any pictures so we can have copies made to help us locate her?"

"Yes, I did, but these are the originals and I have to return them to Von Salzen after we get our copies made."

"That's no problem," replied Scott.

"I also asked Von Salzen if he had any other information about her in his files. He said he had a questionnaire that she filled out when he first saw her. He also made a video of her. I guess it has some interesting information on it and we can have a copy of that also."

"As soon as you make copies of the photos, questionnaire, and video fly back East. We'll have to talk about what we want to do next."

"OK. I'll be in touch with you when I get back."

CHAPTER
11

Dr. Perkins, Dr. Aronson, and Detective Gray had a meeting after Gray returned from Los Angeles.

Instead of reading the questionnaire, Scott looked at the video that Von Salzen had made. It was a professional production. Dr. Von Salzen made a video of Robin before and after her operation. Its title was "The Transsexual Change of Robert to Robin."

"I don't understand why Sousa would allow a video to be made if he's trying to hide from civilization and specifically the cops," said Scott.

"I asked Dr. Von Salzen that question. He said that a lot of these people are exhibitionists. Robin told him that only her first name could be used on the film and that she had to approve the film before it could be used. Besides that, Von Salzen didn't know her last name. She told him she had a different French last name," replied Detective Gray. "She also did not put her address or last name on the questionnaire."

"The story you're telling me sounds fishy. She must have had her surgery in a hospital. She had to pay big bucks for the operation and also to the plastic surgeon. Her name had to be in the records somewhere."

"I asked Von Salzen that same question. He said she paid all her hospital bills with certified bank checks or cash. Her last name was not on the checks."

"You ought to be able to trace her through the bank then," suggested Scott.

"I tried that, too, and got nowhere. Robin is covering her tracks. She's real smart."

"Well, let's put the cassette in the VCR and see what it shows. Is there a sound track?"

"Yes, there is. Von Salzen asks her a lot of questions. He's in the film too with his long white doctor's coat on. I'm sure that's how he plans to get business."

"Start the video and we'll see what we have."

Dr. Von Salzen's voice began the film. "In the film you are about to see you will be shown the dramatic results that can be attained in changing the sex of a male to a female. I have done approximately seventy of these operations. All of them are different and present different problems. Robert had a penis but no vagina and was told that he had bilateral undescended testicles. He received shots and hormones as a child but was never surgically explored to see what was going on. He was an only child. The majority of sex changes have been successful and 40 percent have married after their change. The film you will see today, shows Robert, a former effeminate homosexual, who became a transvestite and then requested a total change to a woman. The patient is first evaluated by a psychiatrist and then has to sign informed consent forms for medico-legal reasons. The first picture you will see is Robert in the nude and then you will be shown the numerous surgical steps necessary to complete the transition. I will narrate the early part of the video and at the end Robin has consented to allow us to photograph her in the nude. She will then answer specific questions that I ask."

Detective Gray stopped the video. "Dr. Perkins, the surgery is kind of gory. Essentially it shows her getting another face-lift and nose job done first. Then she has the breast reconstruction with silicone implants and, last but not least, the amputation of the penis and making of a new vagina. That part is kind of bloody.

"If you don't mind, I'd like to fast-forward that part and get to the question and answer period. I get a little queasy watching that part of the film."

"That's OK with me," replied Scott. "I don't plan to try to learn how to do those operations. Go ahead. Fast-forward the video."

Finally the film got to the part that showed the results of her surgery. It was incredible. The color film first showed her face. She now had beautiful female facial characteristics. Her nose was petite and turned up. She had long, beautiful, blonde hair and her perfect almond-shaped clear blue-green eyes had long eyelashes. Her mouth had full sensuous lips and when she smiled her teeth were perfect pearly white and beautifully proportioned. Obviously an orthodontist had done work on her teeth. She used eye shadow and a small amount of lipstick on her cupid-shaped mouth.

Robin weighed about 120 pounds. The upper part of her body showed two beautifully shaped breasts that appeared to be full, and firm with what appeared to be sharply pointed nipples. She had a magnificent tan body with no bra strap marks. No scars from the recent surgery could be seen.

Her stomach was flat and her hips and buttocks beautifully curved. The pelvis and vagina area looked exactly like any female with normal-looking pubic hair and external reconstructed labia. The film showed closeups of her breasts and vagina. She had long slender legs and the film showed her walking backward and forward wearing high heels.

The professional photographer also took some provocative boudoir pictures of her in the nude which could easily be used as the centerfold of a major magazine.

The most interesting part of the video showed Robin walking into Von Salzen's office in a tight-fitting, low-cut green dress that left little to the imagination. She had the perfect female gait to arouse the male senses and she was obviously enjoying the photography session. Her long blonde hair was done in a French braid, accentuating her long slender neck and low-cut décolletage. She was wearing a short, tight skirt that was cut high above the knees, hugging her hips and revealing long, slender, perfectly shaped legs. She walked into the room with confidence, her head held high, carrying a large black patent leather shoulder bag and wearing spiked black heels.

"You're the man I owe my life to," she said as she sat down in front of his desk and crossed her legs, leaning slightly backward to accentuate her breasts. Every move of her body looked like it was calculated to be sensuous and provocative.

"Robin, I want to ask you a few questions about your past, if you don't mind," said Dr. Von Salzen.

"I'm trying to forget my past completely. I have such a wonderful new life," she said. "However, I'll answer a few questions."

"How old are you and where were you born?"

"I'm twenty-eight years old, and, believe it or not, I was born in Paris, France. My mother was French and my father was Italian. I lived in Paris until I was twelve years old. I received hormone shots as a child and was brought up as a boy. My parents came to America about that time and my father was an international importer for a company in New York City. Later, he was in the diplomatic service. My father and mother are no longer alive. They were killed in an automobile accident when I was a freshman at Yale. I was an only child and inherited a substantial sum of money when they were killed."

"When did you first realize you might be a little different from the other boys?"

"When I was little I used to like to dress up in girl's clothes. I never got to be big like most men. I was always slender and never weighed very much. My mother told me I needed the hormone shots for bone development. My roommate in law school got me involved with the guys. We did everything together when I was in law school; cocaine, the bathhouses in New Jersey, you name it. I enjoyed loving men and they were more successful going up my rear end than I was theirs. I didn't have a big penis. Women never intrigued me. I sort of despised them. In reality, I was in competition with them for the men. I began to lose interest in men and when the AIDS problem came along I decided I had to change my ways or I could die from AIDS.

"I was at a law convention out in San Francisco and went to Finnoccio's—that place where they have males impersonating females. They really put on a great show. I met one of the transvestites at the bar and was propositioned. We got together and he got me a job with the troupe. I found out I enjoyed being a female more than a male and didn't enjoy having sex with another male. It became pretty disgusting to me. That's when I met a transsexual female who was as happy as a lark. I met her at the piano bar at the St. Francis Hotel. She gave me the name of a plastic surgeon to see. I saw him and decided that was what I wanted to do. I wanted to get the best and that's when I came to see you."

"Now that it's been eighteen months since your change, do you have any regrets?"

"Yes. I wish I had done it sooner. I should have been born a woman."

"Usually, when we do transsexual operations the patient has to make some emotional adjustments. Has anybody been seeing you? Just what are you doing with your life these days?"

"After you completed the reconstruction of the vagina I decided to let my new body heal. I decided to go back to Paris. You told me it would take a year or more before all my new parts would be working. I went to a plastic surgeon in Paris. '*Magnifique!*' he remarked when he first saw me.

"I had a few minor problems and adjustments to make because I had taken high-dose estrogens to help fill out my breasts. I had to take some antacids like Tums so I wouldn't get an ulcer."

"What was your biggest problem?" asked Dr. Von Salzen.

"My biggest problem was fighting off all the Frenchmen who wanted to bed me. Young, middle-aged, and old wanted to invade my treasure chest. *Voilà!* My life had changed. I was becoming the center of attraction. It would only be a matter of time before I would succumb. I enjoyed every minute of it and I was beginning to learn how to act like a French woman. My whole personality blossomed.

"*Je ne sais quoi!* I don't know why. The French part of my ancestry from my mother was taking over. My mother had been a stunning blonde who was born in the northern part of France, in Lille. She always said she wanted a girl. I wonder what she would say now?"

"What do you think?" asked Dr. Von Salzen.

"I think she would say I am one of the most beautiful women in Paris or perhaps all of France. At least a lot of Frenchmen have expressed that to me."

"When did you start having intercourse?"

"After about nine months. The plastic surgeon in Paris told me I could have sex anytime I wanted to. For a moment I thought he was interested. He told me my vaginal mucosa looked just like any other female's. I was starting to get frustrated and my juices were flowing, but I was afraid. He told me to keep using a metal stent to keep the opening in my vagina expanded. Every night I dilated my new vagina.

"By this time, I learned to dress with the best French women on the avenues. I went to the best fashion shows and bought the most expensive clothes from Christian Dior and Yves Saint Laurent. I even had a seamstress make some tight-fitting dresses that completely hugged my body lines. There were two or three places I loved to go to in Paris: the Ritz Hotel with its rich decorations, exquisite dining areas, and long corridors; and the Café de la Paris, where I met François. What a man! He's the gentleman I'm with."

"Did you have any difficulty having intercourse?" asked Dr. Von Salzen.

"Oh yes. I almost lost him," replied Robin.

"What do you mean?"

"That's another story. Let's say I accomplished my goal. I'm extremely happy now. I've had sex with François as many as five times in one day. He's the answer to a women's dream."

"Don't you get tired of it?"

"Are you kidding? Not at all! I think any woman could become a nymphomaniac if the right man and lover came along." Robin thought back to her first meeting with François. What a tragedy that had been. The video ended there.

"That's a remarkable video," replied Dr. Perkins. "Von Salzen is really an artist. She's going to be a tough one to catch and put in jail. We know she's in Paris but how are we going to find her? We don't have any evidence that she's killed anybody. Although, she was probably the last one to see his wife and Bill Carroll alive. The police never found the murder weapon. It was a neat, clean job. So far she seems to be healthy, which is a good sign for me and Dr. Aronson. What Sousa did is incredible. She's doing a good job of disappearing into the woodwork."

"I think we have to continue to look for her," said Detective Gray. "However, if we find her, we'll have to deal with the French judicial system."

"What does that mean?" asked Scott.

"French law is different than ours," said Gray. "It's based on the code of Napoleon. The judicial system is independent of all other French systems. The French constitution stipulates that the president of the republic with a judiciary council is the guarantor of the independence of the judges. They have a police court like ours for civil cases where one or more judges preside. The higher civil courts deal with the more serious crimes and act as appeal courts. Usually there are three judges but no jury. The serious crimes are judged by a judge and two assessors and a jury of nine who combine in giving a verdict. There is also a supreme court of appeal, which can order a retrial."

"The problem is what crimes are we going to accuse Robin of?" asked Scott. "You're the only witness who saw him come out of that hotel room in New Orleans and fly to San Francisco after the killing. I think the French will think we're crazy when we tell them what happened. Robin may have committed the perfect crime and no one will ever know about it."

"Except the three of us," replied Detective Gray.

"I wonder if we should go to the Dallas-Fort Worth police and tell them what we know?" asked Scott.

"I'll call Dallas and tell them what we know if you'd like," replied Gray.

"I think I want to wait a while. I might be implicated," replied Scott.

"Whatever you say."

CHAPTER

12

"Do you think we should pursue this Robert Sousa case any further?" Scott asked the anesthesiologist.

"It's three and a half years since our exposure in the operating room," replied Aronson. "Our HIV blood tests have all been negative, although I didn't have one done the last time. I think we can assume that Sousa didn't have AIDS. If he did, we should be testing positive by now."

"So that's why you two guys have been trying to find Sousa. He was a fag," said Gray.

"It's a little more than that," said Aronson. "Dr. Perkins was inoculated with Sousa's blood by a needle stick and I inhaled a snootful of his lung secretions. We were afraid we might get AIDS."

"Well, thanks for telling me about it now! I should have gotten more pay for hazardous duty. It's a good thing I haven't kissed you guys."

"We are all forgetting one important fact and that's that Robert Sousa killed two people," said Scott.

"You're assuming that. All we know is that there are two people dead and Sousa was seen coming out of the New Orleans hotel room where they were shot."

"That's pretty strong circumstantial evidence," said Detective Gray.

"There's one minor correction. Three people were killed! Sousa's wife was pregnant with a viable baby."

"The question we have to resolve is whether we should tell the New Orleans and Dallas police what we know about Sousa," said Scott.

"It could implicate all three of us," said Gray. "We could be cited for withholding evidence."

"I never thought of that," said Aronson. "What do we have to gain by letting the police in on what we know about Robin?"

"That's simple," said Scott. "It's a moral and ethical problem and doctors are supposed to have ethics. Sousa should be brought to justice for killing these people. We're not off the hook yet. You can get AIDS up to eight years after exposure. The good news is that she looks pretty healthy so far."

Detective Gray spoke up. "I think the New Orleans police have kept their files open on that murder case but I'm not sure the Dallas police have."

"You don't know that," said Scott. "A murder case isn't closed until they find the murderer, particularly since it was the assistant D.A. from Dallas who was killed."

"What would you tell those detectives," asked Aronson, "if they ask you about Sousa? Would you tell them that he became a transvestite, had a sex change, and is now a female bombshell living in Paris?"

"They'd say you were as crazy as a hoot owl! Sousa could kill someone else, or could be plotting to kill someone right now!"

"That's right," said Detective Gray. "She's a strange one and very unpredictable. Well, are we going to tell those New Orleans police what we know or are we going to sit on it?"

"There's one other lead we have to follow up," said Scott. "Robin flew in from Paris to see that plastic surgeon, Von Salzen, at least once. Gray, why don't you give him a call and see if he's heard from her?"

"OK. I'll call him tomorrow."

The following day Scott received a call from Detective Gray.

"I think we should have another meeting right away," said Gray.

"Why? What's up?" asked Scott.

"There's been a new development. That plastic surgeon in Los Angeles, Dr. Von Salzen, was killed in a fire three weeks ago. The police think it was arson."

"What happened?"

"That fancy office was burned down, but it wasn't completely destroyed."

"What do you mean?" asked Scott.

"Four people were killed in the fire; Dr. Von Salzen, two of his nurses, and a patient. They didn't die from burns—they died from suffocation."

"What's that got to do with it?"

"It's got a lot to do with it! The fire started in the basement of the three-story office building and incendiaries and suspicious substances were found. The four bodies were found on the third floor, where there wasn't any fire damage. They died from smoke inhalation."

"Didn't they try to open any windows?"

"That's the problem. No one could have opened them—they were all nailed shut."

"Well, that certainly makes it look like a suspicious fire. Someone was obviously out to get him."

"That could be anybody. He took care of so many kooky people. He told me he operated on seventy transsexuals—and we all know those people are nuts."

"They were also out to destroy some of the files," said Gray. "Most of them were burned, although a few were saved. The sprinkler system didn't work either."

"It sounds like a professional job to me," said Scott.

"The whole building would have been destroyed if it wasn't for a patient who was late for his appointment. He saw flames in the basement and called 911 on his car phone. The fire engines responded rapidly."

"Well, at least we know Robin didn't have anything to do with the fire," said Dr. Aronson.

"How can you tell that?" asked Gray. "She could have contracted someone to start the fire—although I don't believe if she was pleased with her operation she would want to kill him. She might have wanted her files destroyed, however. This case is becoming more baffling the deeper we get into it."

"You're right," said Scott. "It might be interesting to find out if she's been in Los Angeles lately. Did you try to check on that?"

"Yes, I did," said Gray. "Von Salzen's appointment book wasn't burned in the fire and her name was in the book. She was supposed to see him the week after the fire."

"That's interesting. She could have been in Los Angeles at the time of the fire!"

"Well, there's one thing for sure."

"What's that?" asked Scott.

"She won't be flying to Los Angeles to see him any more. There's no way we'll be able to pick her up that way. Do you think she could have had someone set that fire?" asked Gray.

"I don't know," said Scott. "If she did she certainly is covering up her tracks. This whole mess is getting more complicated all the time. It's scary. I've given you over seventy-thousand to track Sousa and we still don't have him."

"I haven't exactly been sitting on my ass. We know Sousa's a female now and she's living in Paris somewhere," said Gray.

"Paris has over a million people," replied Scott. "I'm getting pissed off that you haven't apprehended her!"

"If you think someone else can do a better job, hire them!"

"No. I can't do that," said Scott. "We still have to pursue her. I think I want you to check in with the New Orleans and Dallas police to see if they have come up with anything new."

"I was down there six months ago, and I saw the files on the case in New Orleans. They wanted to know why I was so interested. I told them Sousa owed my client a lot of money."

"Well, until they solve the murder, they have to keep the investigation open, right?" asked Aronson.

"They should! I was more impressed with the New Orleans detective squad than the one in Dallas."

"What do you mean?"

"In Dallas, they gave me a hard time. They wouldn't let me look at the files. I think they were disturbed that one of their fair-haired boys, the assistant district attorney, was a homosexual. I don't think they liked the bad publicity they got from the media when he was shot and killed."

"I think someone should go to New Orleans and tell the police what we know," said Aronson. "Someone should talk to that district attorney and show him those pictures we've gotten of Robin. He might be able to talk to the *préfect de police* from Paris and get them to pick her up."

"What are they going to arrest her for?"

"For questioning concerning the murder of three people," replied Aronson.

"If you show those pictures of that nude broad and tell them she is a he, they'll laugh at you."

"I'm not so sure," said Gray. "I'm willing to make the trip to New Orleans again if you'll pay my expenses. I'd also love to see Paris."

"I bet you would," said Scott.

"No salary?"

"That's right. I want to solve this case. It's driving me buggy. Go talk to that district attorney in New Orleans again. I'll pay your expenses."

Detective Gray took the next flight to New Orleans.

He was drawn back to New Orleans by the frustration of not finding out any more about what happened that night at the Hilton Hotel when Sousa's wife and the assistant district attorney from Dallas were shot to death.

He remembered seeing Sousa and the assistant D.A. from Dallas board an American Airlines plane for New Orleans. He got on the next flight to New Orleans and tried to get a room at the Hilton. He wanted to snooze around to see if he might find some new leads. There were no rooms available that night because of a convention in town, so he had to settle for a second-rate hotel five blocks away. The next day, it cost him a $20 tip to get a room at the Hilton and another $10 tip to find out which room Sousa had been staying in. He had read the New Orleans police report about how the two bodies were found by the cleaning lady in the morning when she went in to clean up the room and make the beds.

It evidently had been a professional job because there was no evidence of a struggle and both bodies were nude, stretched out on the bed, and with a single bullet wound behind each left ear.

Detective Gray decided to go downtown to the library at the newspaper—*The Time-Picayune*—to see if he could find anything in the paper he might use for a lead.

He had the librarian pull the newspapers for the three days before and three days after the date on which the crime was committed.

He did find out some new facts. The crime was committed two days after the start of the American Bar Association's Annual Meeting. In fact, the crime was committed on the night of a big banquet that was held at the Hilton. It was a Saturday night and Attorney Sousa and the assistant district attorney had attended that banquet.

The Attorney General of the United States gave the keynote address, discussing the increased problem of drugs and street crimes in the country. In fact, his picture was on the front page of the newspaper. It was a black-tie affair and the society section of the Sunday edition showed pictures of many of the outstanding lawyers and judges dancing with their wives with the names captioned underneath.

Detective Gray read all the names of the prominent lawyers from New York City, Washington, Chicago, and San Francisco.

One of the pictures caught his eye. It showed the assistant D.A. from Dallas dancing with Robert Sousa's wife.

I suppose you could call that the last dance, mused Detective Gray. I wonder where Robert Sousa was when they were dancing?

Oh well, maybe Sousa got mad and bumped them off—it sorta looks that way. There were other photographs of dancers in the newspaper, including the chief district attorneys and their wives from New Orleans and Dallas.

The article stated there were over 1,200 lawyers and judges at the gathering and it was obviously a gala affair.

In one of the middle sections of the Sunday newspaper there was a small headline that read, *Attorney from Dallas and woman shot and killed at the Hilton.* It was not a big article and it stated that the identity of the woman could not be accurately established.

Detective Gray had copies made of all the newspaper articles and planned to read them when he got back to his room at the Hilton.

When he got there, he showed the headlines of the murder article to the clerk. He was an elderly gentleman who looked as though he had worked at the hotel for quite a while.

"Were you working here when this murder occurred?"

"Yes. I was the desk clerk that night," he replied.

"Do you keep track of all the room reservations?" asked Gray.

"Of course we do. They're all put on computers."

"How long do you keep the records?" asked Gray.

"They're kept until the bill is paid."

"Do you know who paid the bill for those two people who were murdered?"

"I'd have to look it up and tap into the main computer. I can't give out that information because of what happened," he said.

Detective Gray flashed his badge.

"That case has gone unsolved. How about finding out who paid the bill?"

"I'll try," he replied.

It cost Gray another $10.

The desk clerk went over to the main counter and tapped into the bigger computer.

"I can give you some of the information," he said. "That bill was not paid. It was for one of the best suites in the hotel. It had two bedrooms and a living room with a conference table. The main suspect, an Attorney Robert Sousa, disappeared and left without paying the bill. The room was reserved for five days. It was for he and his wife and the assistant district attorney from Dallas, Texas."

This is weird, thought Gray. Two former lovers who are homosexuals and a wife sharing a suite. The wife and former homosexual lover get bumped off—clean job—their nude bodies in the same bed. The wife is about five months pregnant. I wonder what else the New Orleans police found in that room?

When he got back to his room Detective Gray took out the New Orleans police file on the case and read through it again. Sousa's wife's negligee had been neatly placed on the chair by the bed and the assistant district attorney's underclothes were neatly piled on another chair. There were a couple of half-empty glasses on the bureau and some Eagle Snacks that were half empty by the night table.

What was Sousa's wife doing crawling into bed with the assistant D.A. from Dallas—she was pregnant. It looked more and more like Sousa was justified in bumping them both off. There was no gun found. However, two bullets were recovered and analyzed.

The report stated the dance ended around 3:00 A.M. Sousa had been seen going down to a bar on the first floor at about 2:00 A.M. He was seen drinking with three or four other attorneys. He was last seen going up to his room alone around 3:00 A.M.

The big question was, what happened between 3:00 and 4:00 A.M. when he left the hotel and went to the airport? He had to have gotten a gun somewhere in order to shoot the other two occupants of his suite.

After spending four days in New Orleans, Gray decided to pay a visit to the district attorney's office.

He had a long wait but finally got into see District Attorney John Harrigan.

"Attorney Harrigan, I'm Detective Gray from New England. I wonder if I could see your files on the murder of that assistant D.A. from Dallas that took place in New Orleans three years ago."

"That's interesting that you're here inquiring about those files. We have been going nowhere solving that case. One week ago the district attorney from Dallas was looking for those files and we have been having difficulty locating them for him. He said the Los Angeles police wanted to look at the files. Now, why would all you people be wanting to look at those files?" asked Attorney Harrigan. "Is there something you people know that the New Orleans police should know about?"

"Yes, there is," replied Detective Gray. "I read all about that murder in the New Orleans newspaper the day after it happened. The newspaper said you were trying to locate a material witness who might have seen the assistant district attorney and the woman before they were shot—an attorney by the name of Robert Sousa."

"Were you ever able to locate Sousa?"

"No, not a trace of him. We've searched high and low for him."

"What would you say if I told you I think I know where Sousa is and that he is no longer a he but a she?"

"Well, I'll be!" said Harrigan. "That's probably why we can't find him—I mean her."

CHAPTER

The next night Gray flew into the Dallas-Fort Worth Airport, got a rental car and checked into the Marriott Hotel. The following morning he drove out to the house where Attorney Bill Carroll used to live. The home was in a nice section in the outskirts of Dallas. He drove up the street and noticed there were three cars parked in the driveway.

He parked his car, turned on the radio, wrote down the license plate numbers of the cars, and waited. All the cars were late models and one of them had a Texas state seal on the door.

At 8:00 A.M. two men came out holding hands and got into one of the cars. It looks like the same gang that had a male whorehouse down here, thought Gray. They must be back in business.

Sure enough, two more guys came out and got into another car. There was one car left in the driveway—the one with the Texas state seal.

I think I'm going to follow that car when it leaves, Gray decided.

At 8:30 A.M. a tall man wearing dark glasses and a short stocky man came out and got into the last car. They drove to the freeway and headed for Dallas with Gray following close behind. They were moving right along, exceeding the speed limit. He stayed right with them in his rental car.

He was doing 75 mph when flashing lights appeared behind him and he had to pull over to the side of the road.

"God damn it!"

As the officer approached the side of his car he said, "You were exceeding the speed limit, Mister. That's a rental car. What's your hurry? I'd like to see your license and registration, please."

Gray pulled the rental car registration out of the glove box and got out his driver's license.

"I guess I was in a hurry to get into Dallas," replied Gray, as he flashed his badge to the officer and gave him the rental car paperwork.

"What's a detective from New England doing down here in Dallas?" he asked.

"Visiting some relatives," replied Gray.

"I should give you a ticket for speeding," replied the officer. "But I won't this time. You're part of the fraternity. Watch your speed. Detectives can get arrested for speeding just like anyone else."

"Thanks a lot!" replied Gray.

As the officer drove away, Gray was mad at himself for being stopped. He felt he might be on to something and now he lost the car he was following.

What should I do now, he wondered? I think I'll go visit that district attorney and see if he's come up with any new findings on the Sousa case. He drove to the district attorney's office and saw the car with the state seal parked outside. He walked into the building.

"Do you have an appointment with the district attorney?" asked the secretary.

"No," replied Gray.

"State your business," she replied, quite curtly.

"I'm interested in discussing a specific murder case with the district attorney that has not been solved."

"What case is that? Was it in our district?"

"No. It was in New Orleans. In fact, it was the murder of the assistant D.A. from this office, Bill Carroll. It happened a few years ago," replied Gray.

"Oh! Oh!" the secretary exclaimed. "You'll have to talk to District

Attorney Joseph Russo about that case. That record is kept in his confidential files in his office. I know very little about it. I do know that it's still unsolved."

"Is the district attorney in?"

"No, he's testifying on a case in superior court this morning," she replied. "He's due to be back here at 1:00 P.M."

"Do you think he'll see me then?" asked Gray.

"That's up to him," she replied. "Why don't you get some lunch and come back?"

"I'll do that."

At 1:00 P.M. Detective Gray returned to the district attorney's office. Attorney Russo had not returned from court. He finally returned at 3:00 P.M.

Detective Gray waited for an additional 30 minutes and then was escorted into Russo's office. He decided to introduce himself.

"I'm Detective Harry Gray from New England," he said. "I used to be a detective from the third precinct in Manhattan."

"Have a seat," said Attorney Russo. "My secretary tells me you're interested in the Bill Carroll murder case. Is that correct?"

"Yes," said Gray. "We're trying to locate Attorney Robert Sousa."

"Well, good luck with that one. We've come to a dead end on that case. The district attorney in New Orleans said the last they knew he was in San Francisco. The California state police have been unable to come up with anything. In fact, we've reached a dead end in trying to find Sousa. He's disappeared from the face of the earth."

"Could I see your files on the case?" asked Gray.

"Why are you still pursuing this case?" asked the district attorney.

"Robert Sousa owes my client a large sum of money. He's also absconded with some confidential tax records from the law firm where he worked."

"Not only is he a murderer—he's a thief," said Russo.

"That's right," said Gray.

"We've more or less closed the files on this case," said the D.A. "If we do catch him, he'll probably claim he caught Bill Carroll making out with his wife in bed so he shot them. It certainly looked that way from the evidence we have. A jury in Texas would probably let him get off scot free."

"It doesn't look that way to me," said Gray.

"What do you mean?" asked the D.A.

"Well, we have evidence that Bill Carroll was a homosexual," replied Gray. "And homosexuals don't enjoy sleeping with girls."

"How did you find out that he was a homosexual?" asked Russo.

"I think we got that from the New Orleans police files on the case," replied Gray.

"I've seen those files and there's no mention of homosexuality."

Detective Gray started to squirm in his chair.

"To be honest with you, I don't remember where we found that out."

"What else have you found out about this case that we don't know?"

"Not too much," replied Gray.

"I could subpoena you and question you under oath if you're keeping information from us."

"You wouldn't believe what I tell you about Sousa anyway," said Gray.

Suddenly the D.A. seemed more interested in finding out about Sousa.

"Do you know where Sousa is now?" he asked.

"We don't know exactly where he is, but we believe he's masquerading as a female in Paris."

"That's preposterous," said Russo. "We knew he was a homosexual just like Carroll, and homosexuals don't like females, they like males. You're on the wrong track, Mac! What name is Sousa using? That's probably why we've been unable to find him—or her."

"He's using the name Robin Cooker," said Gray.

"Have you put that name through the government files and checked the social security numbers?"

"Yes," said Gray. "They're different."

"Then they're not the same person," said the D.A. "Why don't you send someone over to Paris to look for her?" suggested Russo.

"Because that costs a lot of dough," said Gray.

"Notify the French police. Maybe they can help."

CHAPTER

Robin thought back to the June day in Paris when she first met François. She thought that day changed her whole life.

She remembered every detail: I had gone out for a walk on the avenues with my French poodle, Fifi. I was immaculately dressed in a snug emerald-green Christian Dior dress with gold trim, low-cut front, and a bit daring in the derriere. I had taken the pins out of my hair, allowing it to freely flow down my back. My shining gold-blonde hair sparkled in the sunlight. My dress was short—above the knees—accentuating my long slender legs and I wore matching emerald-green high heels. I often took walks along the avenues to observe the populace. I was frequently approached by young dashing Frenchmen and would be invited to lunch or dinner.

I refused their invitations because I didn't feel ready for a serious encounter, although my sex drive was there. I knew it would be only a matter of time before I would select someone to help release my inhibitions. That day quickly came.

It was a beautiful sunny Spring day and some of the flowers were in bloom at the Tuilleries Garden. There were also quite a few other damsels out for strolls but none caught the eye of the Frenchmen more than I. I was the center of attraction.

Out of the corner of my eye I saw an expensive chauffeured Renault limousine slowly following behind me. I walked by the Place de la Concorde and started to walk up the Champs-Elysées. My attention was brought to the car because some of the cabs were honking their horns, trying to get the car to speed up. I noticed a tall, distinguished gentleman get out of the limousine and start to walk behind me.

I became frightened and walked faster. My French poodle would be little protection. The distinguished gentleman continued to walk behind me but didn't get closer. I decided to walk down the tree-lined Boulevard de la Madeleine—perhaps he wouldn't follow that way—then again, maybe he would.

I window shopped, stopping and looking in the windows at all the elegant displays of dresses, shoes, and accessories—they were works of art. Christian Dior and Yves St. Laurent had shops in the area also. I bought some of my best lingerie at Nina Ricci's.

I looked back, out of the corner of my eye, in hopes of getting a better look at the man following me—was he still there? He was. I started walking slower but he didn't approach. I wanted to see what he looked like. I continued to walk more slowly down the Avenue toward a small French restaurant. Perhaps he'll ask me to dinner. I suspected that he was quite rich because his chauffeured limousine continued to follow behind him.

As I slowed my walk, he got closer and I could see him better. He appeared to be very good looking. My heart began to beat faster. Could he be the one? He was watching my every movement. I noticed that he stopped when I stopped. I decided to be bold and turned around quickly and walked toward him.

He didn't move. As I approached him, he looked much more handsome—very athletic and distinguished looking—tall, perhaps weighing over 200 pounds with a black mustache. He wore a beautifully tailored gray pinstriped suit. He looked very prosperous and very French.

"*Comment allez-vous?* How are you?" I asked with a broad smile.

"*Je vais très bien. Et vous, Mademoiselle?*" he replied. "I am very well and you?" He kept repeating himself in French and English, perhaps because he didn't know whether I was French or American.

"*Bien,*" I replied.

"*Parlez vous anglais?* Do you speak English?"

"*Naturelment,* but of course," I replied. "I speak French and English."

"I have noticed you for quite some time," he said. "*Vous êtes très beau*—you are very beautiful and have a beautiful walk."

"*Merci,*" I said as I flashed my best smile and curtsied.

"Are you taken?" he asked.

"*Bien entendu,* why of course!" I replied as I smiled again.

"*Quel dommage!* What a shame!" he replied.

I smiled again and said, "*C'est vous, toi.* It is you!"

The handsome Frenchman's face lit up and he smiled broadly. He took my hand and kissed the back of it. "*Mademoiselle,*" he said.

"*Je vous aime avec tout mon coeur.*"

"I could love you with all my heart."

"*Comment vous appellez-vous?*" I asked. "What's your name?"

"François Bouvier."

"What a nice name! Are you married?"

"*Non,*" replied François. My heart began to beat faster.

"*Bien,*" I said as I took his hand and squeezed it, my crystal blue-green eyes flashing. "*Voulez-vous que je vous à accompagne?* Would you like me to go with you?"

"*Dejeunier?* Dinner?" he asked.

"Why of course!"

"Where would you like to eat?" he asked as he hailed his chauffeur.

"You choose and surprise me. What about Fifi?"

"My chauffeur will take care of the dog. Café de la Paix," he told the driver.

We quickly arrived at the café and the maître d' seated us in a select spot under a large parasol. All eyes were on me as François held my chair. I was the prettiest woman in the café.

"Champagne?" asked François.

"*Un petit,*" I replied.

Charles, the maitre d' produced a wine list and François selected a very expensive champagne.

"*Vous êtes magnifique!*" said François. "You are so beautiful."

My face lit up.

"*Merci beaucoup!* Thank you," I replied.

"*Comment vous appellez-vous?* What's your name?" he asked.

I hesitated for a minute, for I had recently changed my name to Cartier.

"*Je m'appelle Robin.* My name is Robin. Robin Cartier."

"*Magnifique!*"

The meal seemed to take forever. I had decided that François would be my first endeavor for love-making. He was charming, had a magnificent athletic body, dressed perfectly and seemed to truly want to court and charm me. He seemed to be quite nervous and was obviously trying to please. I was sexually aroused and wanted him to bed me. I could hardly wait to give up my beautiful new body to his. After eating, I had had enough of the chit-chat and the sun was going down. Finally, he asked the question I wanted to hear.

"Would you like to see my place in the country or perhaps a suite at the Ritz?"

I hesitated before answering. I didn't want him to know I was anxious. The apartment would be too far away. I was definately in heat and wanted quick sexual satisfaction. It was getting dark.

"Perhaps the Ritz," I replied.

"*Bien.* The Hotel Ritz it will be. I'll have to make a phone call first."

François went to the phone and I went to the ladies room to freshen my makeup. We left the Café de la Paix and François hailed his chauffeur. He held the door for me and got in behind.

"Hotel Ritz, 15 Place Vendôme," he instructed the chauffeur. François put his arm around me and pulled me to him. His mouth sought my lips. They were full, warm, and passionate as I gently parted my lips and quickly darted my tongue between his teeth. His mouth engulfed my tongue as I gently rotated the tip against the back of his mouth. He tried to palpate my breasts but I pushed his hands away.

"*Attendez un moment.* Wait just a moment," I said. "Wait till we're alone."

"Your breasts are very delicate, beautiful and in full flower. *Vous permettez moi à touche*? Do you permit me to touch?"

Rather than disappoint him, I gently took his hand and placed it on my right breast.

"*Pas de soutien-gorge,*" François exclaimed, as he squeezed gently and I arched my back to help protrude my breasts. "*Si tellement ferme*—so firm."

I was getting more passionate as my mouth continued to answer his kisses.

We finally arrived at the Hotel Ritz and François jumped out to open the door and assist me out of the limousine.

I could hardly wait to get to the suite. I mustn't look too anxious, I reminded myself.

François opened the door to the large suite. It could have been the bridal suite by its size and furnishings. Once we got inside I was smothered by his kisses.

"*Allez lentement. Donnez moi le temps de souffler,*" I spoke in French first and then in English. "Slow down. Give me time to catch my breath," I said as I was crushed against his chest.

François was not to be denied. I was picked up like a feather and taken into the bedroom and gently placed on the oversized bed.

I released the straps and buttons behind my dress and slid out of my garment as François raced to take his clothes off. He had more on than I so I lay back in the middle of the bed in anticipation. I arched my back to show off my beautiful breasts.

"*Très beau, très beau,*" he exclaimed as he looked at my nude body. I could hardly wait for the love-making to start and for his penetration.

"*Très beau, Très beau,*" he exclaimed again and again, as he pulled my body to his. I arched my back to raise my buttocks off the bed. His palms took the cheeks of my buttocks in his hands. He drove for my vagina. I couldn't feel him inside me. We wrestled around the bed as I tried to position myself for his entry. Sweat came to his brow as he continued to probe. I could feel him against my pelvis. After an eternity he spoke up.

"*Est-ce vous aux de vierge?* Are you a virgin?"

"*Oui,*" I replied.

He continued to try as I tried to please him. Tears came to my eyes. I wanted him so. I wanted to give him my love. I started to cry.

"*Mon cheri, Mon cheri. Je vous aime.* My dearest, my dearest. I love you," he exclaimed. "*N'ayez pas peu!* Don't be afraid."

"*Eile avert les yeux. Pleu de larmes.*" My eyes were full of tears. I felt that I was like a flower that wanted to burst into full bloom for François.

I continued to cry as François continued to probe. It was no use. Our bodies would not meld together.

"*Sacre fleur et je suis dans la fleur de l'age*. God damn and I'm in the prime of life," said François. "*Pardon! Excusez-moi, Robin,*" he exclaimed.

"I am so sorry," I responded as tears flowed down my cheeks. "*De n'est pas le moment s'aimer, s'entrarme*. This is not the time for us to love one another.

"*Mon cheri, mon cheri,*" said François as he pulled me to him and tried to console me.

"Do you wish to stay here tonight in my bed?"

"*Non,*" I replied.

"Perhaps you should see a doctor to make a small cut?"

"Oh, yes," I replied. "I will find out what's wrong."

François kissed me passionately as I lay on the bed. He then put his head down and kissed the nipples of my breasts.

"*Je vous aime*. I love you," I said. "I will see my doctor in the morning. Will you still want to see me?"

"But of course," he replied. "It's too bad you can't see the doctor tonight, instead of waiting until morning."

CHAPTER

François had his chauffeur take Robin back to her apartment. She sobbed all the way. It was 4:00 A.M. when she got into bed. All kinds of negative thoughts were going through her mind. Would she see François again? He was so tall, athletic and had such a marvelous body, she could easily fall madly in love with him. Tears continued to run down her cheeks. What had gone wrong? She had been assured by two plastic surgeons that her operations were success-ful. The most important operation didn't work! She dilated her vagina with the metal stent and it went in all right. *"Au nom de Dieu sapresti,"* in the name of God—God darn! What had gone wrong? She continued to cry and, totally exhausted, she finally fell asleep.

She tossed and turned all night and into the morning and finally awoke at noon.

Bad thoughts continued to engulf her mind. She decided to call her French plastic surgeon, Dr. Pierre Dubois. She had difficulty getting through to his secretary. Her sobbing on the phone helped to get through.

"Dr. Dubois, I have to see you today. I have an extreme emergency," she said.

It was most unusual for a plastic surgeon to have emergencies but he remembered Robin very well. She was the magnificent transsexual who had been operated on in Los Angeles. He could hear her sobbing on the phone.

"What's wrong, Robin?"

"My sex change is not working."

Dr. Dubois remembered that some transexuals become suicidal and want to be reversed. Robin's operation had been perfect and there should have been no problem in making the change to a woman.

"Come in this afternoon, Robin. You may have to wait for a short time. I'll work you in."

"*Merci beaucoup*," she replied.

Robin got to the doctor's office at 3:00 P.M. and had to wait almost two hours before she saw him. She was agitated and disturbed. Finally, Dr. Dubois' secretary told her that she could go in. She burst into tears when she saw him.

"Calm down, Robin," he said as he tried to console her. "It can't be that bad."

"It's worse," she said as she blotted the tears from her eyes.

"Get yourself together and tell me what went wrong."

"After I saw you last month and you told me everything was perfect and well healed, I decided that if the right man came along I'd bed down with him. Well, this magnificent specimen of a male came along—a tall, handsome Frenchman. He was perfect. He had a pleasant personality and was very rich.

"We bedded down together and my new vagina didn't work! He tried and I tried, but he couldn't penetrate me. It was the most frustrating experience I've had in my entire life. We rolled all around on the bed for a long time with no luck. He had no difficulty getting an erection. It was just that he couldn't get into my vagina. I wanted it so much! He thought I was a virgin—that I had a hymen covering the opening. What could I do or say? I told him I was a virgin."

"Well, you are a virgin, but not in the true sense of the word. You have a new vagina."

"There's something drastically wrong. I want you to check me out."

"All right. I'll have my nurse take you back to the examining room and you can disrobe. We'll put your legs up in stirrups and see what's wrong down below."

After Robin was prepared, Dr. Dubois came into the room. He put gloves on and used a vaginal speculum to look into her vagina. It looked perfectly normal.

That Dr. Von Salzen who did your operation is a true artist," said Dr. Dubois. "In the recesses of your vagina he made a nubbing—it's a hard piece of tissue in the center that feels exactly like a cervix. Everything looks all right here to me."

She started to cry. "I don't understand."

"Your vagina has a normal healthy membrane lining its surface. Have you been taking all your estrogens?"

"Yes."

Dr. Dubois placed three fingers together and put them in her vagina. There was plenty of room within her vault. "I want you to press down around my fingers—strain as though you're having intercourse."

Robin strained real hard and Dr. Dubois felt the muscles tighten around his fingers. "I think I know what your problem is."

"What? What is it? Can I be helped?"

"Quite simply! Why don't you get dressed and I'll explain it to you."

Robin's face lit up and broke out in a smile. She got dressed quickly and went back to Dr. Dubois' consultation room. He was smiling too.

"You're too anxious."

"You'd be anxious too, if you were me and you saw that hunk of a Frenchman who wanted to make love to you."

"Your problem is that you have to learn to relax before penetration so entry can be accomplished. It's sort of like riding a horse. Sometimes it takes a while to break in the horse so you won't be thrown off its back. You have to be persistent to break in some horses. That's part of your problem. You're the new horse and François was trying to break you in so he can ride you while he's making love to you.

"It will take a while, but you'll find out that once you develop rhythm together with your partner you'll be able to use your pelvic muscles to your advantage. In fact, I have a transsexual, not as pretty as you, who says she can end her lovemaking and hasten his orgasm just by tightening up her muscles intermittently. She said you have to be careful though, because you can force him out and he might have trouble getting back in."

CHAPTER
16

François was upset with himself after he dropped Robin off at her apartment. He had always prided himself with his manhood and his ability to perform for the women he loved. From the age of fifteen when he was six feet tall, many girls from all classes pursued him and he had gained experience in the art of making love. However, he had never had a mistress or sycophantic woman. He had been happily married but his wife died in childbirth along with their firstborn—a son.

It was taking him a long time to get over that part of his life. It was also ten years now since he had bedded down with a woman. He was in perfect health and had no difficulty being stimulated by a beautiful woman.

Robin was the first woman he had attempted to have sex with for a long time. She was the most beautiful, delectable maiden he had ever seen. She seemed to be intelligent, irresistibly feminine with the most perfect body—magnificent beyond words. She seemed to want him as much as he wanted her. Her passion and desire for him was overwhelming. He was completely enthralled by her. She was a virgin—he had no doubt about that!

He was in a state of shock over what had transpired. Why did this happen? Was his approach wrong? Was he in too much of a hurry? Would she let him try again? Would she go out with him again? What should he do?

He decided to talk to a close friend and confidant, Dr. Charles Reins, about his problem. Charles lived in Paris so he called him and invited him to dinner, which Charles accepted.

"You sounded like you have some urgency in seeing me, François," said Charles.

"I do. It's a personal matter. I know I can trust you with my problem."

"What is it? Is it serious?"

"You know about the death of my wife, Antoinette, ten years ago. I have not slept with a woman since then."

"*Quel dommage!* You must have had many opportunities. You're still an attractive, distinguished man."

"That's just it. I met this beautiful, magnificent French woman two days ago. I took her to the Ritz Carleton to consummate our relationship, but I was unable to perform properly. I was able to get an erection—everything was working fine—but I was unable to penetrate. She said she's a virgin and I'm sure she is. It was so tight down there—if you know what I mean."

Charles had a broad smile on his face and started to laugh.

"It's not a laughing matter."

"I realize that. I can see that you are really out of practice. What's your hurry? There are beautiful and interesting women all over France, from the northern blondes of Lille to the Mediterranean brunettes of the Riviera. There's quite a few beautiful available French women out there."

"But I want this one," said François. "I could easily fall in love with her."

"Well, François, I've known you for many years and I think it's great that you're waking up. It's about time you *chercher les femmes.* It sounds like this one is for real. What's her name?"

"Robin Cartier."

"Well, you know that love and lovemaking in France is a national hobby—sometimes it's played like a game. She may be playing a game with you. Are you sure she's not just teasing you?"

"I'm sure! She had tears streaming down her cheeks. She was as frustrated as I. If you could see her you'd realize why I'm so disturbed. She dresses with a feminine elegance—oh la la! She has the most gorgeous face and the most beautiful body you've ever seen."

"It sounds like you're serious."

"I am!" said François. "What do you suggest I do?"

"I think you have to use a different approach from taking this pretty young maiden to a hotel room, particularly if she's a virgin. Why don't you take her to your château at Tours and spend a little time with her? Some French women like to be pursued differently. Robin sounds like she is something special—a special jewel. You have to pamper her. You know as well as I do they like to be courted. There's an art to making love. Some of them are like those spring horses that you have on your farm—the fillies. You can't break them in overnight and you have to get them when they're in heat."

"You might be right. I think I'll take your advice."

When he got back to his apartment, he called the florist and sent a dozen red roses to Robin. On the note he wrote, *"Je vous adore, Robin!"* and then, "I believe I was too hasty when first we met. I have a château in Tours and would like you to accompany me there to spend a week or so. I want to show you how much I could really love you," and he signed his name.

When Robin received the roses with the note her tears suddenly dried up and her heart began to beat faster in anticipation of his call. Of course she would go! François was a woman's dream come true. He was so handsome and so ruggedly masculine. He was a giant of a man with a physique beyond comprehension. Tears of emotion filled her eyes, but they were not tears of grief, they were tears of joy. She would not fail this time. She had the secret for her success—she would be sure to relax when giving him her body. She knew that she already worshiped the ground he walked on and would do anything to please him.

The phone call came sooner than she expected. She hesitantly picked it up and it was François.

"Robin, this is François. I just want to tell you that I miss you already and apologize for the other evening. I didn't know you were a virgin. I hope you'll forgive me."

"François, I do. I do forgive you!"

"Did you read my note?"

"Yes! The answer is yes! I will go with you and spend time with you at your château in the country. I'm looking forward to it."

"When is the earliest you can be ready?"

Robin thought for a minute—she wasn't prepared for this question. She wanted to say she'd go right away, but she needed time to prepare. She wanted to pack some clothes and perhaps add a few new things to her wardrobe.

"It will take me a day or two to get ready. Is that all right with you?"

"But, of course. I'll pick you up on Tuesday. *Je vous aime.* I can hardly wait to be with you again."

"And I with you," she replied.

When she hung up the phone, her heart was beating rapidly. She felt like a young girl preparing for her first date. She took a bubblebath with perfumed soap and got out of the bathtub and looked at herself in the full length mirror. She did not look at herself as a whole woman—she looked at each little part of her body—for she wanted it to be perfect for François. She looked at her long, glistening blonde hair with the natural curls and ringlets. She decided she would have to call her hairdresser the first thing in the morning and have her hair put up in a French braid. She turned her head from side to side to see how she looked in the mirror and liked what she saw. She had a perfect cupid-shaped mouth with full lips and when she opened her mouth and smiled, her glistening, white, pearly teeth shone brightly. The nape of her neck was slender and beautifully shaped and her breasts were full, firm, and uplifted, with beautifully shaped nipples. She did a pirouette, like a spinning top, in front of the mirror and looked at her flat stomach and gently curved, but full buttocks.

As she stood on her toes whirling on one foot, her beautiful thighs and long slender legs with beautifully shaped ankles and calves were accentuated.

"I can hardly wait to give François all this," she said out loud, as she cupped her breasts with her hands. "I know I'm in love—so deeply in love, and yet the anticipation of what will happen takes my breath away."

She had difficulty sleeping and awoke early in the morning. She called her hairdresser and made an appointment to have her hair done. She also made an appointment to have a manicure. Then she made arrangements to go to Christian Dior's and Yves St. Laurent's, hoping to add a few new exciting dresses to her wardrobe. She also planned to stop at Rue des Saints-Pères to search for some new shoes. She was anxious to see François but she began to realize that she had a lot to do in a short time.

The day and night passed rapidly. François had told her they would be taking a train from Paris and his chauffeur would pick them up at the station in Tours and drive them to the château.

When François approached the door to Robin's apartment he did so with great apprehension. He rang the bell and was overwhelmed when she opened the door. She looked absolutely beautiful in every way. She put her arms around his neck and gave him a long kiss.

"I've missed you, François."

"I've missed you, too. I've been looking forward to this day and seeing you again."

"Well, then, let's be on our way."

The train trip was uneventful and took much too long for Robin. François held her hand and gazed into her eyes and made small conversation all the way to Tours.

The chauffeur picked them up at the station with the Renault limousine and they drove out into the beautiful farmland of the Loire Valley. Many French kings and noble families had built fortified castles and magnificent châteaus in the middle of the Valley during the thirteenth and fourteenth centuries and some were still standing.

François pointed out some of the châteaus as they drove through the gently langorous countryside. Robin could see the Loire River as it flowed through the Valley. She was captivated by the pristine beauty of the rolling hills and the castles with their round towers that were used as lookouts for protection. A lot of the architecture was Gothic and there was a warm Renaissance charm to the châteaus.

Robin's heart was beginning to quicken as she surveyed François from head to toe. He was more than she had ever hoped for in a man. Her fire had been lit and was slowly beginning to burn. She knew it would burst into a full-blown explosion when he pulled her to him and made love to her. She knew that time was getting closer.

The limousine finally arrived at François' château. It was a mammoth Gothic structure with towers and, by today's standards, still magnificent. François told her it had ninety rooms and had recently been completely modernized with new plumbing, lighting, and a magnificent living room and dining area that could seat more than two hundred people.

The chauffeur and butler brought her luggage in and Robin was introduced to all the servants. She was introduced to Marie, who would be her lady-in-waiting, and Marie was directed by François to take Robin to her room in the east wing of the château.

"You might want to freshen up before dinner," said François.

Robin was a little surprised by that statement, for she thought François could hardly wait to make love to her. She also could hardly wait to be in bed with him. Oh, well, it would be only a matter of time before he wouldn't be able to control himself. She would play his game for the time being.

"Yes, I think I might like to wash up and change into something relaxing after that train ride," said Robin, as she smiled at François.

Marie showed her to her room. In the center of the room was a large oval king-size bed. There was a walk-in closet and numerous chests along the walls. An adjoining bath had beautiful blue and white tile, a huge sunken tub, and full-length mirrors around the entire room.

"This bathroom is beautiful," she exclaimed to Marie.

"This is the new wing of the château," said Marie. "It was completely done over in 1987."

"That door on the other side of the room, where does it go?"

"That goes to the master's bedroom. Master François will be sleeping there tonight."

Robin thought about that. Not if I can help it, she decided.

"Marie, I think I'll take a bath before dinner. You can run a tub for me. Perhaps you can help me pick out some clothes for this evening."

"You have so many beautiful things," commented Marie.

"Thank you. I want to please François."

Robin picked out three tight-fitting dresses to show Marie: pink, chartreuse, and a flesh-colored one.

"Perhaps I shall bathe first and try them on so you can help me decide."

When the bath was ready, Robin put her toe into the water and it was just perfect. She noticed Marie staring at her.

"What are you looking at?"

"I'm looking at you, your face, and your body. I've never seen a more beautiful woman."

"Do you think I might please François?"

"Oh, yes! Oh, yes!" replied Marie. "He has been lonely for so long. All of us in the château have prayed that he might find someone to love and who will love him. He's such a kind and good man. We don't like to see him so sad. Maybe you will be the one to make him happy again."

When Robin got out of her bath, Marie dried her off with large warm towels.

"Your hair is so blonde and beautiful."

"Well, it's all natural," said Robin. "Which dress would you like me to try on first?"

"The chartreuse one."

Robin slipped into the dress. It fit like a glove, hugging each curve of her body. It was low-cut in front with spaghetti straps over the shoulders. It showed the half-moon mounds of her breasts pulled tightly against the thin silk material. Her nipples were easily seen through the cloth. The back was low-cut with a bow just above the waist. The skirt was short with a slit on one side to show off her thigh over her long slender legs. She wore no undergarments.

"Oh, what I would give to have your body and be as pretty as you," said Marie.

"Well, what do you think?" asked Robin, as she swung around.

"I don't think François is going to eat his dinner tonight. You have such ravishing beauty."

"The beige dress is more tantalizing. Would you like me to try that one on?"

"I think you would be beautiful in anything."

"I'll wear what you choose for me, Marie. If it does what you think it will do for me, I'll let you help me choose my clothes every day. What time does François want me to be ready for dinner?"

"Six, he said."

"What time is it now?"

"Five-thirty."

"We mustn't keep him waiting. I want to put a little perfume on and then I'll be ready."

Robin's bedroom was at the top of a spiral staircase that led directly into the dining room. The dining room had partitions that allowed the room to be made larger or smaller depending on the occasion. At this time, it had been made smaller for Robin's visit.

As she slowly descended the staircase, she saw François' eyes riveted on her every move. She decided to allow her body to relax as she came down, showing a flash of her slender legs with the movement of her hips. Her breasts strained against the chartreuse silk as she walked erect, much like a queen or princess with regal bearing.

He met her at the bottom of the stairs and kissed the back of her hand.

"You are so beautiful, Robin. You take my breath away."

"*Merci*," she replied, as she curtsied. "You are quite handsome, François," she said as she sat down on the hand-carved high-back chair he pulled out for her.

For the next hour the butler and the chef brought in delicious food fit for a king and queen. Wine from François' wine cellar was served with each course. The food was not overly filling, but just right.

François couldn't take his eyes off her. In fact, she thought she saw him salivating as he looked at her and it wasn't because of the food.

Robin had enough food and the wine had fully relaxed her. She felt she was ready for François. But, how could she give him the hint without appearing too aggressive? She decided to yawn and put her hand over her mouth. As she did, she said, "François, I'm getting a little tired. I think I'm ready for bed."

That was all François needed to hear. He stood up, walked around the table, picked her up in his arms and walked up the spiral staircase. When they got to the bedroom he crushed her in his arms and kissed her passionate lips. "*Mon ami, mon ami. Je vous adore, Robin.*"

He gently placed her on the large oval bed as he started to undress. Robin gently unzipped the back of her dress and let it slip to the floor. She laid back on the bed and arched her back. François' heartbeat quickened as he looked at her perfectly shaped breasts— two breasts as white as snow, almost like roses coming to full bloom with erect petals in the centers.

François decided to go slow. He felt Robin's breasts were ripe for caressing and holding in his hands as he gently palpated and kneaded them, as they reddened and swelled. He moved his moist lips over their tips, pressing them gently as he used the tip of his tongue and lips to suck the sweetness of her honey. Each sinew of the soft, but firm breast added to his fire and quickened her heart-beat. The tips of her breasts became erect, like roses in full bloom. He couldn't leave them alone, kissing them and caressing them as Robin arched her back to put them more fully into his mouth.

Robin was panting and sighing in ecstasy as she moved her body, gently to and fro, moving ever more closely to his massive frame.

Her eyes were closed and her beautiful blonde curls tossed against the silk sheets. His mouth crushed against hers as her tongue explored his, tantalizing his ardor. Robin was a willing captive of his masculine sexual desires as the palms of his hands reached beneath her buttocks. She could feel his erection against her upper thighs, which only aroused her more as she raised her but-tocks upward to ease his entry. She remembered that she must relax, although she felt her body was out of control. All she wanted to do was to respond to his desires.

She then felt the sensation she would always remember for the rest of her life as he penetrated her vagina and drove deeper and deeper into her. He smothered her lips with kisses as her body arched against his in response.

Soon a rhythm that she had no control over began to quicken ever so slowly. She felt she was in heaven floating on clouds. It was a feeling that was making her breathless and was so enjoyable that she didn't want it to end. His mouth covered her lips and her legs wrapped around his, tighter and tighter. Then she dug her heels into the bedsheets, arching her back upward toward the ceiling as their bodies melded into one. Every movement made it seem deeper and deeper, their passion uncontrollable.

Robin felt she was giving her body to François in the sexual act that was the truest expression of her love for him. Sex was a gift from God. It was the ultimate expression of her inner self and her romantic ethos. Her body was now completely out of her control and her basic animal instincts and desires were being satisfied by François. Her sighs of endearment and love and her groans of ecstasy just seemed to enhance his drive as their bodies drove to an increasing crescendo. Suddenly she felt his body quiver as they both reached the ultimate spasm of an erotic, overwhelming climax.

CHAPTER
17

François was the first to wake up after the lovemaking, even though Robin had completely sapped his strength. He looked at the beautiful specimen of womanhood who was cradled in his arms. She looked so fragile and delicate and so, so, beautiful. Her body was so perfect with such beautiful, voluptuous lines. Just a few days ago he had seen her from a distance. She was the epitome of beauty of the French women, just the way she dressed so classically French. The way her hair was coiffured and the impetuous cupid appearance of her mouth, the way she walked so sensuously, moving her hips and buttocks. Now she was here in his arms, sleeping contentedly and she looked even more beautiful close up. Her hair was so naturally blonde, her eyelashes so long, and the crystal blue almond-shaped eyes with the cute, turned-up nose. Her mouth was perfect and her teeth pearly white.

He looked at her breasts, so erect and firm, along with the beauty of the sharply pointed nipples, her flat abdomen with the curve of her hips and buttocks, and her long, slender, perfectly shaped legs.

As he scrutinized her beautiful body he started to become

aroused. He heard the grandfather clock chimes ringing in the hour. The chimes started to wake Robin up as her eyelashes fluttered and her blue eyes opened.

"*Mon cheri*. Did I hurt you?" asked François.

"Oh, no! Oh, no! That was so beautiful I felt like I was in the heavens riding the waves of the clouds. I feel like the most beautiful flower that has just opened its petals."

"*Mon fleur*, my flower you are," said François.

"*Je t'aime*, I love you," she said.

"*Je t'adore!* I adore you," he replied. "You're so sweet, I could eat you up."

Robin thought for a minute. She felt he had, for his mouth had lovingly kissed and explored all the recesses of her body. His mustache had added to her excitement and enjoyment. His hands were gently squeezing her breasts now and she felt she was getting aroused again.

"I would like to make love to you in many different ways tonight. Is that all right with you?"

"Oh, yes," she replied. "My body and soul are totally yours!"

As he pulled her to him she opened her lips and his mouth met hers. She darted her tongue between his teeth again as a signal of acquiescence and passion. His mouth went to her neck and to her breasts and all the way down her legs. She felt so little and helpless as her body tried to fit into his large, muscular frame.

François turned her over onto her stomach and grabbed the cheeks of her buttocks. He lifted her up on her haunches and probed for her vagina from behind. Robin put her head down and put her arms across her chest and folded them so he could get better leverage for penetration. She was totally relaxed as she felt his organ slide into her vagina.

"Oh, oh, darling," Robin sighed. She moaned in ecstasy as he continued to drive into her. She pushed against his groin, answering his challenges. He put his hands over the back of her shoulders from behind to pull her body against him. There was no way she could move or resist. François was in complete control as he increased his rhythm and penetration and she tried to respond by pressing against his groin.

Robin was again feeling that strange sensation of being suspended in space and loving every minute of it. Her long blonde hair flowed in disarray down her tanned back. François briefly compared it to a beautiful mane of a filly horse when she raised her tail up for the penetration of a stallion. He was the stallion trying to please this gorgeous filly. She was the filly trying to please the stallion. Robin tried to arch her buttocks upward for better penetration.

After what seemed a long time, Robin felt his organ go into spasm and ejaculate intense pleasure into her vagina. He then collapsed on the bed next to her.

That last engagement exhausted them both. They were fully relaxed and tired out. Robin cuddled up to him, purring like a satisfied kitten. There was a brief verbal exchange.

"*Je t'aime*, François."

"*Je t'aime*, Robin."

They both drifted off to sleep, happily exhausted.

Robin dreamed about what it would be like to spend the rest of her life with François. He was so handsome, so strong, so athletic and oh, so French. Would he continue to want her and her body as he did now? Could she satisfy his insatiable desire to make love to her? Robin was in a new life, a new experience, and her heart was filled with joy. She knew she couldn't get enough of him. She felt so wonderful as he caressed her body and kissed her lips. She felt like a complete woman as they locked their bodies together in the sexual encounter.

Again François awoke first and looked at Robin stretched out on the white satin sheets. Her bare body was so tantalizing and beautiful as she lay there. The dim lights in the bedroom sent beautiful shadows across her body. The chimes on the clock downstairs began to ring the hour again.

She stretched, and as her muscles tightened they accentuated her curves even more. She heard the chimes and was waking up. Her arms stretched upward and her back arched as she took a deep breath, bringing her breasts taut against her chest. She opened her eyes and reached for François. He pulled her to him.

He started to become aroused again. Would she let him make love to her a third time? She looked so fragile and tender nestled in his arms. Should he ask her or should he wait for a signal from her?

"François, François, I love you so! You are my first love. I want just you!"

"*Mon cheri, Robin.* I believe you," he replied as he looked down at the white sheets and saw red blood spots on them. She truly had been a virgin.

Robin wondered whether François would try to share their love again. During the past few hours they had spent most of the time with their bodies locked together with only a brief nap in between. She felt totally relaxed and happy. That surgeon in Los Angeles had really done a good job. Her reconstruction was working, although she felt like she had been hit with a battering ram inside her vagina. She hadn't tried the trick with the muscle that Dr. DuBois told her about. She thought she might use it someday. Perhaps she would try to tease François a little to see if he could satisfy her again.

"Why don't you kiss me some more?" she whispered in his ear as she tickled his ear with her tongue. "*Je t'aime, François.* I still desire you."

He pulled her body to his as his mouth sought hers. Her full sensuous lips responded to his as the tip of her tongue once again tantalized his throat.

She arched her back and put her arms around him, compressing her breasts against his chest in a compelling, seductive manner. The tips of her nipples seemed to excite François and ignite his passion. She decided to be the aggressor this time. She bit his lip, tasting his blood and started to grind her hips against his groin. She was diabolically clever in arousing him. As she pressed her body against his she could feel the pulsating mass between his legs probing for her.

"Roll over onto your back, François," she said.

Wanting to please her in every way, he turned over on his back as her mouth kissed his entire body and the tip of her tongue explored his groin.

"Oh, darling, *mon cheri.* I too have never felt so completely happy," as she continued to please him.

She got on top of him and slowly she started rotating her hips in a circular pattern, grinding even deeper against his groin. While still on his back, he responded by arching upward against her. His hands reached up and gently palpated her magnificent breasts. She leaned forward to kiss his mouth and held his tongue against hers.

Her rotation and pressure continued. François wasn't sure he liked this position. She was the aggressor and he felt he should be the dominant one. He rolled her over and faced her with her back now on the bed. He pulled her long slender legs up and placed them over his shoulders as he drove deeper into her. She locked her legs around the back of his neck to increase her drive against his groin. Their rhythm slowly increased as their bodies locked tighter. Robin felt she was out of control as the heat of her passion began to overtake her. Her breathing increased and her heart was pounding. She no longer had control over her body.

"Oh, François, I love it. I love it. Give me all of it. Drive it into me harder. Harder. Oh, darling, I love you. I love you."

François' passion was also getting out of control as he tried to respond to her wishes. He drove harder into her pelvis. He felt her vagina tighten. He never felt anything quite like this before, as her muscles continued to tighten up intermittently. There was a beautiful slight smile on Robin's face as she practiced controlling her muscles. She really had finally learned how to relax and enjoy François.

Both were completely exhausted after this third time of passionate lovemaking and were awakened when the clock struck midnight.

"François, I love you," she said.

"Robin, I love you," he replied.

"Are you tired?" she asked.

"Totally," he replied. "I'm completely satisfied. You're the most extraordinary woman I have ever met. I want you to be mine."

"Oh, François," she said as she kissed him again. "I think I should use the bidet and bathe. You can stay in my bed tonight if you like."

"If I stay in your bed, I won't sleep. I won't be able to keep my hands off you."

"Then you should rest in your own bed, darling. I'm just beginning to get to know you. I might want to find out if you're a morning person tomorrow."

"I'll look forward to that," he responded as he walked toward his bedroom.

CHAPTER

Robin turned and headed for the bathroom to bathe. "François, I might like to see the sun rise with you," she said.

"Just call me, if you want me to join you."

"Could you have the maid wake me at 5:30?"

"I'll have her call you."

After she used the bidet and bathed in the sunken bathtub, Marie was waiting for her as she got out.

"I hope you had a pleasant evening with the master," she said.

"Oh, yes. It was exquisitely pleasant!"

Marie helped to dry off her body.

"You are most pretty," Marie commented. "God made you beautiful!"

If only she knew, thought Robin.

"All the people who work here at the château are happy about what's happening, *Mademoiselle*."

"Why is that?"

"You're the only one he's brought here to the château since his first wife died. He seems so happy again. We're all happy for him. Will you be getting married to him?"

"He hasn't asked."

"I'm sure he will. I can see the way he looks at you. Will you say yes?"

"I would give it very serious consideration. He captured my heart this evening."

"You seem very happy. I hope he wins your heart. What we've seen, we like! He needs to have an heir."

"That's not always easy."

"With beautiful bodies like yours and his, I'm sure you would make beautiful children together."

"We'll see. Marie, I want you to wake me thirty minutes before sunup. I want to shower and bathe before the master awakens."

Marie had a smile on her face. "I'll be sure to awaken you in time."

I think she knows what I have in mind, thought Robin.

Marie turned the lights out and Robin fell fast asleep.

The next thing she heard was a very soft voice saying, "Mademoiselle, it's time to get up. I've prepared your bath for you. Would you like me to bathe you?"

"Perhaps. I probably need a massage rather than a warm bath. All my muscles ache, but it's a good ache."

Marie washed her back with a soft sponge and gently massaged her back. It felt so good to Robin.

"Would you like me to lay out your clothes?" she asked.

"That won't be necessary."

"Will you be eating breakfast at 7:00?"

"No. I'm sure I will be later than that. I think the master will be later also."

"Would you like breakfast in bed?"

"Perhaps. I want you to awaken Master François at 6:30 and tell him I wish to see him."

"Yes, Mademoiselle. Do you wish that I change the sheets on the bed? I have some clean satin sheets."

"Why don't you go and change the bed now while I finish my bath. I have to put my make-up on."

"You look so beautiful. You don't need any make-up. I wish I looked as pretty as you and had as beautiful a body as you."

"A woman's face and body can be her fortune. It seems to be mine."

Robin got out of the bath and surveyed her body in the full-length bathroom mirror again. There were no flaws. Last evening's love-making had no effect on her body. If anything, her eyes were more radiant and her broad smile covered her face. She felt and looked like the cat who swallowed the canary.

He loves me! He loves me! Robin kept saying to herself. I feel as though I'm on top of the world. How can I make myself more beautiful for him? I wonder if he's a morning person. I think I could be a morning, afternoon, and night person with him. And he's so rich and handsome. There's nothing more I'll ever want out of life than François.

Robin started applying light-colored eye shadow. She gently plucked her eyebrows to form a slight curve and used a dark pencil to accentuate her brows. She selected light perfume to put behind her ears and between her breasts. She used a brush and a pencil to accentuate the lines of her lips. She then added a touch of musk oil to her breasts and vaginal area.

I don't think I need any Valium after last night, she muttered to herself. She then went to the closet to select some lingerie and a pretty lounging robe. She picked a light pink, see-through, very expensive French teddy with a snap crotch so it could easily be undone. The bra area had a cute bow that untied easily. The loung-ing robe was pink silk and covered her body completely. Her slip-pers were pink high heels. The robe had slits on both sides so her upper thighs and legs could easily be seen.

After she was dressed she spoke to Marie. "What do you think? Will he like what he sees?"

"But of course. His heart will melt in your hands. You haven't eaten since last evening. You must be starved."

"I think I could live on François' love," she replied.

"You might have more energy to respond to his love," suggested Marie.

"The sun is just coming over the horizon. You can awaken the master now.

"He's already up. He got up when you did and took his bath. He asked me to tell you that he would like to have breakfast with you."

"Downstairs or in my room?"

"Up here. The chef has a portable cooking cart. He can prepare a gourmet breakfast right in front of you in your room. I would suggest you have breakfast first."

"Marie, I think I'm going to like you. Tell François I will see him here."

Robin walked over and sat down on a chaise lounge.

François entered from his room. He had on a lounging robe and slippers.

"Good morning, *mon cheri*," he said. "Did you sleep well?"

"Oh, yes, François," she replied as she got up from the chaise lounge.

He walked over to her and gave her a big kiss. Robin hugged him and pressed her body against his. She thought she could feel a pulsating protrusion in his groin. He kissed her lips and neck and held her tight.

"You are like a beautiful flower that opens its petals to the sun. You look even more beautiful in the daylight."

"*Merci.* Shall we eat?"

"Perhaps we should."

"I'll call Marie and have her tell the chef we're ready."

The chef came to the door and rolled in a cooking cart.

"What would you like for breakfast, my dear?"

"I usually eat a very light breakfast. I'll have half a grapefruit, some of those fancy croissants, and coffee."

François told the chef he wanted a cheese omelet and a small steak.

There was a small table in the bedroom on which Marie arranged a white tablecloth, china, and a small vase with two red roses. She then served the breakfast. As she left, she said, "Have a pleasant morning."

Robin and François ate their breakfast quite rapidly. Robin could hardly wait to get back into his arms. He had such broad shoulders and muscular arms and a thick neck. His face was quite handsome but very rugged looking.

"I'm going to have you for my dessert," he said.

"*Oui, oui,*" said Robin as she stood up and walked toward the bed. François caught her from behind and quickly turned her around. He untied her lounging robe and she loosened his. He pressed her body to his as she responded to his kisses. His hands gently removed the robe from her shoulders as she did the same with his. He had a brightly colored bikini on. The bikini was having a difficult time restraining the pulsating mass between his legs. Robin got excited just seeing it.

François untied the bow restraining her breasts and cupped both her breasts in his hands as he leaned over and kissed their nipples.

François unsnapped the crotch of her teddy and gently removed it over her shoulders. She was completely nude except for the high-heeled slippers. She put her hands around François' waist and gently pulled his bikini off. She slowly leaned back onto the bed, pulling him down with her. Slowly she arched her back and, as she did, he penetrated her vagina. She was completely relaxed now and knew what she wanted to do. Once it slipped in she started to rotate her thighs and hips against his groin in a rhythmic response to his drive.

His mouth kissed her neck and breasts and she responded by darting her tongue in and out of his mouth. The rhythm of their lovemaking was more intense as each tried to satisfy the sexual drive of the other. Their lovemaking was like the best symphony played at a concert. There was more confidence in one another's ability to respond. They were both more relaxed and obviously enjoying each other.

Their mutual rhythm seemed to increase very smoothly as François tried to drive deeper into her pelvis. Robin slowly started to tighten up her vaginal muscle ever so lightly to increase his enjoyment. Her buttocks kept rising higher and higher off the satin sheets as his hands cupped her buttocks in his hands. Their passion was increasing and Robin tried to wiggle her hips and rotate her buttocks harder against him as she moved automatically to his movements. She started to moan and writhe in ecstasy, which only increased François' drive. Her long legs wrapped around him to lock him into her vagina.

"*Oui, oui*, François. I love you. I love you," she kept repeating. "I love all of you."

François' groin seemed to harden even more as she felt his spasmodic climatic orgasm.

This time Robin didn't pass out. She held his body on top of hers to cherish the moment.

After resting a short while, they tried another position and then took a brief nap.

When they awakened, François said, "Would you like to go for another horseback ride?"

"What do you mean by that?" she said as she smiled.

"I didn't mean it that way!"

"I think we should go for a walk! I think I need to strengthen my legs. They feel like spaghetti right now."

"Mine do too," he replied.

CHAPTER

During the three weeks that followed, Robin and François got to know each other better, physically as well as intellectually. After five nights of sleeping in separate rooms, it was their better judgment they might as well sleep together in one bed and, since Robin had the bigger bed, they'd sleep in her room.

Robin liked that much better because she liked cuddling up to François and knowing that he was sleeping next to her. It gave her a feeling of security and love that she wanted.

They became morning, noon, and evening people when it came to lovemaking and it was almost unpredictable when he wanted her. She felt as if she was taking her clothes off and putting them back on three or four times a day. Usually in the evening she'd prepare herself for bed, fixing her makeup and wearing a different negligee or bikini. That would stay on for a short time and then they would end up sleeping the rest of the night in the nude.

She mused that he had an insatiable desire for her body, for he seemed to always want her and there was never a day when they didn't have sex. He must have thought she was a nymphomaniac at times, because she would initiate the action after stimulating him. Her favorite position was to face him with his body on top so she could kiss his mouth and stimulate him with her tongue. He could also stimulate her by kissing her body and breasts. Robin felt more and more like a woman as each day passed and she loved it!

She loved the château because there were so many places they could be alone to enjoy each other. Or was it because the hired help stayed out of sight when they wanted them to?

Not all their days were spent in bed. They often went horseback riding and he would show her the vast land he owned. She found out that he owned four separate farms surrounding the château and that he had general managers or tenant farmers who worked the farms for him. There was a cattle farm, a dairy farm, a wheat farm, and a horse farm.

He met with the managers once a week in the main dining room to discuss any problems that had developed. She also found out that, because he was so successful with his farming, he was put on the Agricultural Board for France by President Jean-Paul Giscard.

He was also a close friend of the prime minister, Charles Delacroix and François told Robin they would socialize with him once in a while. Now that Robin was spending all her time with François, she would meet the prime minister in the near future. There was an international ball that François was asked to attend and he was to sit at the prime minister's table. He asked Robin if she would go with him to the ball.

"I'll have to get a gown in Paris. Are you sure you want me to go with you? I don't know any of your friends."

"I sincerely want you to go with me, and I want you to meet my friends. There's one part of the ball I don't like. I'll have to dance with Bridget, the prime minister's wife. She's a very aggressive woman and I really don't like her."

I wonder what he meant by that, thought Robin. Did that mean they would exchange dances and she would have to dance with the prime minister? She decided to ask François.

"François, when you dance with the prime minister's wife, does that mean I have to dance with the prime minister?"

"If he asks you to, you will. It's to be polite. He's a very important man and he has helped me get subsidies for my farms."

"I'm not so sure I'm going to like doing that."

"It's merely a formality."

"I've never danced with anyone as important as the prime minister."

"You'll see he's no different than any other man."

Robin found a nice riding and tackle shop in Tours that had all sorts of riding clothes. If the weather was warm, she could discard the masculine jacket and wear a brightly colored shirt. She liked it better because her body lines were more visible. François didn't miss the opportunity to congratulate her on how she selected and wore her clothes. She really knew how to dress.

François' wheat farm was used for feeding the cattle and dairy cows and the horses on the other farms. He had thirty top mares that he bred to international stallions for race horses. He didn't race the horses. He sold the yearlings at international auctions for high prices.

"Have you ever seen horses being bred? he asked Robin.

"No."

"Would you like to?"

"I might."

"One of my top mares is being bred with an Irish champion stallion this Friday. It's costing over six-hundred-thousand francs."

"All that for just a few minutes of copulation?"

"They guarantee a standing colt. It's not as simple as that. The veterinarian gets over forty-thousand francs to make sure everything goes well. It's an expensive gamble."

"I'd like to see that event!"

The Irish stallion arrived early in the morning and was allowed to roam out in the pasture for a while. When everything was ready, the mare was brought in and a heavy rubber mantle was put over her back and neck. A teaser horse was then brought in to get the mare ready for penetration. When she was ready, her tail would raise straight up in the air.

The stallion was then brought in to sniff a little and get aroused and then would be guided to mount the mare. He'd get up on his hind legs and a stable hand would guide the organ into the proper place.

Robin's eyes dilated when she saw the size of the stallion's genitals. The copulation was over in a very short period of time. At the end the stallion bit the neck of the mare.

François was standing next to Robin when the breeding took place.

"Not much different from humans," remarked Robin with a smile.

"What do you mean?" asked François, feeling a little insulted.

"You bit me on the neck last night, or have you forgotten?" She loosened the top of her blouse and showed him the teeth marks on her neck. "You gave me a hickey," she said with a smile.

"Are you sorry?"

"Not at all. It's one of the battle scars that I like."

"If you don't watch out, I'll give you another one tonight."

"Is that a promise?"

"You'll see."

"I can hardly wait."

Robin should have been able to predict what was going to happen that evening. Sure enough. He came at her from behind, just like that stallion. He seemed more aggressive, as though he was trying to prove himself. Robin enjoyed every bit of it and hoped it would never end. At the climax he put his mouth over the nape of her neck and bit her. She screamed in pain and in ecstasy.

"You were trying to prove something. Now I have another battle scar."

"It's just another memento for you," laughed François.

"There's one big difference between you and that stallion," she said.

"What's that?"

"You have more staying power!"

"That's an unusual compliment. Or isn't it a compliment? Someday, I'd like to successfully breed you like that stallion and have a son, Robin. Just how are you preventing pregnancy?"

"I take birth control pills."

Oh how I'd love to bear a son for him, she thought. But I know I can't. I so hate to disappoint him. What if he asks me to marry him? What should I do? I know I love him and want to spend the rest of my life with him. I can't tell him about my past. I've got to give it some thought because I think he's going to pop the question pretty soon.

The next morning, when Marie was helping Robin with her bath she asked, "Has he asked you to marry him yet?"

"No. Why do you ask?"

"He's got that look in his eye. He's probably afraid to ask you."

"What should I say if he asks?" said Robin with a big smile.

"*Oui, oui*, but of course! We at the château love you, too."

When Robin finished her bath, she dressed and went down to the main dining room. François was waiting for her. She came back to reality when she heard François say, "Robin, I want to have a serious talk with you very soon."

"Not just yet. But, we must talk. Will we be going back to Paris soon?"

"Are you unhappy here?"

"Oh, no. It's just that I don't have all my clothes here and I'm running out of new clothes to wear for you."

"We could go back for a day or so or I could have my chauffeur pick up your clothes for you. I thought you might like to go with me to southern France to the Côte d'Azur and perhaps do a little gambling at the Monte Carlo casino. The beaches are great and we could do some people watching at the St. Tropez Café on the beach."

"I'm not interested in people watching. Watching you is enough to keep me happy."

"I'll do whatever you want to do."

"Why don't we both go shopping in Paris for a couple of days? You can help me pick out some things that you would like to see on me and I'll help you pick out some clothes."

CHAPTER
20

Robin and François decided to take the train back to Paris. While en route on the train they decided that they would stay in a hotel rather than in the suburbs in François' apartment. The Ritz Carleton was out—Robin had nightmares about that place since her first encounter with François there.

François suggested L'Hotel, the chic hotel on the west bank—small with an excellent restaurant.

Robin had other ideas. "When I was growing up in Paris my parents would always stay at Le Bristol on Rue du Faubourg St. Honoré. I really would like to see that place again."

"That's where we shall stay then!" said François. "I'll call the hotel from the railroad station."

He called the hotel Le Bristol and had no difficulty getting the reservation, particularly when he told the reservation clerk who he was and that he wanted the best suite available for a week.

The hotel was magnificent, with large air-conditioned rooms and authentic Louis XV and Louis XVI furniture. The bathrooms were spacious with gorgeous marble lining the floors and walls. The hotel had all the conveniences for relaxation—pool, sauna, solarium—just what Robin wanted.

"There's a lot of France's history around this place," said François.

"I know very little about French history—I should learn more about it now that I'm living in France."

"Not all French history is pretty," said François. "The furniture in this room goes back to Louis XVI reign—at that time, Paris was the center of European culture and style."

"It still is," replied Robin.

"But, France was in turmoil at that time. The French Revolution and the First Empire took place. The Bastille was stormed—we still celebrate Bastille Day in France—the first French Republic was established."

"Why did they have a revolution?" asked Robin.

"Because the people wanted to be heard. Every Frenchman remembers that day—it was the day the people were liberated from the domination of the people by the kings, queens, and the clergy. All royal authority was abolished. The Marseillaise was adopted as the national anthem. France followed the example of the American revolution and introduced the declarations of the rights of man and the citizen proclaiming liberty, equality and the inviolability of property and the right to resist oppression.

"King Louis XVI and his queen, Marie Antoinette, were guillotined just up the street from this hotel in the Place de la Concorde."

"The guillotine is so brutal," said Robin.

"But death is so quick," replied François.

"Big crowds watched when the guillotine was used. Twenty-six-hundred aristocratic Frenchmen had their heads chopped off during that period of terror."

"I'm surprised," said Robin. "You're a descendent of King François I, and here today you vocally support freedom for the people. Your ancestors could have been on that guillotine."

"I know. However, the world has changed and it's taken centuries to change it. I believe that someday all nations will be dependent upon each other. The people's voices have to be heard or else there would be a revolution with every change in government."

"I agree with you wholeheartedly. You've just reinforced my love for you. Perhaps tomorrow we can visit a few of the historic places in Paris."

"I shall show them to you."

"I realize now why my mother loved Le Hotel Bristol—it's right in the center of the famous couturiers of Paris—most of the fabulous expensive creations are shown here first right on this avenue. I think I'm going to have a nice exhorbitant adventure shopping around here this week."

"The sky's the limit."

"Two of my favorite couturiers are here—Karl Lagerfeld and Christian Lacroix—their dresses are so original and so romantic."

"You ought to be able to find some beautiful new clothes to wear in these shops, Robin," he said with a smile. "Now I understand why you wanted to come to this hotel."

The next morning after breakfast in bed, they went shopping on the avenue—Robin had little difficulty selecting five new couture dress creations—very few, if any alterations had to be made—she was a perfect eight. François also selected three new British tweed sportjackets that Robin liked.

After an exhausting day shopping for clothes and visiting some of the historic areas they decided to have dinner in their suite at the hotel. François seemed quite pensive and seemed to have something on his mind. After eating the gourmet meal and sharing each other's love he spoke up.

"Robin, I love you so much—but I can't understand why you won't say yes to my proposal for marriage."

"François, we have only known each other for a short time. You've swept me off my feet. I've been overwhelmed with your love—both mentally and physically. You have become a dream come true in my heart. I know I love you. I know how much you wish an heir, too. Would you love me as much if we couldn't have children?"

"That's not something we have to worry about," he said. "Just look at yourself. God gave you a beautiful healthy body—I'm in perfect health—we would have no trouble having children."

If only he knew about my past, thought Robin—a past that she wanted to forget totally—her murky past would haunt her the rest of her life—homosexual encounters, drugs, transvestite experiences—tears started to flow from her eyes and down her cheeks. There were other more serious encounters in her past—Robin had been on the run since the murder of Bill Carroll and Robin's own wife in New Orleans when Robin was Robert Sousa—she had suppressed all of this—she knew she could never reveal that part of her past to François—if it became known, the relationship would be totally shattered and could be life-threatening.

After giving François' question a lot of thought and after a long period of hesitation, Robin finally spoke up.

"First, François, I want to tell you that I know I love you. I've known that from the first day we met. You have epitomized everything I have wanted in a man"—then, measuring her words carefully, hoping to get more time to think, she said, "I have only known you for six weeks. I've been swept off my feet by your ardor. I think we have to give ourselves more time together before marriage. We have had no disagreements—I'm sure we will. As for me bearing an heir for you—that would have to be an act of God—only God could bless us with a child. What if God did not give us a child?"

"I would still love you just as much," he replied.

Robin thought about that—would he? As she got older and as they tried unsuccessfully to have a child—it would be a horrible, frustrating experience for both of them. Robin knew there was no way she could have a child of her own. What if François eventually found out about her scandalous past? She wouldn't be able to tolerate that! She was not ready to commit to marrying François—in some ways, she loved him too much. She had so many ambivalent feelings about what to do. She knew that she was madly in love with him and her heart was breaking.

François noticed the tears coming down her cheeks.

"My dear, I'm so sorry I've made you cry."

"These are tears of happiness," she said, "professing your love for me has made me so happy that I'm crying. I love you so, François. Come to me and make love to me again."

CHAPTER

The French International Ball was held at the Louvre, Paris' most important public building, which contains some of the most famous art in the world. You can walk for half a mile, admiring some of the finest works of art. The floors of the museum echo the sounds of immortality and the artwork hanging on the walls the immortality of the artist.

The Louvre was being reconstructed to be the Grande Louvre and President Mitterand was instrumental in its change. The new main entrance is the famous glass pyramid in the center of the Cour Napoleon, designed by the Chinese American architect Leoh Ming Pei which opened in 1989. It is from this glass pyramid that one gains access to the three different sections of the museum.

The flowers from the Tuilleries Gardens were all in bloom stretching westward from the main entrance to the Louvre and the glass pyramid and added to the magnificence for the setting of the ball.

Two orchestras played for the ball—the Orchestre de Paris and the Orchestre National de France.

One of the large palaces of the museum was selected for the ball and was completely redecorated with artwork selected by a committee. A carpeted center aisle for introduction of the various dignitaries led to the main ballroom.

The French National Anthem was played when the French prime minister, Charles Delacroix, arrived, after most of the other dignitaries.

François and Robin were seated at a table near Prime Minister Delacroix and on her dance card, she was to dance with him on the fifth dance.

François was to dance with the prime minister's wife. Robin didn't mind dancing with the prime minister but was upset that François would be dancing with his wife. She was quite younger than the prime minister, a gorgeous brunette with a beautiful figure that one could truly classify as a beautiful woman.

Security was strict for the dance with members of the French intelligence service mingling with the guests and members of the French police in evidence around the Louvre and also inside the palace.

The ladies' washrooms had all been redecorated, enlarged and sanitized for the affair, and there were ladies-in-waiting to help out with their gowns and makeup.

Television security cameras were in place in a side room and were monitored by members of the Paris police. The French government was taking no risks for possible sabotage. There were many prime targets attending the ball: the United States Secretary of State, the British prime minister, and the German chancellor.

There were about 500 selected guests, the men resplendent in their black ties and tails and the women ravishing in magnificent gowns, some having been recently bought in Paris.

François and Robin enjoyed dancing together. Robin's beautiful long blonde hair done in a French braid and magnificent athletic figure caught the eye of the men at the ball. She had spent part of François' fortune on a gorgeous turquoise gown that was cut low in front and back and the skirt was slit on one side. It was quite simple in appearance, but put on the body of a modern Mona Lisa such as Robin, was quite captivating.

A magnificent French dinner was served in a large banquet hall next to the palace ballroom that was to be used for the dance. The cuisine was perfect and the French wines complimented the meal.

François and Robin were seated with the prime minister of France and foreign dignitaries from England, Germany and Italy and their wives. The conversation of French and English was not diction perfect but understandable, and everyone enjoyed the food and music. When it came time for dessert, Robin noticed one of the waiters watching her every movement and she became quite nervous and perturbed. She thought she recognized the man but wasn't sure. She tried to remember where she had seen him before. He was quite tall and heavy with a black mustache. Robin decided to mention it to François.

"François, one of the waiters has been watching every move I make and I don't like it," she said.

"That's because you're the most beautiful woman in this whole room," replied François.

"I don't think so," said Robin. "I've seen that man somewhere before."

"Nonsense," said François. "Half the men in this room have been watching you. Relax so we can enjoy ourselves."

Robin continued to wrack her brain about the waiter. Where had she seen that man before? She kept trying to think where she had seen him. It was kind of scary because he seemed to be watching her so intensely. She wondered whether he was stalking her. Suddenly she felt frightened for the first time in a long time. At least François was with her and she would be with him the entire evening. When they danced, she held him more closely to her.

After dancing a waltz and returning to their table, the Italian minister leaned over at the table and asked, "François, are you by chance related to King François the First, who ruled France in the 1500s?"

"Yes, I am," he replied. The French at one time occupied a part of Italy and François I occupied Milan and at that time tried to obtain the German Imperial Crown but was unsuccessful. Eventually France was driven out of Italy. I know the history of my ancestors completely. My land and chateau that I own now dates back to that period."

"You never told me that you were related to royalty," said Robin.

"Well, now you know, and that's why I want a son. I have a portrait of King François I in my dining room. He's quite a handsome giant of a man—he was famous for his chivalry and was a patron of the arts and letters. He built one of the largest châteaus in the Loire Valley. He called it his hunting lodge. Unfortunately, the French people felt he was a better dilettante than a king. The historians say he neglected his duties but I don't believe it. He wanted to take over and control Italy. Unfortunately, in 1525 Imperial Italian forces routed the French army and captured my relative, François. Charles the fifth of the Holy Roman Empire was his adversary. François was released after promising not to fight anymore. However, he continued to fight until his death."

"Your characterization of King François I fits your description," said Robin. "Particularly in relation to your persistence. I love every minute of it."

Just then the French prime minister and his wife arrived at their table.

The time arrived for the exchange dance with the prime minister and his wife. The prime minister was quite a bit older than his wife and was an excellent dancer. He held Robin tightly as they danced and spoke softly to her in French.

"*Vous êtes très beau, mon ami,*" he said. "François is a very lucky man."

"Thank you," said Robin. "I think I'm lucky to have François."

The light had been dimmed for the dancing and the prime minister had a tendency to drop his broad palm over her derrière.

Robin didn't know quite how to react to that. She couldn't slap the prime minister's face in front of all these people. She tried to wiggle her bottom out of his grasp. It didn't work. He just grasped her a little more tightly. She realized she definitely was the weaker sex. She was sure she wasn't going to enjoy this dance and wished it would end quickly.

The prime minister pulled Robin a little bit closer to him and with his left hand around the nape of her neck, kissed the side of her cheek.

"*Non monsieur, s'il vous plaît,*" said Robin, as she gently pushed him away. She noticed that he had danced her into a dark corner of the ballroom. He had also had too much to drink and there weren't very many people around the area.

"We should go back to our table," said Robin.

"Let's sit down on this bench here," said the prime minister, as he pointed to a large bench in one of the alcoves, "I want to talk to you."

"We really should go back to our table," said Robin. "What will your wife think?"

"She'll be busy with François," said the prime minister. "She's got a crush on him. The longer I stay away from her and keep you occupied, the happier she'll be."

"That's what I'm afraid of," replied Robin. "Please take me back."

"Not before I talk to you about something. I have a proposition to make you. I believe I can give you everything that François can and then some. You can name your price. I see you love clothes and, I might add, you wear them well. I'll be glad to open up an unlimited bank account for you with the best haute couture shops and you can move into one of my villas. You will eventually meet all the important people in France. My wife doesn't travel well so you can be my traveling companion all over the world."

How do you reply to the prime minister of France when he's asking you to be his mistress? he did nothing for Robin when it came to male attractiveness. If it were money she wanted, her answer would be yes. François gave her money and true love. How could she discreetly refuse?

She hesitated before answering.

"I must think about something that is as important as this," replied Robin.

"Then your answer is yes," said the prime minister.

"*Non, monsieur,* my answer is perhaps."

CHAPTER

22

Prime Minister Delacroix was excited about meeting Robin. She was the most delectable morsel of French femininity he had ever encountered and she had said "maybe" to his proposition. How could he contact her at François' château without him knowing what he was up to? He had to figure out a delicate but concise way to meet Robin again. French men had a way of passing around their mistresses once their interest and ardor for her decreased. François was very attentive to Robin—it might be difficult, thought the prime minister. Finally he had a plan.

"François, this is Charles Delacroix. I've decided that I want you to serve on an agricultural committee that is meeting in Cannes in three weeks."

"What's the meeting about?" asked François.

"France has been asked by the common market to reduce the subsidies to farmers and also to cut down on the production of certain agricultural products—I want you to serve on that committee."

"Is it really necessary for me to serve?" asked François. "Some-times those meetings last much longer than planned."

"Absolutely!" said the prime minister. "I want someone on that committee who knows something about French farming—not just a bunch of politicians dreaming up answers to questions they know nothing about. In fact, I'm also going to be there with my wife. You can bring Robin and we can all stay at the same hotel, the Carlton International, on the Boulevard de la Croisette. The meetings will be held in the mornings from 8:00 A.M. to 1:00 P.M. and the afternoons and evenings are free. The four of us can go over to Monaco and do some gambling if you like or relax on the beaches. I'll arrange the accommodations for the four of us."

"I'd like to talk to Robin about it first."

"Nonsense. Any woman would love to gamble on the tables of Monaco or be seen at the most fashionable seaside promenade in the world—along the palm lined Boulevard de la Croisette. There's also some expensive specialty shops there for the girls to shop in!"

"Do I have to give you an answer right now?"

"It would be most gracious if you did."

"I'll be there. However, I do wish to discuss it with Robin. I'm sure you understand."

"Of course," replied Prime Minister Delacroix. "In fact, I want you to chair a couple of the morning sessions so I can be sure the discussions stay on the right track. I won't be able to attend all the sessions myself."

That evening, François told Robin about the prime minister's phone call.

"Charles Delacroix called and wants me to serve on a committee for the French government."

"How nice," said Robin. "What's it all about?"

"As you know, France is the breadbasket for most of Europe. We grow most of the food on our rich farmlands. The farmers, includ-ing yours truly, are subsidized in France. The common market wants us to restrict some of the products we grow in order to help some of the other countries."

"That doesn't sound too good for the French farmers," said Robin.

"That's right," said François. "That's why he wants me to serve on the committee."

"I think you should!"

"I'm glad you feel that way. It involves you somewhat too."

"In what way?"

"The committee is meeting in Cannes in three weeks. He's invited you and I to spend time with him and his wife at the International Carlton Hotel. He suggested that we could do a little gambling at Monaco or relax on the beaches."

Suddenly Robin began to realize what was going on here—Prime Minister Delacroix was very clever. She wasn't ready for another encounter with him—that was the last thing she wanted at this time—or was it? If she acquiesced to Charles Delacroix's wishes, she would have much wealth and earthly goods—but not true love. However, she wouldn't have to worry about not being able to give birth to François' child. She would always be known as the mistress to the prime minister—she might even influence some of his important decisions. Being in the limelight scared her—someone might recognize her true identity. She decided she'd have to give this a lot of thought.

"Are you sure you want me to accompany you to Cannes?"

"Of course! I wouldn't want to go without you."

Robin and François took the TGV train from Paris to Marseilles— the train traveled at 125 miles per hour to the Côte d' Azure. Charles and his wife Bridget were already in Cannes and met them in the lobby of the Carlton Hotel.

Bridget gave François a kiss on the mouth in greeting and the prime minister expected the same from Robin. It was a moist kiss with a mustache in-between. Ugh! thought Robin.

"So nice to see you, Robin," said the prime minister, as he gave her a big hug. "We shall have breakfast together later on in the week."

"François, you and I can get together this afternoon to discuss my feelings about the farm problems in France. The women can go shopping along the boulevard if they wish. Tonight, we'll visit the casinos at Monte Carlo."

"Sounds like a full day and night," said François.

"That depends on our women!" replied the prime minister with a smile.

Bridget and Robin decided to go shopping in the afternoon while the men worked—two beautiful women—one a brunette and the other blonde, walking on the Boulevard de la Croisette—they would be prime targets for the French and Italian men and members of the international jet set.

François had given Robin some credit cards and quite a bit of cash to use if she wanted to—Bridget had also been amply supplied with cash.

Most of the couture shops of Paris had small specialty shops on the boulevard.

Bridget found a pretty, tight-fitting black and gold evening gown that left very little to the imagination. It fit her perfectly. She asked Robin whether she liked the gown on her.

"It's quite charming," replied Robin.

"Do you think François might like it?" . . . she caught herself . . . "I mean Charles?"

"I think they will both like it," replied Robin. "I'd love to find a gown to wear for Monte Carlo also."

Robin tried on numerous evening gowns in the shops and finally found a glistening gold lamé gown that was very expensive and quite stunning.

"What do you think?" she asked Bridget as she pirouetted in front of the mirror.

"It's too many francs for that dress," she replied.

Robin could tell by the expression on Bridget's face that she really liked it and wished she had seen it first.

"I'm going to get it," said Robin. "I'll use one of François' credit cards."

That evening, Bridget and Robin were two of the prettiest women in the casino. The two caught the eyes of all the men. Both wore the gowns they had just purchased on their shopping spree—snug-fitting with low bodices and low-cut backs.

Robin had done some gambling in college—when she was Robert Sousa—and knew quite a bit about blackjack and rolling the dice. She didn't like roulette. She decided to have some fun—François had given her a handful of varied colored chips.

François and Charles decided to play poker. Bridget said she wanted to play *Vingt-et-un* so she and Robin went to the blackjack table and soon the cards came in the right directions for both of them. They were hitting 18 and 20 frequently. They changed the dealer but they still kept winning. In an hour and a half they both had increased the value of their chips to about 50,000 francs.

"Bridget, why don't we roll the dice for a while? It looks like we're both going to be lucky today."

"I'm not as good at rolling the dice," Bridget replied.

"Then I'll roll the dice and you can put side bets on me," suggested Robin.

They went over to the crap table, followed by a few of the men from the blackjack table, who wanted to watch the beautiful young French women.

Robin started placing side bets on the people rolling the dice. Sometimes she'd bet with the house and sometimes against. She was good at guessing the number. The chips started piling up in front of her. She was on a streak of good luck. Other people standing around the table started betting with her. Bridget was raking in the chips.

Finally, it came Robin's turn to roll the dice. More people began congregating around the table to watch the beautiful blonde in the gold lamé gown roll the dice.

Robin put half her chips on the first roll of the dice. The purple chips were worth 2500 francs. She rolled a seven, a natural, and won. She put her whole pot up and rolled the dice again and won. The croupier's forehead was beginning to sweat. Because she had so many chips they were exchanged for more expensive ones. She rolled the dice again and the number was seven. She rolled five sevens in a row.

"Mon dieu!" exclaimed the croupier.

A crowd assembled around the crap table.

As she looked out of the corner of her eye at the opposite end of the crap table she saw a tall, dark man with a mustache wearing dark glasses. She took a deep breath. He was watching her intensely. Could it be? He looked like the waiter at the French International Ball.

"Are you going to roll?" asked the croupier.

"No. I'll pass."

A tall gentleman picked up the dice and took her place.

"Let's go, Bridget. Let's find François and Charles. We'll cash in our chips."

"Why don't you keep rolling the dice? You can't lose!"

"It's better to quit while you're ahead. Besides, I want to get away from this table. I've got a good reason."

The man who picked up Robin's dice rolled snake-eyes. He lost the dice.

"See what I mean?" said Robin.

Bridget and Robin went to the cashier's window and cashed in their chips. They received a certified French bank check for 480,000 francs.

"Wow!" exclaimed Bridget. "I knew there was something about you I liked."

"Are you going to tell Charles about your winnings?"

"Are you kidding? This will be my mad money. I'm putting this check in my bosom. How about you?"

"Not me. That check wouldn't last very long there with François around."

They went to find François and Charles, both had frowns on their faces—they were losing at the poker table.

"How did you girls make out?" asked Charles.

"We had a lot of fun." replied Bridget. "Right, Robin?"

"Right."

The next morning François and Charles attended the agricultural committee's meeting. Bridget called Robin and asked her to have breakfast with her. She accepted—she was beginning to get a warm feeling about Bridget—they had such a good time together at Monte Carlo. In many ways they were quite similar—they were both very attractive and caught the eye of the men wherever they went. After eating breakfast and laughing about what happened the night before they decided to go to the beach in front of the hotel and work on their tans.

"Are you going to wear your bikini?" asked Bridget.

"I have a light robe that I'll wear over my suit to the beach. I'll wear my top to start with."

"It looks like a beautiful day to get a tan," replied Robin.

"I don't want to get any tan lines on my breasts. Charles wouldn't like that," said Bridget.

"Do you have any children?" asked Robin.

"I have one son who goes to preparatory school. He's twelve years old."

"You're so fortunate."

"I'm not so sure," said Bridget.

"Charles is away so much."

"Why don't you travel with him?"

"It's too boring," said Bridget. "I feel as though I'm wasting my life away sitting in hotel rooms or traveling on trains or planes around the continent. How are you and François making out?"

"He's the greatest! He's the best I've ever known."

"I confess—I'm envious of you. François is one man I could leave Charles for. He looks so virile. I'll bet he's great in bed."

"All I would ever want."

"Has he asked you to marry him or does he want you to be his mistress?"

"I'm sure I can answer yes to both of those questions."

"That's what I'm afraid of," said Bridget. "I'm afraid that Charles will find some young pretty French girl to spend some of his money on."

"What would you do if you found out he did have a mistress?"

"I really don't know. I don't know whether I'd shoot the mistress or him. I'm still pretty enough to get all the offers I want."

"You are beautiful," said Robin.

The inevitable happened. Three days later when François was chairing one of the morning meetings, Robin got a call from Charles.

"Robin, this is Charles. How would you like to take a drive in the country with me? I want to talk to you privately."

"I can't do that! Your wife is here."

"No, she isn't. She's gone into the country to visit the vineyards with a group of women attending the meeting. They won't be back until nightfall."

"I've got a splitting headache! Perhaps some other time," said Robin.

"A drive in the fresh country air will help that headache. I've rented a convertible that we can use."

Robin wanted to tell him to get lost, but she thought better of it—after all he was the prime minister of France.

"I will have lunch with you, but we'll have to come back early so I can meet François."

"François will be late today. They've run into some controversies—the farmers don't want the subsidies reduced. His meeting will probably run all afternoon."

It sounded like Charles had an answer for everything. Robin had no intention of sleeping with him, no matter what he said.

"I thought we would drive to Eze, just this side of Monaco, and stop at the hotel Château de la Chevre d'Or—it's got a four-star restaurant with a beautiful view of the coast. I've got a lot of things I want to talk to you about."

I bet you do, thought Robin. The problem is that I don't have all the answers to fend you off.

"I'll pick you up in an hour in front of the hotel. I'll be driving a red Porsche convertible."

Before she left the suite at the hotel, Robin placed an elastic-type garter around her right upper thigh and then put a derringer in a small holster there. This will give me a little protection if I need it, thought Robin. I hope I don't have to use it on the prime minister.

It was a beautiful day as they drove along the highway to Monaco. Charles wasn't the best driver and there were times when Robin wished she were at the wheel. He was a good conversationalist and a clever politician as he repeatedly told her how beautiful she was.

"Please watch where you're driving," Robin said repeatedly as he started the drive up the startling steep hill to the village of Eze. There were times when it appeared that he was going to drive them over a cliff. All Robin could think about was what would François say if she and Charles did go over the cliff? That would certainly hit the headlines! They finally arrived safely at the hotel after much trepidation. It was about noon.

The concierge told Charles that he could use a hospitality suite if he wanted to.

"Perhaps after lunch I might want to use it," replied Robin. "I'm starved right now." Robin had no intention of entering a large bedroom suite at this time with Charles.

Charles was charming during lunch but also asked Robin lots of questions. "Where is your family from, Robin?"

"I'm originally from Paris and I'm also an American citizen. I have an apartment in Paris."

"Have you ever been married?"

"No."

"You are so beautiful, that's difficult to understand."

"It's because I'm very particular about who I consent to go with. Right now I'm enjoying François' company."

"Are you happy?"

"Yes. Very much!"

"I believe that I can give you more than François."

"Rather than talk in generalities, why don't you be more specific?"

"I would give you whatever you want so that I might enjoy your favors. You are one of the most beautiful women I've seen in all of France. Just look around us here in this dining room—everyone's eyes are on you."

"No. That's not true. The reason they are looking is because they know you're the prime minister. François has given me everything I want. What more could you give me that I'm not already receiving?"

"Unlimited bank accounts, world travel—my love."

"What about Bridget?"

Charles began to squirm in his seat. "She would be in the background. I could not marry you because of our catholic religion."

"I have a tremendous headache. I want you to drive me back."

"I want you to answer one question for me. Will you be my mistress?"

"Not until you become more specific about marriage. I have a lot to lose if I say yes to your proposition."

As the prime minister and Robin left the dining area a photographer took a candid shot of the two of them. Charles tried to get the negative but was unsuccessful.

"Charles, I think we really blew it! The society pages of tomorrow's newspapers will have our picture in it. You'll have some explaining to do to Bridget and I to François."

* * *

Robin decided to tell François about having lunch with Charles. She didn't want him to have any surprises—he might think she was working both sides of the street.

She and François decided to have dinner in their room at the hotel. It was much more relaxing and romantic. François told Charles that Robin had a headache. After eating a delicious beef tenderloin with a light bernaise sauce and a flambé dessert, they decided to go back in the bed and take a short nap—it lasted for about twenty minutes.

François reached over and pulled Robin over to him. He reached around her back and gently pulled the zipper on her dress down. She responded to his kisses and shrugged her shoulders to slip out of the top of her dress. She raised her hips so he could remove the dress.

"I'll help you take your clothes off," she said as she undid his belt. François had unbuttoned his shirt and was taking it off.

She continued to respond to his deep kisses as he gently kneaded her breasts. Her nipples became erect as he suckled them in his mouth—his hands went down her back to her buttocks to pull her closer to him as she arched her back against his torso. She had no difficulty relaxing for his entry and let out a moan of ecstasy as their bodies began to meld as one. As their rhythm increased and their passions escalated both were trying to respond to each other. François could not express his love in any better way than to respond to her—the most beautiful female animal he had ever made love to. Her athletic, perfectly shaped body worked to satisfy his sexual drive.

They seemed to be able to respond to one another's movements. Their rhythm increased out of control as they reached the climax.

"I love you, François," she said. "Each time we share our love I feel it gets better and better. You've got to be mine forever."

"If you marry me, I will be yours forever."

After taking a nap, she decided to tell him about her lunch with Charles.

"François, I have to tell you about something that happened today. I'm not happy about it."

"What is it?"

"The prime minister invited me to lunch today."

"Was Bridget with him?"

"No. We drove to a restaurant in Eze."

"Was he a gentleman?"

"Yes."

"I don't object to that."

"A photographer took our picture as we came out of the hotel. It will probably be in the newspapers."

"Having your picture taken with the prime minister does not bother me. However, if he tries to come between our love for each other—that's a different story."

"Do you want to hear anything more?"

"You've told me enough," he replied.

Early the next morning, Bridget called Robin. "How about having breakfast together again—we could go to the beach afterward. The meeting ends tomorrow."

"Fine. I'll meet you in the main dining room at 7:30."

After eating breakfast they changed into their bikinis and went to the beach in front of the hotel.

"I've enjoyed this trip with Charles," said Bridget. "I think I would like to spend more time with you—I think we could become good friends."

"I'd like that, too. It might be awkward, though."

"Yes, I know. Charles has a roving eye."

"You've noticed?"

"Yes I have. He's typical of most aristocratic Frenchmen. You are very beautiful. I thought he preferred brunettes, but in your case, it looks like he prefers blondes."

"I'm very happy with François."

"I would be too, if he were mine."

CHAPTER

When François and Robin got back to the château their lives returned to normal. They continued to do things together every day except when François had to meet with his farm managers. The seasonal weather had been good, and as a result, all the crops were good.

Robin's maid-in-waiting, Marie, was ever present and a close relationship developed between them. François would periodically ask Robin to marry him and her answer was always an evasive no. Marie encouraged Robin to say yes, but to no avail.

Charles had gotten phone calls through to Robin and her answer was always no. She finally refused his calls.

"I can't understand why," was the prime minister's reply.

In Robin's mind there was a simple explanation—his male characteristics did nothing for her sexual drive. She knew she could never really love him or anticipate spending any length of time of her life with him.

François' persistence was weakening her, but she was horribly frustrated by the thought that they could never have children.

It wasn't long before François realized that Robin loved to take part in active health and exercise activities. She was very conscious of her weight, watched what she ate, and often jogged around the château. She was a good tennis player and loved to swim. She felt that maintaining a good healthy body and, in particular, remaining slender with just the right amount of muscle would allow her to respond to François and maintain his amorous attention.

François continued to have a difficult time convincing Robin to marry him so he thought that perhaps a trip away from the château might be helpful.

"Have you ever been skiing?" François asked.

"When I was about ten I used to ski with my parents when we lived in France. I remember going to the French Alps with them. In law school, back in the states . . . ," Robin hesitated—she hadn't told him she was a lawyer. "I skied in Vermont and New Hampshire on weekends—Stratton Mountain, Killington, Waterville Valley."

"I didn't know you had gone to law school."

"Well, I did," said Robin, her eyelids blinking. "I never really practiced law—only for a short time. I've been here in France since I was twenty-five."

"I bet you were an excellent trial lawyer," said François. "You're so beautiful that the opposing lawyers would be watching your every move. They wouldn't be able to remember or to concentrate on what the case was all about."

"You're prejudiced," she replied. "However, I like the compliment."

"I'm finding out more and more about you and what I hear, I like. I always thought you were an intellectual."

"Not really," said Robin. "However, I do want to keep a few secrets," as she smiled and winked at him.

"Everyone has a few skeletons in their closet," said François.

If François only knew about my past, thought Robin, things might be different. I have more than a few skeletons in my closet.

"I used to ski quite a bit when I was young," said François. "Would you like to go skiing in the French Alps?"

"I'd love to. However, I'll probably need some lessons since I haven't skied for a long time."

"That can be arranged. We'll go to Albertville, where they had the Olympics and then to Val d'Isere—the finest ski area in all of

Europe. We'll stay at Mont Blanc, a grand hotel at Chamonix, for a few days and then go to Tignes where I have a friend who owns one of the most beautiful condominiums in the world. You can ski all year round there. The views of both the French and Italian side of Mont Blanc are truly magnificent. Have you ever seen Mont Blanc?"

"I saw it when I was ten years old. I don't really remember anything about it."

"Well, it's the highest mountain in Europe—almost sixteen-thousand feet. Its beauty is breathtaking! There's nowhere in the world for skiing that compares to the Tarentaise Valley of the French Alps. It's a skier's delight! There are unlimited runs available encompassing all ranges of difficulty. They have beginner, intermediate and expert slopes. The skiing is nonpareil.

"Val d'Isere has three of the best ski schools in France. There's one ski area that has a lift that goes six-thousand feet to the top of the mountain in four minutes. If we learn how to ski well, we can try that slope or take a helicopter for a flight across the Italian border and ski there."

"That sounds so exciting! I'd love to ski again. However, I don't have any ski equipment or ski clothes to wear."

"There are all sorts of ski shops in the French Alps with the best clothes and equipment," said François. "That's a minor problem. We can shop in Courchevel at L'Espace Diamant, an indoor arcade that has all the designer clothes and ski equipment. We'll pack and leave in a couple of days."

"How are we going to get there?" asked Robin.

"We'll take the TGV fast train to Albertville, and then by train, bus or taxi to Chamonix to the Mont Blanc Grand Hotel. Then after we get outfitted we'll take some ski lessons for a few days and head to Tignes where they have some intermediate slopes. How does that sound?"

"That sounds great!"

Robin and François bought their skis, boots, pants, jackets, poles, and sunglasses at Courchevel—most of the equipment was Rossignol. After taking ski instructions and trying the slopes, it was quite obvious to François that Robin was really an expert skier. Her instructor was also impressed with her expertise.

"You really don't need any instruction," said Gary Perrillat IV. "You can ski on some of the expert slopes if you want to, right now."

"Thanks," said Robin.

The next morning, François and Robin decided to make a day of it. They decided they would ski on the east-facing slopes where the fresh powder was still light, and in the afternoon head for the other side to catch the afternoon sun.

After skiing in the morning, they decided to stop for lunch in Courchevel, a town with at least a dozen excellent restaurants.

"Where shall we get a bite to eat?" asked Robin. "I'm starved after burning up all that energy."

"We'll eat at the La Bergerie. I need a rest. I'm having difficulty keeping up with you."

"That's the first time I've heard you say that," said Robin, as she smiled.

They plunged their skis upright in the snow and went to a fine table in the enlarged former shepherd's hut without removing their boots. They had a bottle of straw-colored Apremont wine with a huge round loaf of bread. Then they ate some freshly opened oysters on the half shell and some smoked salmon with lime. The desserts were out of this world—crêpes Grand Marnier or a warm pear tart with almond filling and tarte Tatin.

With the magnificent view, the fresh air of the mountains, the great skiing and exercise, François was ready for anything and so was Robin.

"Perhaps I should inquire about a nice inn or hotel in this town where we might stay tonight," he suggested. "This looks like a great place."

"That sounds romantic," said Robin. "But I don't have any clothes with me. They're all back at the hotel."

"Neither do I," said François. "I'm sure we can get toothbrushes here. I've stayed at La Pomme De Pin, a hotel run by the Savoyard family. It's magnificent. I'll see if I can get a room there."

François made some phone calls and got a reservation. They skied all afternoon.

The air was clear and refreshing on the mountain as they skied down the slopes. The temperature was about forty-five degrees and the sun was so bright that they needed sunglasses. Skiing was fatiguing because of the length and sharp descent of some of the slopes. The greenery around the trails and the all-encompassing mountains was awesome. After an exhausting afternoon on the slopes, they went to their hotel. They had a nice room with a fireplace and an open-air terrace. The view of the Alps shimmered in the distance and the snow turned to silvery white under the moonbeams of night.

After making love to her, François again brought up the question of marriage. "Robin, I love you so. Please say you'll marry me."

"I do want to say yes. I will let you know soon."

Then Robin got a surprise question.

"Why don't you stop the birth control pill?"

"I can't believe you said that!" replied Robin. "If we had a child it would be out of wedlock. It would be an illegitimate child. I wouldn't want that."

"You're right," said François. "The church wouldn't look at that very well. Forget I said it."

Robin had tears in her eyes. In her heart she knew she couldn't have François' child, yet she loved him so dearly. She didn't have the heart to tell him.

François noticed her tears. "My darling. I'm sorry I suggested that. Please forgive me."

Robin cuddled up to him. "Someday, you'll know," she said as she fell asleep in his arms.

The next morning, they had breakfast at the hotel. It was a magnificent buffet. François had his telecommunication beeper on and it beeped him.

"I wonder who's calling me?" he asked as he got up to find a telephone. "Maybe there's trouble at one of the farms at the château."

He walked out to the hallway to find a phone.

Robin relaxed as she continued eating her breakfast. She was startled by what she saw in the corner of the dining room. There, seated in the corner, was the tall gentleman with a dark mustache and sunglasses wearing a ski outfit. She thought she recognized him. He looked like someone she had seen at Cannes and at the French International Ball. Suddenly she became frightened. Would he recognize her? She didn't know what to do and she began to panic. Fortunately, just about then, François returned to their table.

Robin spoke up as she appeared quite apprehensive. "I want to leave this place right now!"

"Why do you want to leave? I haven't finished my breakfast."

"That gentleman over there in the corner has been staring at me. I think I've seen him someplace before."

"Nonsense," said François. "He's just admiring your beauty."

"I've got ski clothes on. There's nothing to admire."

"Yes, there is! You look beautiful, even in your ski clothes."

"Let's get out of here! Why don't we ski on the expert slopes today?" suggested Robin.

"OK by me," said François. "I might lose you, though. You're a better skier than I am."

"Not really."

They took the ski lift to the top of the expert slope. The vertical drop was supposed to be the maximum an expert skier could handle.

Robin noticed the man who had been watching her in the hotel had taken the same ski lift. She continued to worry about who he was. Was he stalking her?

She challenged François to keep up with her as she started down the slope. There was some ice on the track, which made it fast. She looked back and noticed the man skiing down the slope behind her. It wasn't long before she had outdistanced François. Looking behind, she saw the stranger had almost caught up to her and it looked like he had something in his hand. As he got closer, Robin realized it was a gun. She dug her poles into the snow to try to increase her speed and went into a deep crouch.

She thought she heard a shot whiz by her ear. Golly, he's shooting at me, she thought. He's trying to kill me! As she crouched down still further, she realized her life was in danger. She tried to increase her speed by going straight down the slope instead of zig-zagging. What a horrible predicament! What better place to kill someone than on a deserted ski slope—no police—no witnesses.

Her heart was pounding as she raced to get away. Why was he trying to kill her? Did it have something to do with François? She descended straight down the icy slope, going into a deeper crouch, traveling at what she thought must have been more than eighty miles an hour at great risk to her life.

Looking ahead, she noticed she was approaching a fork in the trail. The man was catching up to her. She had to do something. François was not in sight. She had to get away. She was approaching some big trees close to the trail. She decided to wait until the last second to choose which fork she would take. Just before she got to the fork, she made a quick turn and barely missed a big tree. The pursuer tried to make the turn behind her and she heard a loud scream as he hit the tree.

She glanced behind her to see what had happened, and then calmly continued down the slope to the hotel. François arrived about an hour later.

"Where have you been?" asked Robin.

"I was delayed. There was an accident on the slope. A man broke his leg right in front of me."

"Did you find out who he was?"

"Not really. The ski patrol took him to a level area on the trail after they put splints on his leg and a helicopter picked him up to take him to a hospital."

"That's too bad. Skiing can be dangerous if you don't concentrate on what you're doing." She decided not to tell him what had happened on the slopes.

CHAPTER

Robin was upset about the prime minister's proposition and François' persistence in asking her to marry him. She wasn't quite ready for any of that. She was getting so frustrated, confused and stressed out. He kept telling her he wanted to raise a big family and most of all wanted to have a son. Robin knew she couldn't have any children. She cried herself to sleep just thinking about it. She was at her wits' end.

She remembered when she was little she had to go to the doctor for hormone shots. Her mother told her the shots were necessary so she could grow up to be a big strong boy. Her mother and father had always wanted a boy and that's what they got. She never did understand her early childhood in Paris. When her mother and father moved to the United States her visits to the doctor stopped. She was eight years old at that time.

She periodically continued to see Dr. Pierre Dubois, her plastic surgeon in Paris. She decided the next time she saw him she'd ask him if he could answer some of her questions.

During her next visit, after he had examined her and told her everything was perfect, she spoke up.

"Dr. Dubois, I wonder if you would try to answer some questions for me."

"Of course. You looked distressed when you came in. Usually you have a big smile on your face. What's wrong?"

"I'm very happy, but I have a big problem."

"What's the problem, Robin?"

"François wants to marry me."

"There's nothing wrong with that," said Dr. Dubois. "It's OK with me. I believe you can get married. Have you talked to François about your past?"

"No, I'm afraid to. I'm so happy with him. I'm afraid he'd leave me. He wants children so badly."

"There are other fish in the sea. You're so beautiful, I'm sure you could be happy with someone else."

Tears started to roll down Robin's cheeks.

"I wish I had been born a real girl," she said. "François wants to have children and I do too, yet I know I can't."

"I understand," said Dr. Dubois. "There are some things that will always be out of reach in all our lives. When you had that sex change in Los Angeles, did Dr. Von Salzen explore your abdomen or do any CT scans or ultrasound tests?"

"No," said Robin. "He asked a lot of questions and was going to do some tests but that never materialized. Why would he do those tests?"

"Sometimes we do those tests to determine the true sex of certain individuals," he replied.

"I told him I had been a homosexual in law school in New York City. I had a very small penis. My mother told me they were giving me hormone shots to make it bigger and it did somewhat."

"What made you start becoming a homosexual?" asked Dr. Dubois.

"I was sort of effeminate, never had much of a beard, and I found I was attracted to the male sex. Women never excited me.

"Did they ever check your blood to do genetic studies?"

"Not that I know of."

"Did they every take a smear from the inside of your mouth for buccal studies?"

"No. I believe I told you my first eight years were spent in Paris and I didn't see my parents very much. I spent most of my time in a French academy school."

"Hold on for just a minute. I have some of your old records from Dr. Von Salzen in my files. Let me take a look in your folder.

"Hmm. This is interesting," he said. "His records show that you had a smaller than normal penis with bilateral undescended testicles, no vagina, and a small dimple above your anus where the normal vagina would be. In fact, he sent me some photographs taken before your surgery. He also has a handwritten notation on the bottom of one of the pages here. 'This patient should be worked up for possible female pseudohermaphoditism.'

"I'm going to ask you some very personal questions," said Dr. Dubois. "When you were a practicing homosexual in law school were you able to penetrate your male partner's rectum?"

"I had trouble because I had a small penis—although if I really got excited my penis would get hard. Sometimes I got complaints from my male partners. I did it, because the rest of the guys were doing it and I liked boys better than girls."

"Why didn't you have the ultrasound test of your pelvic organs or the CT scan done?"

"I was afraid of what they might find. I was afraid to have x-rays. Von Salzen didn't seem to push it either. He was more interested in making a video of my operation."

"Well, Robin, there's an outside chance that a big mistake has been made. I'm going to send you to an endocrinologist I know at the American Hospital, in Paris. His name is Dr. Peter Sullivan. I want him to check you out.

"I'm also going to place a phone call to Dr. Von Salzen in Los Angeles to see if he can send me some more information about you before your sex change. I want to see his operative notes. I wonder if he has any more photographs or close-ups."

"I'm sure he does," said Robin. "I also remember he took some video shots."

"If you have any trouble getting an appointment with Dr. Sullivan, call my office and I'll help you."

"Merci beaucoup," replied Robin.

Robin tried to get an appointment with Dr. Sullivan but his secretary said that it would be three weeks before he could see her. She called Dr. Dubois to have him expedite her appointment.

His secretary asked her to hold and then put Dr. Dubois on the phone.

"Robin, I have some very bad news to tell you. I called Dr. Von Salzen's office in Los Angeles. His office is closed. He's dead. He died in a fire in his office three months ago. Almost all his records were destroyed by the fire."

"Oh, how horrible! I'm sorry to hear that. He was a good doctor. Should I still go through with seeing Dr. Sullivan?"

"But of course," he replied. "I'll call his office for you and call you back with your appointment."

He called Robin back and her appointment was for the following week.

Dr. Peter Sullivan's office was in a professional building next to the American Hospital in Paris. His office was unpretentious but she noticed quite a few honorary degrees and awards posted on his walls. He was a very distinguished, tall, thin gentleman who looked about 55 years of age. He asked numerous questions, some that she had never been asked before. It was the most comprehensive history and physical exam she had ever had.

"That plastic surgeon in Los Angeles certainly did a wonderful job," he said. "Some of those guys are real artists. Have you always been thin like you are now?"

"Yes, but not quite this thin."

"Did you possibly notice any breast swelling when you went through puberty?" he asked.

"Come to think of it, yes. My mother took me to a doctor and he said it would eventually go away."

"Did it?" asked Dr. Sullivan.

"No," said Robin. "In fact, I was teased by the boys in school about it."

"I'm going to take a buccal smear, do some blood studies, and order an ultrasound of your pelvis," said Dr. Sullivan. "One other question; do you ever get periodic cramps in your lower abdomen?"

"Yes, quite frequently. I've had intermittent cramps as long as I can remember. The estrogen tablets I take seem to have some effect on those cramps too."

"When can you have the tests done?"

"The sooner the better. Is there anything you can tell me, doctor?"

"No. Not yet," said Dr. Sullivan. "We need to get the results of the tests first."

"I'll do whatever you say."

CHAPTER

Robin did not want François to know that she had been referred to an endocrinologist by her plastic surgeon. She was to be evaluated concerning her sex status and was extremely apprehensive about it.

In order that François not know what was going on, she decided to tell him a little white lie. She told him that she was going to take a brief trip to the country to visit her Aunt Madeline who lived in Lille in the French Flanders. She had told François about her Aunt Madeline before. She was her mother's youngest sister. Robin had not kept in touch with her aunt—in fact, she didn't even know where she lived in Lille—but François did not know that.

"I'll just be gone for about ten days," she told François.

"You can take my chauffeur and limousine if you like," said François. "I'll be down at the château supervising some of the plantings on the farm. I've also started to build a new horse barn down there for some of my breeding mares."

"That won't be necessary," said Robin. "I'll take the TGV North train to Lille."

"I'll miss you while you're gone."

"I'll miss you too, François. My heart will be with you."

Dr. Peter Sullivan, Robin's endocrinologist, arranged for an ultrasound study of her pelvis to be followed by a CT scan of the entire abdomen. She also had a buccal smear and numerous blood and urine tests.

Some of the medical tests were complicated and time-consuming. She had to collect all her urine in a large jar for 24 hours and numerous vials of blood were taken. She felt as if her arms were being used for pin cushions. She was told that some of her genetic studies had to be sent out for evaluation and testing and that it would take at least a week to ten days before all the results would be in.

Robin was motivated to have these tests done because she felt that she had such a screwed up life, that she wanted to get some answers. She truly didn't know whether she was a male or a female. Although she knew mentally she was much happier as a female than a male. Her love for François was one of the strongest relationships she had ever experienced. Within her heart she felt she was a female but she could not completely fill the obligations of a complete female—the ability to have a baby. She often cried about this in private for she knew how much François wanted to marry her and have a child.

The time came for her to have her ultrasound done.

The radiologist doing the ultrasound kept saying, "Hmm, very interesting. Hmm, very interesting," as he moved the ultrasound machine across her lower abdomen and pelvis.

"Would you mind telling me what's so very interesting?" she finally asked.

"I have to show your films and studies to some other doctors and see if they agree or disagree with my findings," he said. "I'm not even sure of my own findings."

"Well, please hurry up. My bladder's full from all the water I had to drink before the test. I really have to pass my water. Don't you have some idea of what's going on?"

"I do have some thoughts about my findings, but I don't want to make a misjudgment."

"That's not very helpful to me. I don't understand what you're talking about."

"Who's your referring doctor?" asked the radiologist.

"My doctor is Peter Sullivan," said Robin.

"I'm sure he'll be going over these tests with you. He's a very thorough endocrinologist. He looks at all his own patient's studies."

"Just what is this ultrasound test anyway?" asked Robin.

"An ultrasound is high-frequency sound waves that are used to penetrate the tissues of the body and then, with the use of a computer, a picture is made of those sound waves. It's helpful in determining solid from cystic tissue and it can be quite accurate in determining abnormal from normal tissue. It's particularly helpful in gallbladder and pelvic organ studies."

"I wonder why Dr. Sullivan's doing an ultrasound of my pelvis?" asked Robin.

"I can answer that," said the radiologist. "He wants to see if you have normal female organs and whether your uterus and ovaries appear normal."

"Well, can you tell me what you see or what you have found?" she asked.

"I really can't," said the radiologist. "What I see is not normal. I need some experts to look at these ultrasound studies so they can be accurately evaluated."

"You should call Dr. Sullivan tomorrow and have him answer your questions."

"You don't know how important these tests are to me," said Robin. "It's as important as my whole life."

"That's why I can't tell you. I'm not sure of what I see. We might be able to tell more when you have your CT scan."

Robin was getting completely frustrated. Her hands were trembling.

"I don't understand. I don't understand."

"I'm sorry," said the radiologist. "Medicine is not always as simple as black and white."

"There's another question I want to ask you," said Robin. "Why do you have to drink thirty-two ounces of water an hour before the ultrasound exam? I feel bloated and could float away. I was told not to urinate either before the test."

"I can answer that question. That's so the bladder will be out of the way of the other organs. We can evaluate the uterus and the ovaries better if the bladder is sufficiently full."

"Thanks. At least I got the answer to one of my questions."

The next day, Robin had to go for her CT scan. It was quite scary and more complicated than the ultrasound. The night before the exam she had to drink some medication and then again the next morning two hours before her appointment. Her body was then put in a big machine and x-ray pictures were taken all around her body. Transaxial slices or pictures were taken of her body for the study.

Robin then went to a medical laboratory next to the American Hospital. Quite a few vials of blood were drawn and she was given a large glass jar to collect all her urine for 24 hours.

She had been told to stop taking the estrogens she had been taking to increase the size of her breasts before the blood tests and urine tests could be done. Because she had bilateral silicone implants, she noticed very little change in the appearance of her breasts after stopping the estrogen hormones.

It was extremely frustrating for Robin not knowing the results of the tests as they were being done. She had difficulty sleeping and she had no one to discuss her problems with. She didn't want to share what was going on with François. Her anxiety was reaching a crescendo. It was almost like a panic reaction.

Dr. Sullivan told Robin his secretary would call her when all the tests were completed and he would then go over all the findings of the studies with her.

The phone call finally came and Robin was to see Dr. Sullivan the next day at 1:00 P.M.

When she walked into Dr. Sullivan's office, there was a big smile on his face.

"Robin, I have some good news and some bad news," he said. "Perhaps you should sit down."

"What is it, doctor? Do I have a tumor?"

"No," replied Dr. Sullivan.

"The good news is that I have reason to believe you are a real female."

Robin began to cry. All that frustration in her past and now she was being told she is a true female.

When she got her composure she asked, "How do you know that?"

"The ultrasound test shows that you have what appears to be two normal ovaries. The bad news is that you don't have a uterus. You have a congenital agenesis of the uterus."

"Are you sure?" asked Robin. "And what does that mean?"

"It means the place where the fertilized egg can be nurtured and grown inside you is missing. It happens in about one in five-thousand women. It means in all likelihood you cannot have any children."

"Are you absolutely sure?" asked Robin, as she continued to cry.

"No, I am not," said Dr. Sullivan. "We would have to test your ovaries to see if you are making viable eggs. I believe we might be able to stimulate your ovaries with hormones to help you make eggs. We can then fertilize those eggs in the laboratory with sperm from your husband and if we find a proper surrogate mother, you could still have your own child."

"How do they do that?" asked Robin.

"The fertilized egg would be put in the uterus of the surrogate mother and you could have your own child."

Suddenly a big smile shone across Robin's face. Everything that she dreamed about could come true. She'd tell François everything—on second thought, not quite everything. She'd eliminate the homosexual part.

"Dr. Sullivan, I don't understand. What was that thing I thought was a penis down there?"

"That was probably an hypertrophied clitoris. The testosterone shots you were receiving as a child caused it to grow larger and when you became sexually aroused it got even bigger. You also probably had an agenesis of the vagina—that's what that dimple was all about down below. Unfortunately, Dr. Von Salzen is dead and we don't have his operative records. Your vagina was almost normal but it didn't have an opening to the outside. Your country pediatrician didn't recognize your problem. That's why you were brought up as a boy and were given testosterone shots. It's a good thing those testosterone shots were stopped early—otherwise you would have poor bone development."

"What you have just told me is the most wonderful news you could possibly have given me."

"I'm glad you're happy."

"Happy? That's not quite the word for it!"

CHAPTER

Robin felt she was on top of the world. Her fondest dream had come true. She had masqueraded as a male, then a homosexual, a transvestite, and then had what she thought was a sexual conversion to a female—when in reality she was female all the time.

She was madly in love with François and wanted to spend the rest of her life with him. Dr. Sullivan told her they would be doing further testing on her ovaries to see if she made any viable eggs and if she did, with the help of God and science, she and François could possibly have a child if a proper surrogate mother could be found. The next week Dr. Sullivan arranged for her to have a laparoscopic study of her ovaries and some other tests to see if she might be able to make normal healthy eggs.

How was she going to tell François about all this? Would he still love her? How could she tell him she had been married to a female when she was a male and that female had been murdered in New Orleans in bed with the assistant district attorney from Dallas and that she was the prime suspect in that murder. She shuddered at the memory and what had happened that night. Nobody should or would believe her story. She decided she wasn't going to tell him that part of her life. That would be her dark secret that would go with her to her grave.

She decided to go back and talk to her French plastic surgeon. She liked him. He was her confidant. He was the one who had helped her to find her true sex identity. She called Dr. Pierre Dubois' office and made an appointment.

Dr. Dubois was pleased to see her. He had an ulterior motive because he was planning to write her case up for the world medical literature with Dr. Peter Sullivan, the endocrinologist. If Robin and François decided to have a test tube baby with a surrogate mother, it would make their research article that much more interesting. Just thinking about what had happened in Robin's past was mind-boggling.

"Robin, it's good to see you again. Have you told François the good news?"

"Not yet. That's why I'm here."

"What's the problem?" he asked.

"I don't know how much to tell him about my past. It isn't exactly a nice clean story."

"I think perhaps you should just tell him about the recent good discoveries," said Dr. Dubois. "I wouldn't tell him about some of those lurid previous episodes. They should be forgotten. If you embellish your remarks François might take it the wrong way."

"That's what I'm afraid of," said Robin. "I'm afraid I could lose him."

"I don't think so," replied Dr. Dubois. "He adores the ground you walk on. I'm sure if you explain the few important aspects of your past to help make him understand, there will be no problem. If you'd like, I could arrange for you to talk to a psychiatrist before you talk to François."

"I've talked to shrinks before," said Robin. "They said I was nuts. They were the ones who were nuts. They tried to explain everything according to Freud. I've been told that Freud is passé today. Most psychiatrists are old-fashioned."

"What do you mean by that?" asked Dr. Dubois.

"They haven't kept up with modern science," said Robin. "The new breed of psychiatrists have found out that many of the severe mental illnesses are due to chemical imbalances," said Robin. "They use lithium for manic depressives, and Prozac for acute and chronic depression, which has an effect on the blood seritonin in the brain. There's even a new expensive drug for schizophrenics that's working."

"Well, you're right about that," he said. "However, a psychiatrist might be able to predict what François' reaction might be when you tell him about your past. That might be helpful for you."

"I'm going to have to think about what to tell François. I'll let you know if I want to talk to a psychiatrist."

During the following week Robin gave it a lot of thought. François had become even more amorous since her faked return from visiting her aunt. He was much more aggressive in his lovemaking, almost as though he was trying to prove something to her. He continued to profess his love for her and again asked her to consent to marriage.

"Robin, *mon cheri*, I love you so. Please tell me that you will marry me. That you'll be mine. My life would be complete."

"François, I love you more than anything else in this world. I have to tell you about a few things that happened in my past, before I say yes."

"I'm not interested in your past. I'm interested in the present and in the future and spending the rest of my life with you."

"It's not that simple," said Robin. "I want you to relax and to listen."

"I'll try," said François.

"I'm going to tell you about something that happened to me when I was in Los Angeles at the age of twenty-five. At that time, I found out I didn't have normal female parts down below and went to see a Dr. Von Salzen, a plastic surgeon."

"That's preposterous," said François. "Your female parts are perfect."

"Just wait a minute. It's not that simple. I want you to listen to the whole story. My vagina had to be reconstructed and I took medication for a while so I could look more like a female. I really didn't know what I was. I also didn't have a normal menstrual cycle. After our relationship intensified and I fell in love with you, I decided to visit a renown French plastic surgeon, Dr. Pierre Dubois, and have him examine me. I must confess, I told you a small lie when I went to see him because I needed some time alone in order to have sophisticated medical tests done to determine my own identity.

"You see, François, I would like to be the mother of your son or daughter and I wasn't sure I would be capable of doing this. Dr. Dubois sent me to see a Dr. Peter Sullivan, a famous endocrinologist, at the American Hospital. He ordered a pelvic ultrasound and CT scan of my lower abdomen and pelvis.

"By doing those tests, he found out that I was born with normal ovaries but I did not have a uterus. This meant I could not carry a baby to term.

"Since those tests were done, I have been given some hormones to stimulate my ovaries. Using a laparoscopic instrument to look inside my abdomen and some other tests, the doctors found that I can make healthy eggs from my own ovaries. Using your sperm, those eggs can be fertilized in the laboratory and then implanted in a healthy surrogate uterus. It would still be our child but another woman would carry it for nine months."

Robin stopped talking and sat silent for a while. She was extremely anxious, not knowing what François' reaction would be.

"There, I've told you why I'm hesitant to say yes. If, after hearing this, you still want me, then the answer is yes."

"Of course the answer is yes," said François. "Oh Robin, you've made me the happiest man in this world. Of course I want you. We'll set a date. It will be the biggest wedding in France. You have made me so happy."

CHAPTER

27

Robin was riding on a cloud—François was not disturbed about her past—at least that part of it. She felt she was sailing on a magnificent cloud through the deep blue sky. Her heart pounded rapidly against her chest in anticipation of spending the rest of her life with François. Tears came to her eyes, flowing down her cheeks—she was so happy.

"Robin, my darling, please don't cry."

"I'm crying tears of happiness."

François pulled her to his chest.

Robin felt so small and weak surrounded by his massive frame as he kissed her gently on the lips.

"I love you so," she said.

"You've made me the happiest man in the world. We'll set a date as soon as possible for the marriage and have an engagement party so I can show off my beautiful future bride. I love you so much, Robin."

"Must we do that?" asked Robin. "I've loved you ever since I met you. We've been sleeping together, sharing each other for over a year now. We can sign the register at the municipality of Tours and then have the mayor and a priest verify our vows. It would be a mere formality."

"No, Robin. Our marriage cannot be a mere formality! France would demand that our marriage be done in a traditional manner."

"I don't have a dowry and my parents are not living," said Robin. "Besides, I'm not happy about too much publicity."

"Our marriage will make big news in all of France," said François. "It will be a day to be remembered!"

Robin realized that she would not be marrying a French peasant—she would be marrying a member of France's aristocracy. François was related to King François from the fifteenth century. It would be a royal wedding with most of the dignitaries and many of the important French aristocracy present—the prime minister, and others would be attending, including the news media and some of the international press.

Suddenly she became quite pensive and melancholy. She was worried that her true identity as Robert Sousa would be found out. Dr. Dubois had warned her that someone was looking for her—someone had gotten close to finding out her secret. She thought she may have been shot at on the ski slopes of the French Alps.

François recognized the change on her face. He decided to say something about it. "What's wrong, Robin? You look disturbed."

Robin attempted a weak smile and after a short while, replied, "Oh, nothing. Nothing at all. I'm just worried about all the preparations we have to make. I want a promise from you, François."

"Anything you wish."

"I want you to promise that the wedding will not be too far in the future and that the media coverage will be minimal."

"I promise you that, Robin—as long as you give me your hand in marriage."

"That I am sure I will do," replied Robin.

Promises are made to be broken.

François contacted one of the owners of Cartier's in Paris and was given the name of Madame Claudette Bonaparte to contact for help on arranging all the intricacies of the coming marriage. She traveled to the château with her secretary to discuss the plans with François and Robin.

When François introduced her to Robin, she said; "Just call me Claudette. My family and I have handled most of the important aristocratic weddings in France for the past two centuries. I'll arrange everything. Of course, there will be a charge."

"Of course," said François. "Don't spare anything. I must tell you that Robin and I have discussed what we want already."

"I'm here to listen. What church do you plan to be married in and how many guests will attend?"

"We haven't decided whether we'll be married in Paris or Tours. We'd like to have the reception at my château here. In Paris it would be either at Notre Dame or the Saint Dennis Cathedral. In Tours it would be at the main Cathedral."

"Why not have the wedding at Chambord—at François' Hunting Lodge? I'm sure that France would allow you to use it for the wedding."

"No!" said Robin. "I'm interested in a small wedding. That's much too big!"

"Nonsense!" said Claudette. "You're marrying one of the wealthiest and most eligible bachelors in France. There must be a magnificent setting for the wedding. The wedding and reception could both be at the same place. It has over four-hundred-forty rooms and is a magnificent castle. It's got a gorgeous double spiral staircase in the center of the main ballroom. Just imagine yourself walking down that staircase to be married to François."

"Just thinking about it takes my breath away. Do we really have to have such a big wedding, François?" asked Robin.

"I'm afraid we have to do what's proper," he replied.

"When do you plan to announce your engagement?" asked Claudette.

"Robin doesn't want any big announcement or media coverage."

"You'll get it whether you like it or not," said Claudette. "François, whatever you do is big news and this lovely creature you're marrying is a dream of all eligible French girls. The news media will eat it up. Personally, I'm thrilled that you asked me to help arrange your marriage. All the fashion magazines will be interested in what your bride wears. Robin could set a trend in couture for future weddings."

"I'm not interested in all that publicity. It scares me. All I'm interested in is marrying François," said Robin.

"My dear, that's what you will be doing, but all of France wants to see and listen," said Claudette.

CHAPTER
28

After meeting with the wedding coordinator in Paris, François and Robin decided to visit the jewelry stores to pick out her engagement ring. They went to Van Cleef's and Arpel's, which were next door to the Ritz. They also went to Cartier and Gerard on the Avenue Montaigne. François wanted to buy Robin the biggest diamond available in Paris. They finally settled for a six carat round solitaire placed in a platinum setting. Its brilliance was perfect and it cost one million francs.

"You are making me so happy, François. I can't express to you the feeling in my heart and mind about spending my life with you."

"This ring is just a small token of my love for you, Robin," he said as he placed the ring on her finger and gave her a kiss.

That afternoon, François went to be fitted for his wedding suit and Robin went to the St. Honoré fashionable shopping section of Paris to look for her wedding gown. She wanted her gown to have simple lines and not too long a train.

It was to be completely made and fitted for her by one of Paris' famous seamstresses—Madame Joanne Bardot. The transparent veil she was to wear was to be fitted to a delicate diamond-studded platinum crown with diamonds that had been in François' family for centuries.

Most of the plans for the wedding had been completed. She and François had agreed with the wedding coordinator to have the wedding at Chambord where King François I had built the Hunting Lodge. It had been recently refurbished and would be a magnificent setting. Robin and François met with Archbishop Richelieu from the Cathedral of St. Gatien in Tours and he agreed to perform the ceremony. The number of invitees had increased. Seven hundred and fifty guests would be invited to attend the wedding. Magnificent, beautiful fresh flowers would be shipped from the Paris flower market and from Lyon the day before the wedding.

Because of the notables, aristocrats, and distinguished members of the political parties who would be attending, security would be handled by the French National Police Department. The wedding vows would take place at 4:00 P.M. and a dinner with reception and dance would follow in the main hall of the castle. The French National Orchestra would play.

François had obtained a completely refurbished and repainted English stagecoach from one of his aristocratic neighbors, for leaving the Hunting Lodge at Chambord. The vintage was about 1848 and it was brightly colored and emblazoned on the sides with red, gold, and silver painting. The French seal of state was hand carved on both sides and it was able to accommodate passengers on top as well as within. The stagecoach had undersprings which made it more comfortable for the passengers and had originally belonged to King Louis-Philippe, who reigned until 1848 in France. At that time, a public riot and a revolution developed when they had a fiscal crisis, and unfair voting laws reminded the workers of their inferior status.

Suddenly Louis-Philippe had to flee France and he left the stagecoach behind. This beautiful stagecoach had been used on numerous occasions for affairs of state.

François had obtained two experienced coachmen to man the reins. The four horses that were to pull the coach were Clydesdales. They had feathers (long hair at the lower legs), attractive heads, and were high-stepping horses weighing over 2,000 pounds each. They were seven hands tall. They were dark brown with white markings.

It was a magnificent sight to see as they pulled the brightly colored carriage.

The beautiful horsedrawn carriage was to take François and Robin from the Lodge to the main highway where they would get into a limousine and drive to Orleans and Dijon to catch a train to the French Riviera for their honeymoon. They planned to leave the reception at 10:00 P.M. in order to catch the night train to Monaco.

CHAPTER

François and Robin had a serious discussion concerning the fertiliz-ation of one of Robin's eggs by François' semen. They decided to investigate how they should go about this and not wait until the marriage was consummated. Dr. Peter Sullivan, Robin's endo-crinologist, discussed surrogate motherhood with them as well as the limitations of artificial reproduction. They also discussed the medico-legal and ethical problems of assisted conception.

There was no official stand by the French Catholic Church con-cerning the method—it was too new. However, there was no prim-rose path concerning surrogacy and the role of criminal law.

One of the problems was—whose child would it be? Was it truly the child of the partners who supplied the fertilized egg or the child of the surrogate mother who supplied the uterus for the egg to grow in?

The nutrition for the critical development of the child was supplied by the surrogate mother. Some fertility physicians called surrogate motherhood mating of the embryos and gestational mothers—others called it reproductive gifts by the altruistic woman.

All Robin and François were interested in was that the child would be born from her eggs and his semen.

Robin and François learned from Dr. Sullivan that assisted parenthood was happening all over the world and that they were doing it successfully at his hospital in Paris. He suggested that legal papers be signed with the surrogate mother and that an agreed-upon price for carrying the child be decided in the beginning.

Robin knew pretty much when her ovaries made eggs because she got cramps—which she had had for years but never understood what they were.

Dr. Sullivan told Robin that the best surrogate mother would be a healthy relative who had a compatible blood type and who would not reject the implanted egg. The only eligible relative Robin had was her Aunt Madeline in Lille.

Robin had seen her Aunt Madeline when Robin's father and mother were killed in the automobile accident and Madeline flew from France to attend their funeral. At that time Robin was Robert Sousa and was seventeen years old, and had just completed his freshman year at Yale. Aunt Madeline was his mother's youngest sister—he remembered her as being a very beautiful blonde. Later, when he graduated from N.Y.U. Law School, she flew to New York City for the occasion.

Robin couldn't wait to marry François and consummate the marriage by having their baby. Of course it would have to be a boy! Dr. Sullivan had told her that if her ovarian eggs were healthy, François' semen could be used to fertilize her eggs and they could even pick out the sex of the child. Robin didn't want to wait for the marriage ceremony to take place in order to set in motion their ability to have a baby. She and François had talked about this and they decided to go ahead with the fertilization project even though the wedding would not take place for six months.

Robin had created a problem for herself, however, when she lied to François and told him she was going to Lille to meet her Aunt Madeline, when, in reality, she had all those medical tests done to determine her sex. She didn't even know where her Aunt Madeline lived. The last time she had contact with her was five years ago at the law school graduation and Madeline knew nothing about

Robin's sex change. She would be the ideal candidate to be the surrogate mother, if she was willing. She would now be about forty-six years old. Once she found her Aunt Madeline, what would she tell her? How could she explain that the boy she knew as Robert Sousa was really a woman named Robin Cartier? How could she prove all this so her aunt would believe her?

Robin had some childhood pictures showing her as a boy. She also had a copy of the video that Dr. Von Salzen had made when he did the transsexual operation.

Robin wondered what Dr. Von Salzen would say if he were alive? Did he know more than he let on? Why didn't he recognize that she was really a girl when he did the sex change operation? Why didn't he send the tissue he removed to the laboratory for examination? They would have known that the hypertrophied clitoris he removed was not a penis.

She decided the next time she saw Dr. Pierre Dubois she would ask him that question along with many other unanswered questions she had.

Two weeks later, she went to see him.

"Dr. Dubois, I would like to ask you some questions about my body."

"Well, Robin, you're fortunate that you now have such a beautiful one—fire away—ask your questions."

"I'm surprised the doctors who examined me and operated on me, didn't realize I was a female."

"I am too!" said Dr. Dubois.

"When you do a transsexual operation—converting a male to a female—do you send the tissue that's removed to the laboratory for study?" asked Robin.

"When I first started doing transsexual operations I did," he replied. "But since there's no going back after that operation and it's considered a cosmetic operation that's paid for in advance, I no longer send the tissue to the laboratory for study. It just adds to the patient's bill."

"That answers one of my questions."

"Maybe Dr. Von Salzen knew you were a female," said Dr. Dubois. "Anyway, you were being converted into one, so he probably didn't bother to explain it to you."

"I would have liked to have known," said Robin.

"Well, he's dead now. No one will ever know what he knew."

"It certainly took the doctors a long time to figure out I was a female. I ought to sue all of them."

"What you have is so rare—one in five-thousand. I think they should be excused. You fooled me until you asked me all those questions. I was trying my best to help you."

"I know, Dr. Dubois. I should thank God for what has happened. It could be much worse. I'm not going to sue anybody for malpractice. I'm so happy! I'm going to be marrying François and hopefully having his baby."

Robin made some phone calls and finally located her Aunt Madeline in Lille—she hadn't moved and still lived at the same address.

When she called her aunt and tried to explain to her that Robert Sousa was now a woman—Aunt Madeline hung up. Just before she hung up, she screamed, "No relative of mine would ever do that or be that crazy!"

Robin decided to talk to Dr. Dubois again—she explained what happened when she called her aunt.

"I'll give you a letter that explains exactly what happened to you. You probably should deliver it in person or, if you'd like, I can mail it to her."

"I think I'd rather deliver it in person," said Robin.

She decided to take the TGV train to Lille and confront her Aunt Madeline directly—face to face. Trying to explain what had happened over the telephone was a disaster and obviously not the right way to do it.

Robin would take a subdued wardrobe when she met her aunt. She'd wear a dark manish-appearing suit, a classic pantsuit look with a vest that she had from Yves Saint Laurent. It was conservative in appearance. She would wear low shoes and forget the high heels she frequently wore.

Her Aunt Madeline might recognize her if she dressed that way—more like Robert Sousa than Robin Cartier. Robin felt that if she could tell her some of the key episodes in her life without embellishment—perhaps her aunt would believe her. However, she decided not to tell her about her past homosexual experiences when she was a male and also her transvestite experiences in San Francisco. She read the letter that Dr. Dubois had given her explaining the fact that she really had been born a female but that she had numerous congenital abnormalities, particularly related to her genital organs, that were never recognized by her parents or her doctors.

François wanted to go with her to meet her Aunt Madeline and to add support to her quest for Madeline to be the surrogate mother but Robin would have no part of it. She wanted to go alone.

She packed enough conservative overnight clothes for her stay in Lille and promised to keep in touch with François.

She took the TGV train to Lille and arrived early in the morning and then took a cab to Aunt Madeline's home—a three-story brownstone dwelling in an affluent section of the city.

She paid the cab driver and told him to wait just in case her Aunt Madeline would not let her in.

She pushed the doorbell and her Aunt Madeline opened the door.

Robin spoke up, "I'm Robin Cartier . . . your nephew Robert Sousa . . . I'm really your niece now. I beg you to let me come in so I can explain what has happened . . . It's so important to me!"

Her aunt stared at her. She was hesitant to accept this attractive woman as her former nephew. She did recognize a slight resemblance in the facial contours of the woman in front of her. Finally she spoke.

"Why don't you come in? I'm willing to listen to your story."

Robin dismissed the cab and walked into the house. Aunt Madeline told her to sit down in the living room.

"What proof do you have that you're Robert Sousa?" she asked.

Robin took out photographs of her parents and some of when Aunt Madeline had come to her graduation at New York University Law School. She handed her the pictures.

"I think you'll recognize these pictures," said Robin.

"Oh my goodness. I can't believe this!" was her response.

"Well, it's true!" said Robin. "My mother, father and the doctors did not realize that I was born a female. Actually, I was born a female pseudohermaphrodite. I thought I was being made into a female when I was operated on in Los Angeles by a plastic surgeon by the name of Rudolfo Von Salzen, when in reality, I already was a female."

Madeline looked at Robin with a quizzical, confused gaze as she listened to her tale.

"I'm planning to get married in the near future to a wonderful man by the name of François Bouvier. I fell madly in love with him after meeting him in Paris. When he told me he wanted to marry me and have a son, I cried myself to sleep every night because I thought I was a man posing as a female and could not have children."

"Go on, I'm listening," said Madeline.

"A plastic surgeon in Paris, Dr. Pierre Dubois, sent me to Dr. Sullivan, an endocrinologist, at the American University. He did CT scans and ultrasounds of my pelvic organs, blood tests and buccal smear tests of the lining of my mouth. These tests confirmed that I am really a woman."

Robin had tears in her eyes now and was trembling as she related her past to her aunt. Her aunt moved over to the sofa where Robin was sitting and put her arms around her. The tears were flowing freely now and her cheeks were wet.

"The ultrasound tests show I have normal ovaries but I wasn't born with a uterus for a baby to grow in."

Robin's head was now on her Aunt Madeline's shoulder.

"Oh, my poor dear. What you've been through. It's truly unbelievable!"

"The worst part of the story is yet to come. François wants an heir and I would like to give him one."

"But that's impossible!" said Madeline.

"I thought so too!" said Robin. "But, it's not impossible!"

"I don't understand."

"They've developed a new method for women like me. Healthy eggs can be taken from my ovaries and matched with François' semen to be fertilized and then implanted in a surrogate mother's uterus. The baby would then grow to term there."

"That's truly a miracle!" said Madeline.

Robin didn't know whether she should ask her aunt outright or wait for another time. She decided to take a chance. "Would you be willing to carry my baby for me?"

Madeline hesitated and then spoke. "I'll have to think about that. I'll have to talk it over with your uncle. I know I'm in excellent health and I had no trouble having my two children. However, it's been over twenty years since I had my last child and I'd want my own doctor to check me over to see if my health is good enough. I certainly will consider helping you."

Madeline invited Robin to stay at her home overnight and she accepted. She met Madeline's husband, Louis, for the first time. She liked him very much and got along quite well with him.

Madeline made an appointment with her doctor the next day and passed the examination with flying colors. She told Robin she would be happy to try to carry her baby.

"Oh, Aunt Madeline! You don't know how happy you've made me! I now have someone to talk to and to love and to help me bear my child. I love you so much!"

Three weeks later, Robin and her Aunt Madeline began taking fertility drugs to synchronize their menstrual cycles. A month later, Robin and François went to the American Hospital in Paris and her eggs were collected along with François' semen. A fertilized egg was then transferred to Robin's aunt's uterus. Six weeks later an ultrasound test revealed the transfer had been successful.

Four months later it was determined that the fetus was a boy.

Madeline was visibly pregnant and would be attending the wedding at Chambord. On the wedding date she would be six months pregnant. Robin and François were ecstatic!

"Don't you worry about marrying me and having a child three months after the wedding?" asked Robin.

"Not in the least! I'm so happy I met you and with modern-day science we'll be able to have a child of our own."

CHAPTER

The murders of the Dallas assistant district attorney and Sousa's wife still remained unsolved. Detective Harry Gray, Dr. Scott Perkins, and anesthesiologist Paul Aronson seemed to be the only ones interested in pursuing Robert Sousa—Robin.

Harry Gray talked to Scott about going to Paris to try to find her. His ego had been tarnished by his inability to locate her and bring her to justice.

"Are you still interested in finding Sousa?"

"Of course I am," said Scott. "It takes two to eight years sometimes to know if you have AIDS. I'd like to get that monkey off my back."

"If you'll pay half of my expenses, I'll go looking for her in Paris."

"How do you plan to go about finding Robin in Paris?"

"I talked to some of my former colleagues at the Manhattan Police Department in New York City and I was given the names of two individuals who work at the Palais de Justice and French Police Nationale.

"One is Judge Louis Labrecque and the other is the Commissioner of Police, Phillipe Soucier. I also learned a little bit about the French justice system. The central police authority for all of France is the Sûreté Nationale, which is under the Ministry of Interior. Paris and the Seine Department come under the Préfecture de Police, which is responsible for the security of the state, and in particular, the supervision of foreigners. I ought to be able to get some leads from them about Robin."

"It's not that simple. Robin was born in France so she may have retained her citizenship. She may have had her name changed when she had the sex change."

"I never thought of that," said Gray. "However, at least I know her first name and there can't be too many Robins in Paris."

"She could've changed her first name too, you know? What do you plan to tell the police in Paris about her?"

"I'm not quite sure yet. How do you tell the police that the person you're looking for committed a crime when he was a man, made his wife pregnant and is now a female?"

"I'm sure you can tell them that, but I'm not so sure they'll believe you."

"That's what I'm afraid of," said Gray.

"What else are you planning to do?"

"That's what I want to talk to you about. I want you to get me a list of the plastic surgeons who do sex changes in Paris. I'm sure Robin has seen one or two of them."

"I'll see if I can get you that list from the secretary of the Society of American Plastic Surgeons," replied Scott. "You'll probably have more luck trying to find Robin by locating her plastic surgeon in Paris than with the police."

"Well, I'm all for trying to find Robin. She made me age prematurely and I don't like playing Russian roulette with AIDS."

"When are you planning to go to Paris?"

"Next week," said Gray. "I've already got my ticket. I'm flying on Air France into Orly Airport in Paris. I'm looking forward to seeing some of those beautiful French women."

"I hope you concentrate on finding Robin and don't get waylaid by some good-looking French coquette."

"All work and no play makes Jack a dull boy," remarked Gray. "Besides, I'm a bachelor so that makes me eligible."

"You'd better remember that Robin's already murdered three people. She could be as dangerous as a rattlesnake."

"I realize that. For all we know, she may have killed a few more. She could have been involved with that Los Angeles fire."

"That's right. I almost forgot about that."

"Are you going to be able to carry a gun?" asked Scott.

"I've already applied for a permit. With my credentials, I think I'll be able to."

"Remember, I want her alive, not dead," said Scott.

"I'll remember that. But if she starts shooting at me, I'm going to return the fire. I'll remember to get a blood sample for you if she gets shot."

"Thanks a lot. How do you plan to speak the language?" asked Scott.

"I know how to speak some French. I took it in college. I contacted the University of Paris and I plan to hire a student part time to aid in my search. Besides, a lot of the French people speak English."

"Where do you plan to go first?"

"I plan to see the commissioner of police, Phillipe Soucier."

"Where are you staying in Paris?"

"I'll be staying at the Le Bristol Hotel. It's supposed to have a good bar and excellent service."

"That's an expensive hotel," said Scott. "I'm not paying that bill!"

"Don't worry, I'm paying half of it," said Gray.

"Well, keep in touch."

Gray got on the Air France plane at Kennedy Airport in New York and had a pleasant flight to Paris. He checked into the Bristol Hotel and took a cab to the Commissariat de Police to look up Commissioner Phillipe Soucier. He gave the receptionist a letter addressed to the commissioner and a few minutes later was escorted to the commissioner's office.

Commissioner Soucier was a robust man with a black mustache who spoke fluent English. When Gray entered the room, the commissioner gestured with his hand for him to take a seat.

"How may I help you?" he asked.

"I'm trying to locate a beautiful blonde woman who lives in Paris," said Gray. "Her name is Robin."

Soucier smiled, his eyes seemed to sparkle and then he said, "Many other Frenchmen are trying also."

"You don't understand. The blonde woman I'm talking about is wanted for questioning about the murder of the assistant district attorney from Dallas, Texas and a woman who was found dead with him in a hotel room in New Orleans four years ago. Robin is the prime suspect and was the last one to see them alive. Her name is Robin Cooker."

"Does she have a criminal record?" asked Soucier.

"Not that I know of."

"Do you know where she lives in Paris? Do you know anything about any of her friends? Do you have any identification. Any pictures?"

"I do have some pictures,"said Gray as he pulled out some five by sevens from a manila envelope and laid them out on the commissioner's desk.

"My! *C'est magnifique*! This woman you call Robin is a beautiful woman. I can't believe this woman is a criminal."

"Well, she is and she might be a vicious one! We need your help in trying to find her in Paris."

"I'll call my secretary and have her run this woman's name through our files. Do you have her fingerprints?"

"I think I do," said Gray. "Someone's fingerprints were all over the room at the scene of the crime in New Orleans. Here's a copy of the prints. We think they're hers."

"Well, it will take us a few days to run this information through our files. Where are you staying in Paris?"

"At the Bristol."

"Elegant hotel. Incidentally, just what is your interest in finding this Robin Cooker?"

"She has a bounty of twenty-thousand dollars on her head. Also, she ran off with some expensive documents that we're trying to get back."

"Before we do this search, I need to see your credentials and your passport," said Soucier.

Gray showed Soucier his passport and his detective license.

"We'll see if we can help you. I too believe that if a murder has been committed, the guilty party should be brought to justice."

With that comment, Detective Gray was excused.

Soucier called his secretary in.

"We have another person looking for Robin Cooker now," said Soucier. "Get me the file on that individual who came in inquiring about her last week. I believe it was a young French female medical student."

CHAPTER

After talking to Commissioner Soucier, Gray felt he would get little help from him. He seemed to be very complacent and disinterested. Before he left the police station, he was advised by one of the French policemen to seek help from the judicial police who carry out criminal investigations and hunt down suspects. He was given the address for the judicial police headquarters and saw one of the underlings, Inspector Henri Rousseau.

"Who are you trying to locate?" asked Inspector Rousseau.

"I'm trying to locate a man masquerading as a woman," said Gray.

"We have many people trying to do that here in Paris," said Rousseau. "This is the sex capital of the world. You see everything here."

"This one's different. Robert Sousa underwent a sex change to become a woman. He's changed his name. We don't know his new last name. We think it's Robin Cooker. He's wanted for the murder of the assistant district attorney from Dallas and a woman. The murders took place in New Orleans four years ago."

"Could you give me some more details?" asked Rousseau. "There are many Robins in Paris."

"Here's a copy of the New Orleans police report. It's got pretty much everything in it. There are also some photographs of Sousa after the sex change."

Rousseau leafed through the documents.

"My," said Rousseau. "Plastic surgeons can do wonders these days, can't they?"

"Yes," said Gray. "I believe she's hiding from the law. She's cleverly changed her identification and really covered her tracks."

"The way she looks, I don't believe she'll be able to hide her tracks or whereabouts very long. She is most beautiful. Have you searched the police files?" asked Rousseau.

"I spoke to Commissioner Soucier three weeks ago," said Gray. "I haven't heard from him. He was going to search the French police files."

"He works with the public security forces," said Rousseau. "He's not a member of the specialized police armed forces. I'll see if there's anything about Sousa on my computer right now."

Rousseau tapped the keyboard and entered information in the computer.

"There's nothing on the computer under the name Sousa," he said. "I'll try looking under Robin Cooker."

"Hey, here's something under Robin Cooker. Our police records show there is no Robin Cooker registered in the whole country. There's something interesting on the computer though. Evidently, you're not alone in trying to locate Sousa. A woman from Paris checked in with us three weeks ago at the main office inquiring about Sousa and Robin Cooker."

"Hmm, that's interesting," said Gray. "I wonder if she's found out anything. Do you have her name and possibly her address? How could anyone else be looking for a Robin Cooker? Not too many people know she exists."

"We do," said Rousseau as he scribbled the information on a piece of paper and handed it to Gray.

"Maybe she's a bounty hunter like I am," said Gray.

"What's the amount of the bounty?" asked Rousseau.

"Twenty-thousand dollars."

"That's a lot of French francs. Now I understand why you're looking for her."

Gray thought back to when he went to New Orleans and talked to the district attorney about Sousa. He had told him all about Sousa's sex change and that he felt Sousa was in France.

"Damn it!" he said. Then he thought to himself—did someone come over to look for Sousa in Paris?

"What's wrong?" asked Rousseau, as he looked at Gray's puzzled face.

"Nothing, nothing. I'm just thinking about what you just said."

Harry didn't hear from Commissioner Soucier. It looked as though he was not going to be of any help. Gray decided to try to find the plastic surgeon that Robin might be dealing with in Paris. He decided to contact the American Hospital in Paris because they had English-speaking health services. Rather than trying to talk on the phone, he took a cab to the hospital.

When he got there he went to the reception desk and asked if he could see a list of the doctors who worked at the hospital.

"What in particular are you looking for?" asked the receptionist.

"I'm looking for a list of your plastic surgeons," said Gray.

"We have four plastic surgeons who practice at this hospital," she replied. "Dr. Roland LaDuke is the chief of plastic surgery."

"How can I get to see him?"

"You should be referred by another doctor."

"That's impossible," said Gray. "I'm from the United States."

"What is your problem?"

Gray thought for a minute and then said, "I want to see him about a face-lift."

"I'll write his name and phone number down for you and you can give his office a ring."

"That's fine," replied Gray.

During the next three weeks, Gray tried to call the phone number for the woman that Rousseau gave him. The phone rang continuously but no one answered.

He also talked to the head of plastic surgery at American University and was given the names of ten doctors who specialized in sex changes in Paris.

God! They must be doing a lot of sex changes over here, thought Gray. He found it difficult to get an appointment with the plastic surgeon—he wasn't interested in any sex change for himself.

Finally, he got in to see a Dr. Alexander Rodin, one of the leading sex-change plastic surgeons in Paris.

Gray flashed his detective badge to Rodin's secretary and she obliged by talking to her boss and then letting Gray in to see him.

"Is there a problem with one of my patients?" asked Rodin.

"Not that I know of," said Gray. "Why do you ask?"

"I have operated on quite a few Americans. One or two of them were paranoid. I thought maybe they got into trouble with the police."

"No. That's not why I'm here. I'm looking for a patient who had a sex change in the States and is wanted for murder. I have some pictures I'd like to show you."

Gray handed over the 5 × 7 photos of Robin.

"Hmm. Hmm," said Rodin. "I've seen this woman somewhere. What's her name? Do you have any copies?"

"No, but I'll get some made," said Gray.

"Good. I'll show the pictures around to some of my colleagues."

The next day, Gray went to a specialty photography shop and had duplicate copies made of Robin's photos. He dropped the pictures off at the plastic surgeon's office.

Three days later he received a call from Dr. Rodin.

"Mr. Gray, one of my plastic surgery colleagues has taken care of Robin. However, he hasn't seen her in nine months. He thinks she might be married now. The doctor's name is Pierre Dubois. He's one of the best plastic surgeons in all of France."

"Will he see me?"

"Yes," said Rodin. "However, he doesn't believe Robin is a killer."

"That's what everyone says," said Gray.

After Dr. Dubois received the call from Dr. Rodin, he decided to call Robin. He finally got through to her at François' château. He wanted to tell her about the detective.

"Robin, this is Dr. Dubois. I have to talk to you about a personal matter."

"What is it?" asked Robin.

"There's a detective from the States who's looking for you, a Detective Gray."

There was a long silence on the other end of the phone.

"Are you sure he's a detective?" asked Robin.

"I haven't met him yet," said Dubois. "One of the other plastic surgeons identified your pictures. I presented your case to our plastic surgery seminar here three months ago."

"Please do me a favor and deny you know me," said Robin. "I have done nothing wrong. I'll be forever indebted to you. I don't want the fact that I'm a woman now disclosed to anyone! I believe you promised to keep everything in strictest confidence when I first saw you."

"That's right," said Dubois. "I'll abide by my commitment."

"Thank you," said Robin.

Two days later, Detective Gray entered the plush office of Dr. Pierre Dubois. After a short wait, he was escorted into the doctor's office by the secretary.

"What can I do for you?" asked Dubois.

"I'm looking for a Robin Cooker. I believe she is one of your patients. She had a sex change in the States. I have a few pictures I can show you."

He handed over the pictures.

Dubois looked at them.

"I have a patient who looks somewhat like this, but this is not the same person. I'm sorry I can't help you."

"Dr. Rodin said it was your patient," said Gray.

"Well, it's not. Rodin saw a few projected slides on a screen. He's mistaken!"

"Gosh, I thought I had something," said Gray. "If you see anyone resembling these pictures, I wish you would contact me. This bisexual individual is wanted for murder."

Gray was disappointed when he left Dr. Dubois' office. So close and yet so far away. He decided to try to find the woman who was also looking for Robin. Maybe she found out something.

He dialed her phone and a woman's voice answered in French.

"*Oui? Qui est-ce*? Who is it?"

He responded by saying, "Harry Gray, an American tourist." He then spoke in French. *"Quel est vôtre nomme?"* What is your real name?

She replied in English. "My name is Daphne St. Claire. I'm a third-year medical student at the university. Why are you calling me?"

"I understand you're looking for Robin Cooker? I am too. I thought we might compare notes."

"How did you find out I was looking for Robin Cooker?"

"Commissioner Soucier from the Police Nationale told me. I would like to meet with you. Perhaps we could arrange a meeting place."

"I have examinations at school right now. Give me your phone number and I'll ring you back in a couple of days. Where are you staying?"

"At the Bristol. I'll look forward to our meeting."

CHAPTER
32

Three days later, Harry Gray received a call from Daphne St. Clair.

"I'll be happy to meet with you Friday at your hotel, Le Bristol. We can have dinner together and discuss the search for Robin Cooker. However, I'm sure I have very little information to give you."

"I'll meet you in the lobby of the hotel," said Gray. "Dinner will be on me. I don't have too much information. Perhaps by pooling our resources, we'll be able to come up with something. How will I recognize you?"

"I'm a brunette, five feet, seven inches tall, and I'll be wearing a black suit with a white blouse. *À quelle heure?* What time?"

"How about 7:00 P.M.?"

"That's fine."

Gray made a reservation for two in the fancy main dining room. Who knows, Daphne sounded pleasant on the phone and he was a bachelor. He was somewhat intrigued. The big question was why was she looking for Robin? Until now, he hadn't met any real attractive French girls. But, he hadn't been looking either. Who knows? Let's wait and see.

Gray took a shower, shaved, put on a dark blue suit and a white shirt with a narrow tie and went down to the lobby at 7:00 P.M. It was quite crowded and there were quite a few attractive women there. Most had escorts. He decided to sit on a sofa near the entrance. At 7:15, a tall stunning brunette with a cropped haircut got out of a cab and entered the lobby. She was beautifully dressed in a black silk suit that hugged her body lines. She looked like one of the Mediterranean brunettes from the Riviera. Her black heels and long slender legs made her appear much taller than she was. She certainly didn't look like a medical student. She walked directly to Gray as if she had known him for a long time.

"Mr. Gray, I'm Daphne. So nice to meet you!" She had a broad smile and a sparkle that was combined with good looks and allure. She held her hand out to him.

Gray took her hand and kissed the back of it.

"You are most gracious," she said.

"Young lady," said Gray, "you're typically French and beautiful. If I were younger, I wouldn't mind spending the evening with you."

"We'll see," was her reply as she smiled. "Do you dance?"

"A little," said Gray. "I can learn in a hurry."

"Most Americans I've met really know how to dance. I've yet to see one who doesn't. I love to dance!"

"Perhaps after dinner you could suggest some place we might try."

"Perhaps," replied Daphne.

"Where have you made arrangements for dinner?"

"In the main dining room of the hotel."

"I'm not happy about that. That's not very original," said Daphne. "In Paris on a Friday night, there are lots of exciting things to do and nice places to go to eat."

"What do you suggest?" asked Gray.

"I'd love to go to a night club; the Lido or the Moulin Rouge or listen to some American jazz, or do some dancing at Le Palace. Are you on a corporation account or a limited budget?"

Gray was getting an education in a hurry from this pretty French damsel. She obviously knew her way around.

"I'm on a corporate account. We can have a good time and not worry about the expense."

"Splendid!" said Daphne, as she grabbed his arm and gave him a slight peck on the cheek and a hug. "I love Paris at night."

"Where shall we eat?" asked Gray. "What kind of food do you like?"

"I like to eat fish so I can keep my slender figure," she said as she pressed her hands beneath her breasts.

When she did that, Gray realized she had a white peek-a-boo blouse on. It left nothing to the imagination.

"Why don't we go to Maxims at Rue Royale?" suggested Daphne. "I've always wanted to go there but can't afford it."

"Fine. We'll go there." Gray was beginning to be caught up in the enthusiasm of this young lady. He was looking forward to an interesting evening.

"I do want to talk to you about Robin Cooker before the night is over, however," said Gray.

"I'll talk to you about that at the end of the evening," said Daphne.

They took a cab to Maxim's and Daphne ordered her fish and salad with a complimentary delicious white wine. Gray had a sliced tender beef dish with bernaise sauce. He had a few dry martinis. The food was excellent and Daphne was as refreshing as a spring flower in bloom. She was intelligent and their conversation was both animated and candid. She told Gray all about herself; how she grew up near the Riviera and how her rich uncle was paying to put her through medical school. She eventually wanted to be a radiologist and planned to apply to the Radium Cureé Institute for a postgraduate residency.

After dinner they went to the Lido and fortunately were able to get two good seats in the center section. Gray tipped the head usher generously.

The Lido show was excellent, with beautiful French women dressed in gorgeous revealing beaded costumes dancing in unison.

"My, those girls can dance. They have beautiful bodies," said Gray. "They're also real artists."

"It's because they don't have any clothes on," said Daphne. "A woman's body is her fortune if she is beautiful."

"You've got quite a bit of it in your own bank then," said Gray.

"*Merci beaucoup*," said Daphne, as she gave Gray a big smile.

"After the show," asked Gray, "what's next?"

"I'd love to dance," said Daphne.

"You name it," said Gray.

"Let's go to Le Palace at Rue du Faubourg Montmartre. It's a super disco and they play all sorts of music."

Gray had been a good dancer in his college days—he had some second thoughts about his present potential dancing abilities. Oh, hell, he'd give it a try. He had a young gorgeous French *femme fatale* with him and she was being cooperative. They took a cab to Le Palace and before he knew it, he was out on the dance floor doing all sorts of dances with Daphne. She really knew how to dance—both to the slow music and to the fast. She was really enjoying herself. She cuddled up real close to Gray during the slow music and really knew how to throw her body around on the fast numbers. After dancing for quite a while, she slipped out of her black jacket, revealing her well-proportioned youthful breasts through the peek-a-boo blouse. Gray was beginning to get some ideas about her for later in the evening. I wonder, he pondered. It was after 2:00 a.m. and Daphne was still enjoying the music and the dancing.

Gray finally broached the subject.

"I don't suppose," he started to say.

"Yes," said Daphne. "I've already decided. There's a saying in France—French wine as it ages and gets older, gets better and better and eventually tastes better."

"I'd like to find out if that's true. Why don't you buy a bottle of good French champagne from the waiter and we'll take it back to your room at the Bristol."

"Wow! You think of everything," said Gray, as he hailed the waiter and told him what he wanted.

"No problem, Monsieur," he replied.

"Daphne, we never did talk about your going to the French National Police Department and inquiring about Robin."

"I told you I know very little," replied Daphne. "I was given two thousand francs to go to the police department to inquire about Robin Cooker—who I know nothing about. I was an intermediary. The parties did not want to identify themselves to the police. Commissioner Soucier told me that he would call if he found out anything—I have received no call."

"The same thing happened to me," replied Gray.

The waiter returned with the champagne and they left. Gray hailed a cab. Daphne snuggled up to him as he pulled her to him. Her lips met his without resistance and she arched her body against his. Their tongues intertwined as he reached for the buttons on her jacket.

"Just a minute," said Daphne, as she quickly unbuttoned her jacket and the top buttons of her blouse. She had no bra on, which was quite common with the young youthful French women. Gray kneaded her breasts as they kissed.

"Oh, I could love you," said Daphne, as Gray kissed her ears, her cheeks and her neck. The cab finally arrived at the Bristol.

They took an elevator directly to Gray's room on the eleventh floor. When they got into his room he placed the bolt on the door.

Daphne had already slipped out of her tailored jacket.

"Why don't we have just a little bit of that champagne first?" she said, as she started to unbutton her blouse.

"OK," replied Gray. "However, I'd rather drink the sweet honey from your lips."

Gray opened the champagne bottle and poured two full glasses of champagne.

Daphne unbuckled his trouser belt as she kicked her high heels off and unzipped her skirt.

Daphne raised her glass of champagne; "Here's to you and I, Harry. May this be the beginning of a beautiful friendship. I might even want to be your mistress," she said, as she winked at him and gave him a big smile.

She slipped out of her bikini panties, revealing the flower of her womanhood. Her beautiful youthful body took Gray's breath away. She was gorgeous! He raised his glass of champagne and said; "*Vive la France,*" as he walked over to her, lifted her up in his arms and gently dropped her on the king-size bed. Just looking at her youthful beauty made his mouth water. His body hormones and juices were overflowing with desire as his male animal instincts took over. He started kissing her from head to toe as she moved her body, tantalizing him with the voluptuous curves of her buttocks and breasts. She responded to his full-mouth kissing and he quickly learned what a true French kiss was. He had no trouble in penetrating her as she sighed and moaned in ecstasy. She quickly became the aggressor as she rolled him over and got on top of him, pushing her hips into his groin. He started to feel weakened by this aggressive feline who was in obvious heat. He had gone down rollercoasters and had once ridden horses in a rodeo but those experiences were nothing like this. He started to feel dizzy from her sexual drive—something was happening to him that he had never experienced before.

He felt most peculiar, he felt as if he might be losing consciousness. He tried to talk and push her off but was unable to. That was all he remembered.

Daphne got off him. "That will be the last fuck Mr. Gray will ever have. It's a shame! He was good, very very good." She went to the phone and dialed a number and said; "He's all yours! He's in room 1137. Those knock-out pills in the champagne worked great! I'll leave the computerized door key taped to the outside lower left-hand side of the door."

Three weeks later Commissioner Soucier received a call from one of the detectives in the crime investigation department.

"Commissioner, do you know an American detective by the name of Harry Gray?"

"That name is familiar. Why do you ask?"

"There was a death over at the Bristol three weeks ago. Gray, an American detective, shot himself in the mouth with his own gun. It looked like a straightforward suicide. He had a high alcohol level in his blood—high enough to kill a horse. There was blood all over the bed and his own fingerprints were on his gun by his side. It looked like he got drunk, depressed, and then committed suicide."

"So? Why are you calling me?"

"We searched his room. Nothing was missing. However, we did find something interesting."

"What did you find?"

"Under his mattress we found a black hardcover book—it was a diary and it was kept up to date. The last notation was written the day he died. He wrote that he had a date with a French medical student by the name of Daphne St. Clair. He was going to discuss something about a Robin Cooker case with her."

"He must have been worried about something to include that

notation in his diary before he went out. Did you check out the French medical schools for Daphne St. Clair?"

"We did. There's no one registered by that name in any of the schools. We called you because your name is in that diary, too. Evidently, you saw Gray six weeks ago."

"Hmm. I do remember that guy. Tall, good-looking, gray-black mustache, middle-aged, seemed to be in good health. I thought he looked like a stable guy."

"If you read the diary, you might not think so."

"What do you mean?"

"Two doctors hired him to find an attorney by the name of Robert Sousa. One of the doctors, a surgeon, had his finger pricked by a needle when he was operating on him. The tissue he removed from Sousa was suspicious for AIDS."

"So?" replied Soucier.

"The patient was told that he might have AIDS and took off when he was told about it. The two doctors hired Gray to find him. They wanted to do a blood test to see if he really did have AIDS. Gray must have been a pretty good detective because he found out that Sousa was a homosexual, transvestite, bisexual killer. He tracked Sousa through San Francisco, Los Angeles, New Orleans, Dallas, and finally Paris."

"You've got to be kidding me."

"What I just told you is in that diary. He came to Paris to look for a Robin Cooker, alias Attorney Robert Sousa."

"You'd better bring that investigative file and that diary over to my office right away. I want to see it."

CHAPTER

Inspector Rousseau personally brought the investigative file and the diary to Commissioner Soucier's office. Rousseau and Soucier had known each other for a long time. They were seasoned detectives who had grown up in the ranks together and had excellent records. They had pursued some of the most difficult crime cases in all of France.

Rousseau handed the diary and file over to Soucier. As he did so, he said, "After you read this diary and look at this investigative file, you're going to be really mystified and shocked. I've never seen anything like this before and I'm willing to bet you haven't either!"

"Well, sit down," said Soucier. "In France, anything can happen."

Soucier started to read the diary. He kept uttering *"mon dieu—my* God! This is the most fascinating and intriguing diary I've ever seen. If all this is true, you could write a book about it. Unfortunately, no one would believe you.

"It says here that Gray was trying to locate Robert Sousa to get a blood sample because Sousa might have AIDS. The surgeon who got his finger pricked while operating on Sousa and an anesthesiologist were financing his pursuit. This Sousa guy—or whatever you want to call him, or it—was a lawyer.

"He started out as a homosexual in law school who later got married. His wife got pregnant. That's the crazy part—was he trying to hide his past? Then he catches his pregnant wife in bed with a friend while they are all attending the American Bar Association's annual meeting in New Orleans. He kills them both and takes off for San Francisco where he becomes a transvestite. Then he makes the supreme male sacrifice—he gets his genitals chopped off and becomes a woman—ugh! He's either sick or trying to change his identity or he's nuttier than a fruitcake—or all three!

"Then, according to this diary, he may have killed the plastic surgeon who operated on him in Los Angeles—a fire of suspicious origin. He could have been trying to destroy his records. Maybe someone else did it for him or maybe he had an accomplice. Now he's here in Paris, masquerading as a female, to give us all headaches. Gray, who's hot on his trail, gets bumped off or commits suicide. The suicide story doesn't fit too well in the scenario."

"Rousseau, we've got to find this character. We've got to find this homosexual, transvestite, bisexual killer before she kills again!"

"What did you find at the scene of the crime in the hotel room?"

"What we found was most interesting. Robbery was not a motive. There was nothing missing. It looks like he probably had sex in his bed before he was killed or before he killed himself. The sheets were examined for semen and it was there. We also interrogated all the hotel personnel who worked that evening. He was seen by more than one witness in the company of an attractive brunette."

"Well, that'll give us some lead," said Soucier. "It looks like we have to find that Daphne St. Claire."

"She's a brunette, and in the diary he said he was going to meet her. If we find St. Claire she might be able to tell us something. For all we know, she could be the killer."

"Not really," said Inspector Rousseau. "It still looks like he committed suicide. There's no evidence of a struggle. He shot himself in the mouth with his own gun. That's weird too! If you read the beginning of the diary he contemplated committing suicide over a coed who gave him the cold shoulder while he was in college. He was also a bachelor all his life. Maybe that's why he was a bachelor."

"So, what you're saying is that this Daphne St. Claire was a one night stand. She was out for a good time," said Soucier.

"That's right!" said Rousseau. "I called in and got his credit card expenditures for that night. They went to Maxim's, the Lido, and Le Palace."

"Hmm, expensive taste," said Soucier.

"The waiter at Le Palace remembered Gray," said Rousseau, "and in particular, the young lady. He said she was a beautiful brunette. Gray bought a bottle of expensive champagne before he left there. He obviously had some plans for the evening. He also gave the waiter a big tip."

"Well, he had an interesting evening from the looks of his credit card records. Daphne St. Claire was probably the last one to see him alive."

"What about the champagne?"

"The bottle was half empty and there were two empty champagne glasses."

"Have they done any toxicology studies on Gray's blood yet?"

"Yes. He had a very high alcohol level—enough to kill him. He also had some other chemicals in his blood which our laboratory has been unable to determine."

"Put out an all-points bulletin for Daphne St. Claire," said Soucier. "We're not going to be able to find her very easily."

"Why not?" he asked.

"I forgot to tell you a very important piece of evidence."

"What's that?"

"There was a beautiful expensive brunette wig made of human hair in the bathroom wastebasket."

In the front of Harry Gray's diary there was an identification card with his full name, address and phone number. Beneath the sticker was a notation:

'In the event of my death, the following people are to be notified:

Emily Gray (sister)
1521 Hoboken Avenue
Brooklyn, NY

George Gray (brother)
1793 York Avenue
Manhattan, NY

Scott Perkins, M.D.
    and
Paul Aronson, M.D.
c/o Jefferson Hospital
Box 84
Middlecity, CT

Instructions for burial: My bodily remains are to be cremated. After six weeks the ashes are to be put in the Hudson River by releasing them from the George Washington Bridge.'

Scott received a cablegram from Inspector Rousseau twenty-four hours after Gray's death. It read: 'This is to notify you that Harry Gray died suddenly on June 13, 1992. Our office will be contacting you with further information as soon as it becomes available. If you wish to discuss what happened you can call: Inspector Rousseau, Commissariat de Police, Paris, France. Phone 47-77-13-12.'

Scott was shocked by Gray's death. He immediately called Paul Aronson, the anesthesiologist. Paul's wife Karen answered the phone.

"I'd like to talk to Dr. Aronson."

"My husband is in Europe," she replied.

"What's he doing over there?"

"He's attending an anesthesiologist's medical meeting in Rome."

"I've got to get in touch with him right away," said Scott.

"He's in France now. He's flying in tomorrow morning from Paris. I'm picking him up at Logan Airport in Boston at 6:00 A.M.," she replied.

"Do you know where he's staying in Paris? It's very important I get him right away. A good friend of mine died in Paris and I want him to check to see what actually happened before he leaves to come back."

"I can't help you. He didn't have a reservation for a hotel in Paris. He was only going to be there for two or three days. He said he was going to stay at a bed and breakfast."

"If he calls, find out where he is and call me right away," said Scott.

Karen never called. Aronson called Scott from Logan Airport.

"What's up? What's so important?"

Scott could hardly talk. His speech was tremulous. "Harry Gray is dead!"

"Oh, my God!" said Aronson. "What happened?"

"I don't know," said Scott.

"I got a cablegram yesterday from Paris. I tried to get you. He died in his hotel room two days ago. I have a phone number I can call for more information. Because of the time zone change I plan to call later on this evening. He died in Paris while you were there and I wanted you to find out some of the details."

"God damn it! Too bad you didn't get me. I'll come over to your house. I want to be present when you make that call," said Aronson.

After he got there, Scott made the call with Aronson present. It was then 9:00 A.M. in Paris.

Inspector Rousseau's secretary Cecile answered the phone.

"*Bonjour*. Who's calling?" She obviously had a phone that told where the call was coming from.

"Dr. Scott Perkins from the United States. I'd like to speak to Inspector Rousseau."

"Hold. *Si'l vous plait*."

Inspector Rousseau picked up the phone.

"Dr. Perkins, this is Inspector Rousseau. I was expecting your call."

"What more can you tell me about Harry Gray? He was on an investigation for me to try to locate someone in Paris."

"Yes, I know," said Rousseau.

"Did he die of natural causes?" asked Scott. Then he hesitated for a minute. How did Rousseau know Gray was on a mission for him to locate someone in Paris?

"I can't answer that right now," said Rousseau. "He may have committed suicide—an autopsy has been done. We don't have all the results yet."

"How did he do it?"

"He shot himself through the mouth with his own revolver."

"I can't believe it," said Scott. "He was a stable guy. Something else must have happened."

"That's possible, but it looks like suicide at the present time."

"Is there anything else that you can tell me? How did you know to notify me?"

"Detective Gray maintained a diary. He kept a daily log of what he was doing. Your name was in that diary. In fact, there was a lot of information in that diary."

"Oh!" That revelation took Scott by surprise. He turned white with apprehension.

"We may wish to interrogate you about some of the entries in that diary," said Rousseau.

Scott was shocked by what he had just heard. It was no longer a secret about what was going on.

"Is there anything else you can tell me?"

"Not at the present time," said Rousseau.

When he hung up the phone, Scott turned to Aronson.

"Well, Gray's dead. The French police say he committed suicide. He shot himself through the mouth. I don't believe it."

"Why did they notify you?"

"Gray left a diary and our names were listed to be notified if anything happened to him."

"That's great!" said Aronson. "I wonder how much he put in that diary." Aronson looked quite disturbed by that revelation. Beads of sweat broke out on his forehead.

"Knowing Gray, I'm sure it's got everything in it."

"Well, if it does, we're in trouble. They can get us for obstructing justice and not notifying the police about what we knew."

"I'm not worried about that," said Scott. "I'm worried that there's a real serial killer on the loose and we may be his next target."

CHAPTER

A month later Commissioner Soucier and Inspector Rousseau met to discuss the Gray case. They were beginning to accumulate more evidence and were in pursuit of the possible killer.

"Rousseau, do you think Gray committed suicide?" asked Soucier.

"Probably not, but I'm not sure."

"You're the chief inspector on this case," said Soucier. "Do you have any more evidence?"

"Yes, I do. In Gray's belongings we found some 5 × 7 pictures of this Robin Cooker. She's beautiful. She looks as pretty as Bridget, our beautiful French movie star. We know Sousa's now a blonde, gorgeous-looking female."

"Did you find out anything else?"

"Yes. Evidently there was a complaint about the noise in Gray's room that evening. The television was turned on loud and a patron in an adjoining room complained to the main desk at 4:00 A.M. Nothing came of that except that the T.V. was on full blast when

Gray was found by the maid. I'm sure that helped to cover the noise from the gunshot."

"What about the gun and the bullets?"

"Gray had a .38 Smith and Wesson with a shoulder holster. It was right beside his body at the bedside—recently fired—one bullet missing. We got the bullet out of the wall. It was determined that he was alive before he was shot and he didn't die immediately after the bullet wound."

"How can you tell that?"

"The bullet went through the brain in the cerebellum—the back part of the brain. He probably bled and aspirated and choked to death from his own blood. There was a lot of blood all over the bed."

"What about fingerprints on his gun?"

"The only prints we got looked like his."

"Someone could have worn rubber gloves," said Soucier. "That Daphne was supposed to be a third-year medical student. I'm sure she's worn rubber gloves before."

"That's right!" replied Rousseau. "We did get some other prints that might be useful. There were thumb and forefinger prints on the champagne glasses."

"Have you checked them out?"

"One champagne glass had Gray's prints. The other's could be Daphne's. However, her prints are not registered in the French police files."

"What else have you checked out?"

"Gray's diary has a list of plastic surgeons whom he saw trying to find Robin Cooker. All of the plastic surgeons on his list were sex change artists."

"Have you interrogated any of those plastic surgeons?"

"Not all of them. I'm going to see a Dr. Pierre Dubois tomorrow."

"Call me if you find out anything," said Soucier.

"Can you think of anything else we should be doing?" said Rousseau.

"Yes, there is. That brunette wig has me baffled. Why would somebody throw it in a wastebasket if they were trying to hide? We have to look for either a blonde or a brunette by the name of Daphne St. Claire. The wig could have been thrown there to throw us off the trail."

"This case really intrigues me. I wonder if that Daphne St. Claire had a sex change? I wonder if Daphne is a male now masquerading as a female?"

"I'm beginning to see what you're driving at. You're saying that this Daphne St. Claire could be Robin Cooker. She bumps off this detective Harry Gray, who's hot on her trail before he discloses her real identity."

"That's right," said Soucier. "She may have made one mistake this time, however."

"What's that?" asked Rousseau.

"Just think for a minute."

"I've drawn a blank."

"That thumb and forefinger print that you told me about on the champagne glass."

"But those prints are not registered under anyone's name."

"I want you to call the district attorney's office in New Orleans today. If Robin Cooker killed those two people at the Hilton in New Orleans, I'm sure they found lots of fingerprints around the scene of the crime. We'll see if Robin's fingerprints match up with Daphne's."

"But, even if that incriminates her, we still don't know where she is here in Paris," said Rousseau.

"That's right. But if those prints match up, it puts her at the scene of the crime of two murders. We also have her picture. We think we know her first name and we know that she's a bisexual killer. We'll get her. Justice will prevail!"

Scott called Paul Aronson about a month after Harry Gray's death. "Paul, I want to get together with you and talk to you some more about what happened to Harry Gray. I don't believe he committed suicide."

"Neither do I. I wish you could have contacted me before I left Paris. I could have talked to Commissioner Soucier and Inspector Rousseau and gotten all the facts. I'm quite disturbed that Gray kept a diary."

"I am too! If that diary was found back here in the States, you and I would probably be behind bars by now."

"The trouble is, we don't know what Gray put in that diary."

"Commissioner Soucier did say it was kept up to date," replied Scott.

"That's what's worrying me. Do you think we ought to call Paris and ask Soucier what was in that diary?"

"He probably won't tell us anything because it's considered evidence—they might want to ask us about some of the things he wrote in that diary. They also might want to know why we're asking."

"It's one of those situations where you're damned if you do and you're damned if you don't," said Aronson.

"I don't like what I see on the horizon," said Scott. "We send Gray looking for Sousa and he discovers two murders in New Orleans. He traces Sousa through San Francisco and Los Angeles, and a transsexual body change in which the plastic surgeon who does the change gets bumped off. Now it looks like Gray's getting close to finding that transsexual female and the French police tell us that he may have committed suicide. You and I know that ain't so! I think we've got to find out more about how he died."

"Aren't you a little frightened about delving deeper into this case? Look what happened to Gray."

"I think we have to continue to try to find Robin even though it may put our own lives at risk."

"What you're saying is that we ought to call Commissioner Soucier and find out what's going on in their investigation of Gray's death."

"That's right," said Scott. "Also to try and find out what Gray put in that diary."

"Well, why don't we call Soucier early tomorrow morning in order to get them in their office. There's a time change, you know."

Scott called Commissioner Soucier the next day—Aronson was on another phone listening to the conversation.

"Commissioner Soucier, this is Dr. Scott Perkins from the States."

"I was expecting your call. We have some questions we would like to ask you and Dr. Aronson."

"Are you making any headway in determining what happened to Detective Gray? We would like more information as to what took place over there in Paris," said Scott. "How did he die?"

"We now feel that Gray was probably murdered. He did not commit suicide! He had such a high alcohol content in his blood that he couldn't have gotten the gun up to his mouth to pull the trigger," said Soucier. "His stomach contents were full of alcohol—also a narcotic drug was found in the blood samples taken after death. Besides the alcohol, he must have been given something to knock him out."

"Do you have any suspects?"

"Yes, we do. Gray was out on the town in Paris with an attractive woman who slept with him before his death."

"Do you have any ideas who she would be?"

"We do. Her name is Daphne St. Claire and she is supposedly a third-year medical student in Paris. However, we have been unable to locate her. We have reason to believe that she does not exist under that name."

"How did you find out who she was?"

"Her name was in Gray's diary. He put a notation in the diary the day he died. In fact, she came to see me here in the police station three weeks before Gray's death inquiring about the whereabouts of Robin Cooker. I personally met her. She was a very attractive brunette—we think."

"You met her? Why do you say it that way? Don't you know?"

"Because Daphne St. Claire, who was with Gray the night he was killed, left a brunette wig in the bathroom wastebasket. Daphne St. Claire could have been a blonde for all we know."

"Hmm. That's interesting. What you're saying is that Daphne St. Claire could have been Robin Cooker."

"That's right!" said Soucier. "Daphne St. Claire and Robin Cooker can be one and the same person."

"Brother, this gets more complicated every day," said Scott.

"We'd also like to ask you and Dr. Aronson a few questions."

"Fire away. Dr. Aronson is on the other phone."

"Why are you two spending so much money trying to find Robin Cooker?"

"How do you know that we've been spending a lot of money?"

"In the back of Gray's diary he has an itemized list of funds that he has received and also expenditures. It's over one hundred thousand dollars right now. That's a lot of money to spend just to locate someone. What's your reason?"

"Doesn't Gray have it listed in the diary as to why he's being paid?"

"No, he doesn't. That's why we're asking."

"I'm not at liberty to tell you right now," said Scott.

"We can ask that you be extradited to France. We can subpoena you if we need to."

"If it gets down to that we'll be glad to give you that information."

"We have one other big question to ask," said Commissioner Soucier. "We looked through the register of all the occupants of the hotel the night that Detective Gray was killed. Your friend Dr. Paul Aronson was listed as one of the occupants. He was registered at the Bristol."

"Dr. Aronson's on the other phone. Is that true, Paul?"

"It's true, but it's strictly a coincidence," he replied.

CHAPTER

The week of the wedding came all too soon. Extra phones had to be put in at the château in order to handle the phone calls. Newspapers, fashion magazines and television kept requesting more passes for entrance to the wedding. Robin emphatically opposed giving them out. However, the media would not accept no for an answer. Eventually, the media won out and the French security had to be notified about the additional passes that were to be issued.

The French government, including the prime minister, got involved when the world press wanted pictures of the bride and groom for publication. Robin again refused, but François and the French government prevailed—after all she was marrying an offspring of former French King François I.

Robin also was asked to submit to an interview for one of the major talk shows in Paris. She finally agreed, but she did so with the stipulation that it be taped and shown after the wedding.

Robin was deathly afraid that something would go wrong to spoil the wedding. She knew that someone was looking for her and was trying to get her—so far they had been unsuccessful. That shot at her in the French Alps while she was skiing was not an accident. Someone was stalking her. She had seen him from a distance but had not recognized him. She thought there was much too much publicity for the wedding.

She was so much in love with François—now that she had found out she really was a woman. She felt that if she had to, she could easily kill anyone who tried to prevent her marriage.

As far as she was concerned no one in France really knew who she was except the plastic surgeon, Pierre Dubois. Dr. Dubois had told her that someone had inquired about her but he had revealed nothing—he had been sworn to secrecy.

Robin was afraid someone might recognize her at the wedding and then her past identity would be disclosed. What could she do to prevent that? She worried about the news media and television who would be taking pictures.

She finally came up with a plan. She thought she'd better discuss it with François but she was afraid he might not understand.

"François, what would you say if I colored my hair for the wedding?"

"I think your hair is beautiful the way it is. Why spoil it?"

"I could be a redhead or a brunette."

"I love your gleaming blonde hair. It goes well with your skin coloring and your beautiful eyes. You have tremendous natural beauty."

"Would you still love me if I colored my hair?"

"Of course," replied François.

"Thanks. You've reassured me. I feel better now."

Three days before the wedding, Robin tried on her wedding gown to see if any final adjustments had to be made by the seamstress. The gown fit perfectly. It was a dreamy white satin and tulle gown embellished with hand-beaded lace, modified sweetheart neckline—cut low in front and off the shoulder—with short sleeves and a hand-beaded basque bodice that flowed down to the skirt. The back was cut low, showing her bare back, with a dazzling butterfly bow at the waist. She had a cathedral train with hand-beaded lace. The delicate fingertip veil was attached to the platinum crown, jeweled with large diamonds. She had a beautiful white pearl necklace with lustrous pearl earrings.

Marie, her maid-in-waiting, watched as Robin tried the gown on in front of a full-length three-dimensional mirror.

The seamstress was ecstatic about Robin wearing her masterpiece. "Mademoiselle, you are the most beautiful bride I have ever seen. The gown is perfect for you."

"Amen to that," said Marie. "It took François a long time to find someone and he finally picked the best! He is a very lucky man. All of us who work here at the château are so happy he found you."

"I feel I am very lucky, Marie. I want to look beautiful for François. Have you packed my luggage for the honeymoon?"

"Yes. Everything except the outfit you'll be wearing when you leave the castle at Chambord."

"I'm thinking about having my hair colored for the wedding."

"What color, Mademoiselle?"

"Either red or brown. I could even wear a wig."

"I like your hair the way it is. Your blonde hair is so beautiful and glistening when the sun shines on it."

"I know, Marie, but I have a specific reason for changing it."

Later that afternoon, Robin went into Tours to a specialty beauty salon called Madame Jeanne Antoinette's. It was the most expensive beauty salon in the whole area. Marie wanted to go with her but was told to stay at the château. François' chauffeur drove her to Tours in the limousine and waited for her while she had her hair done. She was given a choice of various tints by the beautician. When she came out of the beauty salon, Robin wore a fine tightly-laced covering over her hair that tied in a bow beneath her chin—a babushka. She had her hair tinted and done up in a French braid. When she got back to the château Marie was waiting for her.

"Did you have your hair tinted?" Marie asked.

"No one will know until just before I walk down the aisle," said Robin with a smile. "Not even you."

Commissioner Soucier alerted the French National Security Forces to increase the number of security personnel for the Bouvier-Cartier wedding. Inspector Rousseau called all the local and Paris newspapers to see if they had any recent photographs of the prospective bride. He was surprised they had none. He also called the marriage licensing bureau to see if any pictures were taken when Robin and François came in to get their license. Rousseau did obtain a copy of a photograph of the bride at the municipal building in Tours but the photograph was so poor it was difficult to visualize any resemblance.

"This woman looks like an old French gypsy with a babushka over her head," said Rousseau, as he showed the picture to Soucier. "Do you still want to go to the wedding?"

"Of course," said Soucier.

"How are we going to dress?"

"I'm glad you asked that."

"We're going to be dressed like the rest of the guests—the aristocracy. We're both going to wear dark formal suits. We will also be going through the receiving line to get a real close look at that Robin."

"That receiving line is just for the aristocracy."

"I know," said Soucier. "You and I are going to be the mayors of two of the local townships."

"What if we find out that Robin is the one we want? We can't just go up to her and arrest her."

"I know. I've thought about that. If we arrest her and she's the wrong one, our careers are over. They might even hang us from the gallows or use a guillotine if they have one around. The prime minister attending the wedding would sign the papers."

"Well, what do we do?"

"If we believe this Robin is the one we want, we'll put a tail on her and wait for her to make her next mistake. Once you become a serial killer, it's like a disease—most of them are on an ego trip. The lust for killing gets into their blood. They usually strike again."

"If this Robin Cartier is Robert Sousa I wouldn't want to be François. Once she tires of him—poof—she'll bump him off."

"And then she'd own one of the biggest châteaus in France," said Rousseau.

"That's right," said Soucier. "This whole mess is kind of scary when you think about it."

CHAPTER
37

Commissioner Soucier and Inspector Rousseau met every month to discuss the difficult crime cases they were tracking.

"Are you getting any more leads on that Robin Cooker case?" Soucier asked.

"Not too many," said Rousseau. "We found out there are over one-thousand Robins in the Paris environs and they're not the fine-feathered kind—some of them are males and some are females. Not one of them fits the description of the one we're looking for."

"Have you tried to locate where Robert Sousa was born in France?"

"Yes, I did. When he became an American citizen, he listed Paris as his birthplace. We looked up his birth certificate. As you know, the official evidence of births, marriages, and divorces are recorded by the mayor of each city or by one of his assistants in France. He was born in Paris on July 9, 1963 and was delivered by a midwife. He weighed six pounds, eleven ounces."

"Have the documents been changed or altered?"

"No, but there was something unusual about the records. There was a typed notation under the name Robert Sousa. It said: 'See confidential files in the mayor's office.' "

"Well, did you look at the confidential files?"

"Yes, I did. However, I had a hard time getting to see them."

"What did you find?"

"It was most peculiar. The outside file was there and the name Robert Sousa was crossed off. Beside it was written in the name Robin Cooker."

"What else did you find?"

"There was nothing else in the file."

"No address or phone number?"

"That's right."

"Well, that information doesn't help us very much. Did you talk to the mayor about the file being missing?"

"Yes, I did. He's not the same mayor as when Sousa was born. He said that there must have been a misfile by one of the clerks. He had the clerks check all the Cs looking for Cooker and all the Ss looking for Sousa but he can't find the file."

"About all that tells us is that Sousa is a female by the name of Cooker living in France somewhere. That's not much help."

"Have you had any luck in locating that French medical student Daphne St. Claire?"

"We've had some luck. If you remember, when she came into the police department and talked to you asking for help in locating Robin Cooker, she left her phone number so she could be notified if we got any information."

"Yes, I remember."

"Through the phone company, we traced where she was living in Montmartre, the site of the Moulin Rouge. She must have been one of those artistic types—she lived on Junot Avenue where the city rents out studios to artists from all over the world.

"We found out she was living with a guy. She was the artsy one— she was a painter.

"Her neighboring artists said she was never around and when she was, she kept pretty much to herself except when she needed art supplies. The guy was around more than she was."

"Did you ask whether they noticed if she was a blonde or a brunette?"

"We did ask that question. All the replies were the same. Evidently, she was quite a dish. She changed her hair color quite often. She was a gorgeous blonde, a ravishing brunette, and a stunning redhead."

"Did you find out anything else?"

"We talked to the landlady to see how she paid the rent."

"Yes?"

"She paid in cash or sent a bank cashier's check. She checked out of her apartment the day after Gray's death."

"What about the guy?"

"He left too!"

"That information helps a little bit but not a lot," said Soucier.

"How about the plastic surgeons? Have any luck with them?"

"None. Although I thought I was on the track for a while with one of them."

"Which one?"

"Dr. Pierre Dubois—the one who's in the news all the time and on television. He's that sex-change specialist. I showed him the photographs of Robin Cooker. He got a little bit shook up when I showed him her pictures."

"Did you tell him why you were looking for her?"

"Yes. That's when he got shook up, but he denied ever seeing her. He really got upset when I told him that a detective from the States might have been killed trying to look for her. I told him it was recently on the front page of the newspaper."

"What was his reply?"

"He said, 'Oh yes. I read about that gruesome mess in *La Monde*. He shot himself through the mouth. What a bloody way to go.' "

"Maybe we ought to subpoena his files," said Soucier.

"You've got to have just cause."

"Let me see those files again on the Gray case," said Soucier. "Did you make a copy of the diary?"

"Yes. It's all in there. In fact, it's on the computer."

Soucier tapped into the computer. "Just what I thought. Gray has a notation in his diary that he saw Dubois also. He's got an asterisk by Dubois' name."

"I think you'd better go back and talk to Dubois again. He may know something. Put some pressure on him."

"That won't do any good. Doctor's records are confidential.

Those sex-change people don't want anyone to know what's happening."

"Damn it! A crime has been committed. If he knows something, we've got to find out. Did those fingerprint reports come in from New Orleans? Did they match the crime at Le Bristol?"

"That's another story. The New Orleans police say the only prints they found at the crime site at the Hilton were those of the two victims. There were a few other prints from former occupants of the suite."

"I thought you said we had Sousa's prints?"

"Evidently I was wrong."

"That's great! Either we're dealing with a clever diabolical murderer who may have worn rubber gloves, or he or she didn't commit the crime."

"Maybe we ought to commit a little crime of our own."

"What do you mean?"

"Just what I said. Maybe we ought to break into Dubois' office and see if he has any records on Robin Cooker."

"We could get into big trouble if we don't find anything."

"I know," said Soucier, as he threw his arms into the air.

"Go in and interrogate that SOB again. Think of something. We don't have any other leads. There's a serial killer out there on the loose."

The next day, Rousseau went over to Dr. Dubois' office at noon. He flashed his badge to Dubois' secretary.

"Dr. Dubois will see you in a few minutes. He just finished a case in the operating room and is eating his lunch."

"Thanks," said Rousseau.

He finally was told to enter Dr. Dubois' consultation room.

"What brings you back so soon?"

"I just want to show you that picture of Robin Cooker one more time. Are you sure you've never seen her? Rousseau looked at him eyeball to eyeball. He noticed there were some fine beads of sweat on his forehead. Dubois hesitated for a long time before he answered.

"I'm absolutely sure! I'll repeat what I said before. Sex changes are protected by law. You're wasting your time. If I did see her, I wouldn't tell you."

"That may be true, Dr. Dubois, but if we find out you're lying, you could go to prison."

"I realize that!" replied Dubois.

Rousseau turned around and walked out of the office.

Dubois called his secretary in. "Diane, I want you to pull three charts for me out of the locked confidential file. I'll be taking them home this evening for review." One of those charts was Robin Cooker's.

When Dubois got home that evening, he threw Robin Cooker's chart into his burning fireplace.

Inspector Rousseau called Commissioner Soucier and told him he had gotten nowhere with Dr. Dubois.

"Do you think he knows something?" he asked.

"Yes, I do."

"Come up to my office and we'll work out a plan. There can be no foul-ups."

Soucier called three of his best officers into the meeting. A plan was worked out to enter Dr. Dubois' office in the evening and to search the files for Robin Cooker's chart. An inspector posing as a patient would first case the office that afternoon.

Everything worked according to plan. The main patient files and confidential files were rifled through—but no Robin Cooker chart was found.

The marriage of Robin Cartier to François Bouvier was announced in the French newspapers on Sunday before the wedding—La Monde and others carried the announcement in the society pages. The wedding was to be held the following Saturday in the late afternoon. It was to be at the Hunting Lodge in Chambord, France and many of the French royalty and aristocracy would attend, including the prime minister.

The Sûreté Nationale, the central police authority for France, were to provide security for the wedding. A directive to all of the major chiefs of police (prefects) in the area was sent including some of the commissioners. Commissioner Soucier received one of the directives. He paid little attention to it.

The directive contained a list of over seven-hundred-fifty guests who were to attend the wedding including those who were coming from outside France. Each registered guest was to receive a numbered gold engraved invitation and metal detectors were placed at all the entrances and exits to the castle.

Anyone of importance in France and Europe would be attending the wedding. No one would be admitted without the gold engraved numbered invitation.

A copy of the special gold engraved admission card was photographed and sent on a sheet of paper with the letter to the police. Soucier casually looked at the list of guests. His eye caught one name he recognized—Dr. Pierre Dubois. His eyes perused the invitation card more closely. It read: 'You are cordially invited to attend the marriage of François Bouvier IX to Robin Cartier on Saturday June 19, 1992 at 4:00 P.M. at the Hunting Lodge at Chambord, France.'

The invitation had the French Seal of State embossed in the middle of the card and in fine print it read on the bottom: 'Admittance is limited to only those carrying the registered numbered invitation card.'

Soucier let out a whistle. I wonder, he thought? It couldn't be! Had this Robin Cooker changed her name to Robin Cartier? Was she or he going to marry one of France's aristocracy? No!

He decided he'd better look into it. If it was Robin Cooker, then some of France's finest might be in trouble.

He called Inspector Rousseau. He had to work fast. Here it was Thursday afternoon and the wedding was to be held in forty-eight hours, on Saturday afternoon.

"Inspector Rousseau, you and I are going to a wedding Saturday in Chambord. You're to call the Sûreté Nationale Chief of Operations and get passes for you and I to attend."

"What wedding are we going to?"

"The François Bouvier—Robin Cartier wedding. I think we may have found our prey."

CHAPTER

Robin and François drove to Chambord the day before the wedding in François' limousine. Marie and other personnel from the château had left the night before with luggage for the honeymoon and essential clothing and material for the wedding.

When they arrived at the Hunting Lodge, newspaper and media personnel with photographers and TV cameras photographed Robin and François as they entered the lodge. Robin was still wearing her camouflaged hairnet and was not in her best mood. She snapped at one of the photographers who wanted to take a close-up of her face.

"Get out of my way. No pictures please."

"Just one," said the photographer.

"That's one too many!" she replied as she held her hand over her face.

François was going to say something to Robin but held back. He didn't want to challenge her the day before their wedding.

When they got into the lodge, François showed Robin how they had set up the main ballroom for the wedding services.

Robin's and François' rooms were at the top of the double spiral staircase. A maroon royal carpet had been put on the stairs and connected with the aisle that led to a newly constructed chapel-like structure at the end of the big ballroom. A magnificent large gold-jeweled cross was at the top of the three-tiered altar. Silk and betasselled cushions were on the top step of the first of two shallow flights leading up to the high altar. It was here that the archbishop would conduct the wedding ceremony. There were over seven-hundred chairs placed around the center aisle. Off to one side of the altar was an elevated stand for the choir which would consist of forty choir boys and their director. On the opposite side was an-other elevated area for the French National Orchestra—they would play the wedding march and the recessional.

François had selected the prime minister to be his best man and Robin had selected her aunt from Lille, who was six months preg-nant, to be her maid of honor. There were twelve ushers and twelve bridesmaids. Robin hardly knew any of the bridesmaids—they were selected by her aunt to fill in the void.

A rehearsal was held at 4:00 in the afternoon with a sit-down dinner served in the Lodge. The archbishop had given them special license to be married at the Lodge and not in the cathedral. Since part of the wedding would be televised, the archbishop announced that he would have a short dissertation for the audience. Robin gave out an almost audible groan when she heard that. The rehearsal party broke up about 1:00 and Robin and François retreated to their rooms.

"I can hardly wait for all of this nonsense to be over with," said Robin as she kissed François goodnight.

"I know, Robin. It's necessary for God to give his blessing to our marriage. He has already blessed me by allowing me to meet you and to court you."

When Robin got back to her room she took a bath in the large sunken bathtub and Marie massaged her back and anointed her skin with sweet-smelling oils. She had difficulty falling asleep but when she did, she slept soundly until almost noon.

"Why didn't you wake me?" she admonished Marie.

"You have a big day ahead of you, Mademoiselle. I wanted you to be well rested to truly show off your natural beauty."

"There's so much to do and so little time. I'll take my bath first—a long beautifying bath. You can lay out my wedding clothes for me, Marie. Is François up?"

"Yes. But you're not to see him before the ceremony."

"Oh, yes. I almost forgot."

Robin spent a long time taking her bath. Marie massaged her back, feet and legs and perfumed her entire body. A beautician helped her apply her eyeshadow and penciled her lips. After she finished, she left the room.

"I'm going to show you a little secret, Marie, but you're not to tell anyone about it. Do you understand?"

"Oh, yes, Mademoiselle. I promise."

Robin put on her pantyhose and then took out of her pocketbook, a leather strap that had a small holster attached to it. She tied the strap around her upper right thigh and placed a fancy snug garter over it. She then placed a small derringer in the holster.

"How did you get that through security?" asked Marie.

"I put it in the middle of all my metal jewelry and walked through. I knew they wouldn't stop the bride going to her own wedding."

"Why are you wearing that?" asked Marie.

"Because I don't trust anybody—except perhaps François. A pistol can be your best friend at times and I'm not afraid to use it."

"You don't need that gun. The security here at the Lodge is fantastic. Everyone has to go through a metal detector and no one will be admitted to the Lodge without a gold numbered invitation with the French State Seal on it. They practically made the help take off all their clothes before they were admitted."

"The security isn't that great. Look what I did. I got through security with my pistol. Marie, you're not to tell anyone about that. Not even François. Do you understand?"

"Explicitly," she replied.

Robin then put on her white satin high-heeled shoes. It was 3:00 P.M.—one hour before the wedding ceremony.

She could hardly wait to get into her wedding gown. The gown caressed her body lines and she loved it. It was made of a clear chantilly white lace and silk satin with a low-cut sweetheart neckline and a closely fitted bodice. Her breasts almost seemed to leap out of the tight-fitting gown. Her thin waist accentuated her breasts and the beautiful curvature of her buttocks.

There was a large white bow on the back and the lower part of her gown had a slit at the thigh level to expose her long slender legs. The train was white lace and silk with a white ermine trim.

Marie reminded her that she had to wear something old, something new, something borrowed and something blue and a silver sixpence in her shoe.

Robin decided that the something blue would be a ribbon of royal blue silk draped over her left shoulder. The blue ribbon signified purity, love, and fidelity in ancient times.

Robin put the gown on. Her diaphanous beauty shone through the thin white lace and silk satin. She looked radiant.

"Marie, I want you to untie my camouflaged hairnet now and take the pins out. I'm not a royal bride but I am marrying into a royal family. I understand that royal brides often had their hair flowing loose off their head and down their back in a maidenly manner—so that's what I'm going to do."

Marie gasped when she removed the hairnet and pins.

"Mademoiselle, you've dyed your hair bright red! It is most beautiful! It's so brilliant and long."

"Thank you, Marie. Do you think that François will like it?"

"Of course. He adores you!"

"Marie, I want you to help me place the platinum crown of diamonds on my head now. You'll have to fix it in place with pins. How much time do we have?"

"Fifteen minutes," said Marie.

"Before I descend that spiral staircase, I want to look at myself in the full-length mirror again." Robin walked over to the three-dimensional full-length mirror.

"I like what I see," she said.

"You are the prettiest bride ever!"

The door was opened to the room and her train was attached. Two small girls were to carry the end of the train. The French national anthem was being played.

"Are you nervous, Robin?" asked Marie.

"Not at all. This is the day I've been waiting for since I was a little child. Now that I know that I'm a woman—I can walk proudly down the aisle."

"What do you mean by that, Mademoiselle? I don't understand."

"Oh, Oh," said Robin. "I made a mistake. I shouldn't have said that."

Marie looked at her with a puzzled look. "It's your time to be the center of attention," said Marie. "I am so happy for you and François."

Everyone was watching, as Robin descended the spiral staircase in her beautiful white wedding gown with her red hair glistening behind her back. She held her head high topped with the glistening diamond tiara. Mary, Queen of Scots would have indeed envied her beauty as she held her bouquet of white orchids. She had a broad smile on her face as she walked confidently down the aisle.

The orchestra was playing the processional march as two flower girls strew flower petals in front of Robin as she approached the altar where François was waiting. Photographers were taking pictures and television cameras were rolling.

Since her father was dead Robin had chosen to walk up the aisle by herself. The maid of honor, bridesmaids, and ushers were all in place. Her eyes focused directly on François as she drew nearer to the altar. His eyes met hers. Small droplets of tears started to come down her cheeks. Suddenly, she realized that everything she wanted in life was coming to fruition.

François took her hand and they ascended to the high altar together. There was silence. Then the archbishop spoke: "We are gathered here before God to bring together Robin Cartier and François Bouvier in holy matrimony."

Robin didn't really hear what the archbishop was saying and neither did François. They kept gazing into each other's eyes, the most spiritual of senses—their eyes reflected their inner feelings—their deep love for each other.

She vaguely heard François saying: "I François Bouvier take thee Robin Cartier to be my wedded wife, to have and to hold for richer, for poorer, for better, for worse, in sickness and in health, from this time forward till death do us part. I plight thee my troth."

And then he placed a ring on the third finger of her left hand.

"With this ring, I thee wed and with my body I thee worship, and with all my worldly goods, I thee honor."

Robin repeated the vows to François.

A nuptial mass was then said and the boys' choir sang *Ave Maria*.

Robin came out of her daze when she heard the archbishop say:

"I now pronounce you man and wife."

François leaned over and kissed her. The recessional was played by the French National Orchestra. Photographs were taken and a receiving line was formed.

Commissioner Soucier and Inspector Rousseau were in the receiving line. After they went through and shook hands with Robin and François, they talked about what they had just seen.

"Robin Cartier is the real thing," said Inspector Rousseau. "As far as I'm concerned we can cross her off our suspect list. She's the most beautiful woman I have ever seen. Her face and body could never have been created by man—a plastic surgeon—only God could have created a woman with a body like that."

"I agree with you," said Commissioner Soucier. "Well, we might as well enjoy ourselves and have a good time."

Three separate rooms were used for the wedding reception until they were able to clear the main hall of the chairs. Robin had her first dance with François and then with the prime minister. The prime minister's hands still had a tendency to travel downward to her derriere as the music played soft and slow. She had to wiggle to get out of his grasp.

"I'm a married lady now," she told the prime minister, as she took his hand and placed it on her waist.

"I realize that," he replied, "but you are a most beautiful married lady and being married doesn't make you less desirable."

"*Touché*," said Robin. "Your proposition for me becoming your mistress is dead. I never gave it a thought. I have everything I want in life by marrying François. I also like your wife, Bridget—one of these days you'll realize how valuable she is."

After dancing with practically everyone in the political hierarchy of France and drinking numerous toasts to their good health, Robin and François retreated to their rooms to change and get ready to go on their honeymoon. It was almost 10:00 P.M. and they had a time schedule in order to catch the late night train to Monaco and the Riviera.

François had arranged for the carriage to take them from the Hunting Lodge in Chambord toward Blois. About seven miles down the road, Robin and François were to change to the motor-driven limousine.

When Robin got to her room, she quickly changed out of her wedding dress. Marie was there to help her get into her going away clothes. After she took the gown off, Marie noticed that the leather strap holster was still attached to her right upper thigh and the pistol was still there.

"Well, at least you didn't have to use that," she said to Robin.

"No, but if François didn't marry me, I was prepared to use it on him," she replied with a smile.

"You would never do that!"

"You're right. He's the only exception though. Marie, I'm so happy. I'm the luckiest girl in the world!"

"I agree," said Marie. "François is a wonderful man."

Robin took a quick shower and looked at herself in the mirror again. She perfumed her body and put on a snug-fitting chartreuse dress cut high above the knees. The edges of the dress were trimmed with gold. It had a low V-neck with simple, straight lines. She wore no underclothes. She said to Marie as she pirouetted around. "What you see is what you get."

"*Très beau!*" exclaimed Marie.

"Why are you still wearing that holster around your upper right thigh?" asked Marie.

"It brought me good luck so far," said Robin. "That's why."

"You don't need it. You could hurt yourself with that gun!"

"Don't worry, Marie. I assure you that if I need to, I would know how to use it."

Robin suddenly became more serious. "Marie, you've been a dear. You've been so helpful to me for so long. I don't know how to repay you. I want to give you something for being so nice."

"I love my job and I love working for you," said Marie. "That's not necessary."

"You shall work for me as long as I live," said Robin as she handed her a white beaded purse. "There's ten thousand francs in that purse. That's for you to spend."

"Thank you," said Marie with tears in her eyes.

François and Robin got into the 18th century carriage with rice and confetti being thrown at them. It was dark outside and the brilliant lights on the outside of the Hunting Lodge were lit up. The beauty of the Lodge was breathtaking. The carriage had been decorated with bright-colored streamers, and a large sign saying "Just Married" was hanging from the back.

"Driver, let's go," said François to the coachman.

The coachman hit the reins and the carriage took off.

Robin quickly came into François' arms.

"Alone at last," said Robin.

François caressed her and kissed her lips. He gently palpated her breasts through the thin clothing she wore. Robin responded to his kisses and cuddled up safely in his arms.

"Why don't we just go back to our own château for tonight?" said Robin.

"No. We've made plans to go to Monaco. I can wait," replied François. "It's not as though this is our first night together."

"I know," replied Robin. "But you are legally mine now and I'm yours. I am so happy! I feel that I'm in heaven and haven't awakened."

Just then, the carriage abruptly stopped. François looked outside. It was dark and he noticed they weren't on the main road. Where were they?

The coachman got down from the driver's seat and opened the carriage door. The other coachman got down on the opposite side.

"Monsieur. You're to get out! I have a gun in my hand. No harm will come to you if you do as I say. All we are after is the young lady with you."

"Who are you? What is the meaning of this? Are you from the police?"

"Yes! You can say we are from the police."

When he heard that, François got out of the carriage.

"There must be a mistake. This is an outrage! I've just been married. We're on our way to our honeymoon."

"I realize that. That's why we're here."

Before François could react, the other coachman crept up from behind and hit François over the head with the butt of his gun. He knocked him unconscious. Profuse bleeding could be seen coming from a deep cut on the back of his scalp.

"Want me to finish him off?" asked the coachman as he looked at the prostrate François and pointed the gun at him.

"Naw. You probably have already. You may have fractured his skull. He's not going to bother anyone for a long time."

The revelry and partying continued at a busy pace at the Hunting Lodge. Champagne, the best French wines, large sumptuous meals with soup, fish, venison, pheasant and several other elegant dishes were served. There were different foods for every particular taste to tantalize the palate. The best French chefs had prepared the food well.

There were three different orchestras playing in the smaller ballrooms for dancing and a much larger orchestra in the main ballroom.

Commissioner Soucier and Inspector Rousseau joined the revelry and partying and had even danced with some of the beautiful women who had been abandoned by their husbands to play cards in some of the side rooms of the Lodge. They were having their share of wine, too and enjoying the food from the main dining room and the buffets. They were eating from the magnificent buffet table when they were approached by one of the gendames.

"Monsieur Soucier?"

"Yes."

"You are wanted immediately by the Chief of Security, Jacques Marcel."

"What's the problem?"

"There's been a stabbing here at the Lodge."

"What happened? Did someone drink too much and have a fight?"

"No, Monsieur. The two coachmen who were to drive the carriage were found without their clothes on, in the back stables. One was dead and the other is probably going to die. The one that was still alive said a man and a woman accosted them, beat them up, and took their clothes and the carriage and then took off."

"*Mon dieu*! They must be kidnapping François and his bride. We've got to find that carriage immediately! Notify all the police surrounding this area to send out search parties."

"Tell the new bride to get out of the carriage," said the coachman with the gun.

"Are you going to kill her?"

"Yes. But not right away. I'm thinking about raping her first. She's a bisexual just like I am. I've done it both ways before but this one looks like it might be more interesting."

"Why don't we just shoot her and get the hell out of here. They might find those two guys back at the Lodge and come looking for us."

"No. They can't find us way up here in the hills. There's no way they'd know where to look. There's too many roads they'd have to search. Besides, it's dark as hell out here and there's no moon tonight. You go on the other side of the carriage and force that new bride out."

"What if she won't budge? She may give us a fight."

"Then pull her out. It can't be too tough. She's a skinny little thing."

Robin heard the entire conversation. She decided if she was going to survive she had to get the coachman with the gun first.

"I'm coming out! I won't resist! If you want to rape me, I'll let you. It's all over now if François is going to die."

"Now that's what I call a cooperating broad. You don't know me, do you?"

As Robin slipped out of the coach, she looked closely at the coachman. She finally recognized the assailant. She pulled the trigger of the derringer, aiming at his belly.

He was taken completely by surprise as the bullet hit him. The gun dropped out of his hand as he slumped to the ground. Robin picked up his gun. She saw the second coachman come from the other side of the coach. She turned and fired again. The bullet hit him in the chest and he fell. She went over and picked up the gun from the second assailant. She looked over at François. He was groaning and holding his head. He was coming to.

"Robin, my dearest. Are you all right?"

"Yes, François."

"I think our problems are over," said Robin.

"How will anyone find us up here?"

"We'll light a fire," said Robin. "We'll burn up that carriage. I didn't like that idea anyway."

CHAPTER

Fortunately, the security for the wedding was tight so there were
lots of gendarmes and personnel from the French security forces
present at the wedding when they found the two coachmen stabbed
in the stables.

One of the coachmen was still alive, moaning, groaning, and
begging for help as he was trying to make noise by hitting a ham-
mer on an anvil iron used for shoeing horses. A stable boy found
him and notified the French gendarmes.

The coachmen's uniforms had been stolen. The dead coachman
was lying face down in the stable with a knife still stuck in his chest.
The other was still alive and conscious with a bleeding belly wound.
He had taken his undershirt off and was trying to hold pressure on
his abdomen to prevent further blood loss. The French security
forces had paramedics on the premises—they quickly applied first
aid and started an intravenous so he could maintain his blood
pressure and not go into shock.

Commissioner Soucier ordered the police to man their vehicles and search every road around the Hunting Lodge at Chambord for the carriage. An all-points bulletin was sent out over their telecommunication system. They were warned that the disguised coachmen were dangerous and were wanted for murder.

The French police were dealing with clever assailants—the kidnappers were smart. They realized that the security at the Hunting Lodge was tight so they waited for their prey to come out of the Lodge.

At the carriage, Robin focused all her attention on François, but not until she made sure there were no more guns. He seemed to be all right, and would make it. He was fully awake and alert but would need some stitches in his scalp. The bleeding had stopped but he had a horrible headache, and was holding a handkerchief to his head. The two coachmen who were shot by Robin were alive but were lying helpless on the ground. The one who was shot in the belly was moaning and groaning, asking for help. There was a big, bright red blood spot on his shirt where the bullet had penetrated his abdomen. The bleeding had taken all his strength away and the bullet had gone through his bowel, releasing the fecal contents into the abdominal cavity and causing excruciating pain. The other assailant had difficulty breathing because the bullet had perforated his right lung—he wouldn't go very far! He gasped. "Get help! Quickly! I'm dying. I can't breathe."

"It would serve you both right if you did die!" said Robin.

"We have a car hidden over there in the bushes," he said. "Get me to a hospital!"

Robin gave one of the guns to François and told him to keep them covered and she dashed to the edge of the woods to look. Sure enough—there was a Renault sedan parked there. She started the motor, turned the lights on and started blowing the horn. Within ten minutes, the police and local residents arrived and an ambulance was called.

Commissioner Soucier and Inspector Rousseau joined the police on the scene.

"What happened here?" asked Soucier, as he saw the two coachmen moaning on the ground and François holding his bleeding scalp wound.

"These two men tried to kill us," said Robin. "They comman-
deered the coach and drove us out here in the woods. The one over
there with the belly wound said he was going to rape me and then
kill me. The other one hit François over the head and knocked him
out. He was going to shoot him, too!"

"How come you're not hurt?" asked Rousseau.

"Because I shot them before they could shoot me."

"Where'd you get the gun?"

"I had it on me."

"A new bride carrying a gun?"

"That's right."

"Well, that takes the cake. I'd like to hear a little more about that,"
said Soucier.

A second ambulance arrived and the two coachmen were admin-
istered to by the paramedics. They were both taken under guard to
the nearest hospital for emergency surgery.

François was also taken by ambulance to a hospital in Tours. He
had x-rays and a CT scan of his skull done, which revealed a mild
concussion but no fracture. He was admitted to the hospital for
overnight observation. Twenty-five stitches were placed in his skull
wound. Robin spent her wedding night sleeping in a chair next to
François' hospital bed.

Before he went to sleep, Robin gave him a big kiss and said,
"You're going to owe me one hell of a honeymoon after this wedding night."

"You shall have it," he sheepishly replied.

François was discharged the next day and they went back to the
château.

The two coachmen were hospitalized and were operated on. The
one with the abdomen wound had to have part of his small bowel
resected and his belly washed out with an antibiotic solution and
was given massive intravenous antibiotics for two weeks.

The one with the perforated lung had his chest explored and a
lobe of his lung removed—he had chest tubes in place for three or
four days.

Both of the coachmen survived and lived to confess to their
crimes.

*   *   *

Two weeks later Commissioner Soucier and Inspector Rousseau made a visit to François and Robin at the château.

"Mademoiselle, would you be so kind as to help us decipher just what was going on here? Why was the district attorney from Dallas trying to kill you?"

"If I told you the true story, I don't think you'd believe it," replied Robin.

"Well, we want you to try. Whatever you tell us will be in strictest confidence."

"Now that it's over, I have nothing to hide. I'm so relieved. The reason the district attorney from Dallas was trying to kill me was because I was the only witness who saw him kill my wife and Bill Carroll, his assistant district attorney, in New Orleans."

"That's the part that's difficult to understand," said the police commissioner. "You're a female. Why did he want to kill your pregnant wife and how could *you* have a pregnant wife?"

"That's where it's going to be difficult for you to understand. It's a complicated jigsaw puzzle."

"It definitely sounds that way, since you are a woman who, I understand, is expecting a son. Yet I am told you were married in the past to another woman when you thought you were a male and your wife was pregnant. I thought I'd seen everything in France when it comes to sex, but I must tell you, young lady, this one takes first prize! Please try to explain exactly what happened."

"I'll try, but you won't believe me. My problems started in high school in New York City. I always liked men more than girls and yet I couldn't understand why. I had been brought up as a boy in Paris by my parents where boys wore boy's clothes and eventually dated girls. That didn't happen to me.

"My father and mother were career people, both working, with much traveling and little time for children. They finally decided they wanted a child but it had to be a boy. That's when I came along. When I was an infant in France, I was taken to a pediatrician who lived in the country. My parents were told that I had undescended testicles and by giving me hormone shots, the testicles would descend to their proper place in the scrotal sac as I grew older. I received testosterone shots for a few years. All it did was make what I thought was my penis bigger. What I thought was my penis, was an enlarged clitoris. When I got sexually aroused, it got bigger. I also had a dimple where my reconstructed vagina is now.

"In law school my roommate was a weirdo. He loved to party and have good times. It wasn't long before I realized he was a homosexual when he propositioned me. We were both drunk and the next thing I knew we were kissing and one thing led to another and he became intimate with me, having sex the homosexual way.

"He wanted me to do it to him, but I knew I couldn't do it even if I tried. I had tried it a few times at the New Jersey bathhouses but I wasn't very successful. In fact, I got punched in the face one time.

"We remained good friends even after I left law school and he was my best man when I married a wealthy woman. It was a marriage of convenience, to help my career. She was the daughter of one of the senior partners in the law firm where I worked.

"The marriage was on the rocks from the beginning because I couldn't consummate the marriage. I tried hard to satisfy my wife. Here's where my law school roommate comes in. One month after our marriage, he came and spent a week with us. I thought he was quite attentive to my wife. The shocker was three months later when she told me she was pregnant and wanted to leave me. I had tried to have sex with her quite a few times and it was useless. Then when she told me she was pregnant, I knew it had to be my friend, the assistant district attorney from Dallas, Bill Carroll, who had impregnated her.

"What I didn't know, but found out later, was that Bill Carroll and District Attorney Joe Russo, back in Dallas, were both homosexuals and were having a heated affair. They were also partners in a homosexual ring for hire in Dallas that was quite profitable.

"When I developed a large swelling in my groin and had to have an operation at Jefferson Hospital I was worried. I was furious when I found out later what it was, because I knew I hadn't been fooling around sexually, although my wife and I had repeatedly tried to consummate our marriage.

"When Dr. Perkins told me that I might have AIDS, I blew my stack. Since I didn't use intravenous drugs, the only genital contact was with my wife, if you could call it that, and she was pregnant by my best friend, who was a known bisexual. If I had AIDS it had to come from Bill Carroll or her.

"I confronted Bill Carroll with the facts and he confessed that he was the father of my wife's child. I didn't tell him that I might have AIDS.

"I flew to Dallas to discuss it with him and then we went to New Orleans to the American Bar Association Convention to discuss options with my wife. She said she wanted to marry him and he was hedging because of his homosexual relationship with the D.A.

"Russo, the district attorney, didn't know his assistant district attorney had a baby in the oven of Attorney Robert Sousa's wife. He also didn't know about the AIDS problem.

"The assistant D.A., Bill Carroll, finally agreed to break off all relations with District Attorney Russo and try to get another job. However, he was afraid that his life might be in jeopardy because of the profitable on-call homosexual ring they both ran in Dallas. He knew too much and was afraid of what Russo might do.

"He agreed he would tell Russo what was going on at the American Bar Association Convention in New Orleans that all four would be attending. He hoped that the district attorney might be understanding because of the pregnancy, but he wasn't sure. I agreed to divorce my wife, since it was not a normal relationship. In fact, at that Bar Association meeting, we had two adjoining suites of rooms. Bill Carroll and my wife slept together in one suite and I slept in the other.

"At twelve o'clock the night of the big formal dance, Bill Carroll took a walk to the men's room with Russo to confront him with the facts. When Bill came back to our table, it looked like he had a black eye and the district attorney wasn't with him.

" 'What happened to you?' I asked.

" 'I ran into a door in the men's room.'

"I'll bet you did. It looks like Russo has a big fist.

"Bill Carroll didn't want to talk about it. We had a few more drinks and he asked my wife to dance. I wasn't having a good time, so I decided to go up to bed.

"I couldn't sleep so I decided to watch one of those pay TV movies. At about 4:00 A.M. I heard a commotion in the next suite. I walked over to the door of the connecting suite and saw Russo with a gun with a silencer on it in his hand, pressed against Carroll's head. He pulled the trigger and then turned around and saw me. I shut the door quickly and heard the impact of bullets against the wall. I ran out of my suite and luckily caught the elevator before he came out of the room.

"The rest is history."

"Not quite yet," said the French police chief. "There are still some unanswered questions. Do you have AIDS?"

"No! I had repeated tests after Dr. Perkins told me that I might have AIDS and they were all negative. It turned out that I had cat scratch disease that caused a swelling of my groin glands. A blood test and a positive intradermal skin test confirmed this. I never got or had AIDS."

"Dr. Perkins and Dr. Aronson will be happy to hear about that. Why didn't you go to the police when you saw the murder?"

"There were a lot of reasons," replied Robin. "The murderer was the district attorney in Dallas. He was also running a homosexual and bisexual prostitution ring. If I went to the police, they wouldn't believe my story. In fact, I felt that no one would believe my story. I decided to disappear into the woodwork. The sex change would also make it more difficult for him to find me. It was the best thing I ever did, because I was finally able to find out my true identity. I really am a female. François came into my life and made it complete."

Commissioner Soucier and Inspector Rousseau listened intently to every word Robin spoke. The look on their faces expressed an amazement that was incomprehensible. Finally, Soucier spoke up.

"Are there any unanswered questions that you would like us to explain?"

"Yes, there are," said Robin. "I would like to know why Detective Gray and why Dr. Von Salzen, the plastic surgeon in Los Angeles, were killed."

"Dr. Von Salzen was killed because there was a contract on his life. A firebug was hired by Russo to bump off Von Salzen because he was afraid you might have told him about the killing in New Orleans. He also wanted the records destroyed."

"Why was Detective Gray killed?"

"Because he was getting too close to finding you. Also, Russo was over here in Paris looking for you and was getting closer to your trail. He felt that Gray knew too much and that he would find you before he did. He was afraid that you would tell him the true story about the murders in New Orleans. Gray also knew Russo was running a homosexual ring in Dallas and might blow the whistle on that, too."

"Who actually killed Gray?"

"Russo did. He used Gray's gun to make it look like a suicide."

"What about the woman who was with Gray before he was murdered?"

"Daphne St. Claire was a bisexual lover of the district attorney's. She, or he, or whatever you want to call it, had been surgically converted from a male to a female and was a part owner of their house of ill repute."

"Who was the guy who shot at me going down the ski slopes in the French Alps?"

"That was Russo. He was lucky he wasn't killed when he hit that tree. He had a compound comminuted fracture of his left femur that laid him up for six months in a cast. He was put on blood thinners so he wouldn't toss a pulmonary embolism from his leg to his lungs. Luckily he didn't. He was in a hospital for three months. That slowed him down from trying to catch up with you."

"How did you find out about all of this?"

"Russo and Daphne St. Claire were the imposter coachmen. They both survived those gunshots that you pumped into them. They confessed to everything they did, including the stabbing of the real coachmen. One of the real coachmen died, so they will face murder charges in France for Gray's death, the coachman's death, and the murder charges in the United States. Indirectly or directly Russo was responsible for the deaths of nine people."

After François was released from the hospital they took the limousine back to the château in Tours. They had postponed their honeymoon so that François' concussion and head wound could heal. Once he felt better their love relationship intensified—both were deeply in love. Robin exuded confidence in her femininity now that her true sexual identity had been established.

They finally had their honeymoon on the French Riviera and took a cruise on the Mediterranean with visits to Italy and Greece.

Robin and her Aunt Madeline became very close as the pregnancy progressed. Three months after the wedding Madeline had the baby at the American Hospital in Paris. She gave birth to a healthy 8-pound, 14-ounce boy—François X.

Robin checked him over to make sure he had all his fingers, toes, and sexual parts—they were all there in the proper places.

Madeline had no difficulty with the delivery and told Robin that after a period of rest, she would be willing to carry another child for her and François.

Joseph Russo, the district attorney from Dallas, and Daphne St. Claire were extradited to the United States, stood trial in New Orleans, and were convicted of their crimes. They were each sentenced to life imprisonment with no chance for parole.